2—

BACK TO YESTERDAY

D1710361

BLEEDING HEARTS BOOK TWO

WHITNEY BARBETTI

BACK TO YESTERDAY

Cover Photography by Dave Kelley
Cover Model: Katrina Coon
Cover Design by Najla Qamber
Interior Design by The Write Assistants
Editing by Murphy Rae
Proofreading by Alexis Durbin at Indie Girl Proofs, Amanda
Maria, and Ginelle Blanch

Epigraph poem used with permission by J.R. Rogue

NOTE TO THE READER

Please be aware that *Back to Yesterday* is not a standalone romance. To understand this story, you must read *Into the Tomorrows* first. This book completes that story; there will not be another novel with Trista and Jude as the main characters. The next book in the Bleeding Hearts series is still untitled, and will feature a character from this book.

If you would like to be notified as soon as the next book releases, please subscribe to Whitney Barbetti's newsletter at http://www.whitneybarbetti.com/signup.

Thank you for reading!

DEDICATION

To those who feel deeply

The world opened
her mouth,
bared her teeth,
swallowed me whole.

She wasn't ready for me.

Said she wanted me to feel
the sadness inside her.
Said she wanted to marry it
to the melancholy in my marrow.

She wasn't ready for it.

Said sorrow stings,
I tasted of borrowed bitter,
spat me out, made me
into something new.

I just want to be ready for you.

- J.R. Rogue

CHAPTER ONE

JUNE 2013

I breathed in the gentle wind, let it burn my nostrils. The sun was warm on my skin, bringing with it a memory of one of my yesterdays, of the man who made me look forward to my tomorrows.

I closed my eyes, imagined his face. Imagined how I'd touched his skin, how he'd kissed mine. How his words had made me feel loved, needed.

It was all I'd ever wanted.

One step forward, one breath out. One dream gone, one hope forgotten. A thousand wishes lost once they'd left my lips. He'd been in almost every one.

A breeze fluttered my oversized shirt, flapping its frayed edges against my bare legs. My arms rested at my sides, my fingers clenched around my phone. How long had it been since my hands had held his? Since I'd felt the very definition of human connection? Too long.

"I miss you," I heard myself say, but my words were a whisper from cracked lips, a tremble from my feeble jaw. My heart was a drumbeat in my head, and I repeated one word in time to each beat: no, no, no.

Goose bumps lit my skin as the sounds of my surroundings broke the trance I was in. People laughing, televisions blaring their afternoon *Judge Judy* as they ate from chipped dollar-store china. The world moved around me as I stayed still. Dawn flooded the horizon, driving away the gray and warming the buildings as it made its approach to where I stood.

As the sun touched first my toes and then my legs, I closed my eyes. From my feet to my head, it warmed my skin, and I imagined it washing away my sins. A baptism performed on the edge of a building.

I loved you, I thought to myself, his many faces like a slideshow behind my eyelids. I still do.

Bring me back to yesterday, to the man who made me feel worth something.

I no longer wanted a tomorrow. I wanted him, but he was gone. He was my tomorrow, all of my tomorrows, and he was gone.

And as I took another step to the edge, I looked down at the cars below me.

Trista, he whispered. *Are you ready?*

God, his voice. It'd been so long since his words had caressed my ear. My knees trembled, their knobby bones the only thing holding me together.

I shook my head, willing him away. He was gone.

I swallowed the saliva that had pooled in my mouth. How had I gone from being someone with a schoolgirl crush to someone standing on the ledge of my shitty apartment building, contemplating taking one extra step and falling through the air to what awaited me below?

I'll wait for you.

It hurt, his voice. His memory was an open wound. I had nearly been ready. And here I was, back to who I'd been before all of it.

The phone in my hand rang. The number was unfamiliar—but they all were. My heart was crumbling inside my chest, but I answered and waited.

There was a rumbling, a cough, and a breath. And then, a ghost spoke, giving me the shiver he always did when he said it.

"Trista."

CHAPTER TWO

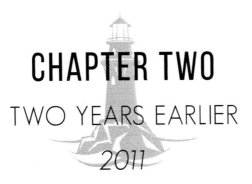

TWO YEARS EARLIER
2011

I told myself I was okay.

Breathe in, breathe out, was my reminder as I drove away.

I looked in the rear-view mirror more than the front windshield as the apartment building shrank to a tiny speck and the mountains turned into little blips, so far from my touch that I was sure I'd imagined them.

A few days later, I followed my grandfather's request, one that led me down a long, neglected road.

I shouldn't have gone there. I knew it the moment my car pulled down the bumpy drive, as the potholes jostled me against the window and the beads hanging from my rear-view mirror clanged loudly.

But despite her apathy toward me, I was easily called back to her.

Each trailer was more decrepit than the one before, with the color fading as I drove closer to her house on the uncomfortably familiar road. Some were missing paint on several boards that had been used to patch holes, and most had more than one broken window fixed with duct tape.

My mother's trailer sat at the back of the lot, just a few steps from the river behind it. Once, we'd had a freak rainstorm that had caused the river to rise up and spill across the grass toward the trailer. The shed in the back of our lot had taken the brunt of the damage and had been only partly fixed by my mom's incapable hands.

At one point her trailer must have been navy, judging by the small fleck of color that stained the cinder block below the siding. But now it was pale blue, with spots that showed its age after spending decades baking in the sun, exposed to the elements.

Mom's car was gone, but that didn't necessarily mean she wasn't home. Her boyfriend—the flavor of the month, really—could have borrowed it, or, more likely, it could've been towed. Like it often was.

I pulled into the space next to where she usually parked her car and turned off the engine, but made no move to get out.

The shutters on her trailer were missing slats and the white paint had cracked and chipped so badly that it was hard to tell which was the original color between the white and the brown that showed equally throughout.

My gaze moved to the door, which had been kicked in by more than one of her boyfriends and even by her once, in a drug-fueled craze. Duct tape had been applied haphazardly over the crack, but you could hardly see it through the screen door that was barely clinging to its hinges. Everything here was duller, like you'd stepped into a period movie, like a sepia-toned curtain had come down over every good thing there had ever been.

A movement out of the corner of my eye alerted me to my mother's neighbor's presence as she scuttled past my car and to the back, where the dilapidated shed had begun sinking into the old mud. I remembered the little old lady, who liked to dig into everyone's trash the day before the trash men came.

A recent rain shower had left puddles throughout the pock-marked lawn, and I watched as she nearly lost her balance in one such hole before pulling her foot out and moving without preamble to the trash. Many

4

mornings, I'd woken to see her white hair moving along the bottom of my bedroom window as she made that walk to our trash. I never waited to see what she found—no doubt she'd come across packs of cigarettes and drug paraphernalia at the bottom of the bag, under the moldy food and bottles holding dregs of rancid beer.

I sighed when she disappeared behind the back of the trailer, and pushed myself out of the car, stretching as I stood up, finally.

I'd driven straight here from Colorado, all because my grandfather had asked me to check on her. Not that he'd come out and said it, but his "Have you heard from your mother recently?" in his scratchy voice had told me he was concerned for her. I wondered when he could finally stop worrying about the person his spawn was growing into, and when he could just live the rest of his life in peace.

Closing the door softly, I took in the neighborhood again now that I was breathing the same air. Everything was muted, like a whisper of what it had been at one time. It was quiet—not even the squeal of a child's laughter to break the thick fog that settled over the area like it was a graveyard.

I turned back to the windows on my mother's trailer, took in the darkness behind them. It was too quiet, too dark, for her to be home.

After trying the doorknob and realizing it was locked, I reached under the bottom wooden step on the stairs and retrieved the key she kept there. I let myself in and blinked in the darkness. The light switches didn't do anything when I flicked them, which was typical of her—she probably hadn't paid the electric bill in a while.

I had a feeling then, a feeling that I should leave and tell grandpa a lie. But instead, I opened a curtain and let the light pour in before I wiped down the counter with a cleaning wipe I found under the sink. More dust than food covered the wipe and I scrunched my nose. The whole place looked like it'd barely been lived in for weeks. Not that my mother kept a neat home—far from it. But from the layer of dust that covered nearly every surface, I figured she'd been gone for a while.

I picked up the dirty clothes that littered the living room and shoved them in a basket I found by her washer and then wiped down the rest of the kitchen. I couldn't tell you why I felt it necessary to do these things other than the fact that I couldn't stand to spend more than a few minutes in such a dirty space and not do something to make it better.

I flopped onto the couch, and a second later my phone rang.

Stilling, I stared at it as it vibrated across the glass coffee table. It rolled past cigarette butts and pennies, along with some unidentifiable substances before I finally picked it up.

Seeing his name on the caller ID made my heart thud painfully in my chest.

Jude.

Gliding my fingers over his name, I debated answering it. But I couldn't. It was too soon. It had only been a day. After leaving Colorado, I stopped at a hotel for the night before waking to my grandpa's call. And now I was in my mother's dusty living room, staring at Jude's name as the phone rang in my palm for two solid vibrations before it stopped.

I set it carefully on the table, hoping he wouldn't call back.

But he did.

It was like he knew I was staring at his name as he called, as if he suspected with enough persistence I'd answer. But I wouldn't.

When the phone stopped ringing that time, I sucked in a breath and stared at it, almost wanting it to ring again.

But it didn't.

Sighing, I rubbed at the center of my chest, where the pain of leaving him hadn't dissipated. I looked out the window, at the gray that surrounded me, and wished for a different yesterday, one where truths had never needed to be defined as such, because they'd been things I'd known all along.

Colin hadn't tried to call me once, but, strangely, Mila had. I'd ignored it like I'd ignored Jude's and suddenly, I'd never felt so alone as I did right then, on my mother's garage sale couch as I looked at my many missed calls.

I set my phone down on the coffee table and stared out the window again, waiting to see the familiar tan car roll down the lane, to hear its backfire as it turned off the main drive to her corner. I remembered years of doing this, from age ten to age seventeen, waiting for my mom to come home. Most of the time, I waited with dread—watching for her arrival so I knew whether to hide from her or to embrace her and hope she would remember to love me the way I wanted her to.

I blinked away the tears that formed at the corners of my eyes. It wouldn't do, to cry tears over her neglect now. Years of listening to her endure abuse at the hands of the boyfriends she'd brought around had harvested a lot of sympathy for her, but I couldn't give in to it. She brought them back in, repeatedly, after kicking them out or calling the cops.

When I was younger and fully grasping that I didn't have a dad to rescue me, I'd tried hard to make her love me. It would sound pathetic to a lot of people, the many breakfasts in bed I'd prepared for her or the homemade cards and coupons promising to help her around the house. But nearly every breakfast in bed had ended with her too hungover to eat, and I always helped around the house without prompting because I'd been embarrassed of the condition of it while growing up. After finding maggots in one of the kitchen cupboards once, I'd decided to take care of her in the hopes that she'd take care of me too.

As I looked around the room, I saw the things I'd done for her had fallen by the wayside. It wasn't just the amount of dust, but the fact that I could curl my fingers into the carpet and come away with an ashtray's worth of ash or food crumbs. The room had an odor of smoke—of the illegal variety, mostly—and something sour, like milk spilled and not cleaned up. If I'd had more energy, I might have searched for the vacuum and a clean washcloth, but I was tired from being in the car for hours. From crying. From the constant aching, the weight in my chest that reminded me of who was waiting for me and why I couldn't go to him.

I felt betrayed that he hadn't told me about his heart condition. After I realized the gravity of his condition, and I reflected on our climbs at Yellowstone, cold ran through my veins. He could have died from over-exerting himself. And where would that have left me? I wanted to be angry that he hadn't told me what was going on between Mila and Colin, but the truth was that it wasn't his fault. And I'd been no better, kissing Jude on the roof of the apartment he shared with my then-boyfriend.

A thousand times since I left, I thought about turning around. I could have ran back to Jude, back into the arms I knew he'd hold me with. But jumping from a six-year relationship to a new one immediately wasn't healthy. I reminded myself of this every time I thought about returning.

A text blinked across my phone and I knew it was Jude.

Jude: Trista, God, I'm sorry. Please call me.

But I couldn't. And I wanted to. I wanted to, so badly. My hand had felt empty for the last twenty-four hours. And when I'd curled up on my motel bed, I wished to hear his even breaths more than anything. The aching for him was a solid presence, a burning rock in my chest.

I pressed delete, knowing I would only taunt myself by looking at it when I was feeling weak.

I must have fallen asleep on the threadbare couch, because the next thing I knew, the screen door was slamming with a racket loud enough to rock me off the couch.

It'd only been a month since I'd seen her, but my mother looked different. She was thinner, the skin in her cheeks sagging in the cavities below them. Her blue eyes were red-rimmed and her hair was greasy and limp, recently dyed blonde. An at-home job, judging by the way it stopped halfway down some strands, and by the varying shades throughout her hair.

"Look what the cat dragged in," she drawled, a cigarette hanging from the corner of her cracked lips.

I pushed my hair away from my face. "Grandpa asked me to check in on you. He hasn't heard from you in a while."

She laughed, but it sounded like a cackle and it set my jaw on edge. "My old man is having my daughter do his dirty work?" She flipped the light switch, bathing the room in yellow light.

I blinked. "I thought your power was out."

After sucking in on her cigarette she gave me a once-over. "I was out paying the bill." She sniffed and rubbed a hand under her nose. "Don't judge me, Trista. You left me here alone."

As I watched her, I wondered what she had expected of me. For me to stay with her, long term, supporting her as she wasted her life being a slave to her many vices? "I'm not judging you, Mom. I was just surprised." She was slouched as she stood by the door, facing me just a few feet away. She had a curve to her back from an accident she'd been in years before, and it always struck me how very fragile she was.

"I thought you moved to Colorado," she said casually as she dropped a plastic grocery bag in the chair by the door.

I hadn't really moved; it'd been more of a stopping place before I knew what my plans were. I wasn't sure how to explain that, so I just shrugged and stepped into the kitchen to run the dishwasher I'd filled earlier. "I haven't settled anywhere just yet."

"You did the dishes?"

I nodded and grabbed a can of soda from the fridge.

"You're not better than me," she said, stepping around the connecting island that separated the tiny kitchen from the living room. "Don't forget it."

Flicking my fingernail on the soda tab, I said, "I never said I was. I just did some light cleaning to help you out."

I met her gaze, seeing as she peered at me, looking me up and down. "You're getting fat," she finally said, poking me in the stomach.

Flinching back, I ground my teeth together. "I'm perfectly healthy," I told her, not really believing it. It'd been so easy to see my flaws when they were reflected in my mother's eyes. I hadn't realized until now, as I stood on her sticky vinyl floor, just how easily influenced I was by her. I'd always wanted to make her proud, to make her happy to have me as her daughter. I worked so hard to make her see me, that sometimes I sucked up the criticisms she gave me because at least she was giving me attention. At least she was acknowledging my presence, as troublesome as it was for her.

"Did that boy dump you for gaining your spare tire?"

I would not touch my stomach and come away with loathing, I told myself. I hadn't ever been in love with the body that carried me through life, but in the last week, I'd learned to respect it. For what it endured, from the mountain climbing to the heartache. Even if my insides shook under the trauma I'd delivered it, my skin still held me together. I couldn't hate the body that Jude had loved, I told myself.

"You don't have any food in your fridge," I said instead of answering her question. "Do you need groceries?"

Her eyes took on a twinkle and I wished I'd said anything else. "Why, got some cash burning a hole in your pocket?"

"No." I thought of the backpack with grandpa's cigar box. "But I can pick you up some dinner if you want."

She eyed me carefully. I could sense she was deciding what to do with the little bit of knowledge I'd given her. Finally, she said, "Sure. Athen's Pizza has a deal right now—free breadsticks with a large pizza."

Athen's Pizza was nearby, but because it was a mom-and-pop style business short on employees, the service was slow. Which meant I'd have enough time away from her to breathe. "Okay."

"And get me a six-pack. Not the cheap stuff, since you're buying."

I closed my eyes briefly before giving her a smile that didn't reach my eyes and slinging my backpack over my shoulder. "I'll be back," I told her on my way out the door.

When I was younger, grandpa would slip me money here and there—to help pay for my school lunches when my mom hadn't been grocery shopping in a while. It had continued into high school, when he'd slipped me money for school supplies and new clothes when my jeans had begun to climb to my calves. My mother had never been a provider except for the roof over our heads, and even that had been in jeopardy more than once.

And I'd learned after the first time she found my cache of twenties to hide them in separate places. So if she found one hiding place, she wouldn't find them all. I'd hidden money in a pillow that I'd opened along the seam, in textbooks and in *Jane Eyre*, under the mattress, inside an empty hairspray bottle, and had even safety-pinned money on the inside of my curtains. She often found one of my hiding places, but the cost was usually just a couple bucks here and there. I knew better than to keep money on myself.

So, as if I had an ominous premonition, I shoved a stack of bills in my car's glove box and then slipped a few under the frame that held a photo of Ellie and me. A smarter person would leave and not return, but I always felt obligated to provide for her like she was the child and I was the parent.

I hid a good amount of money around my car and left just a thousand in the cigar box in my backpack just in case. After tucking a few more twenties in the back pocket of my jeans, I pulled into the grocery store first and grabbed her some essentials—milk and bread and cheese and bananas. I'd lived on that exact diet for several years, so I knew it would do for my mom.

When I returned with the pizza, there was an unfamiliar car in the parking space I'd occupied before. I stared at it uneasily as my car ticked after turning it off. I wondered who it could be, but resigned myself to spending at least dinner with my mom before leaving to see grandpa.

The sounds of laughter and a deep masculine voice caused my skin to prickle. The hair on the back of my neck stood as I paused at the threshold into the house. The voice was familiar, but not in a way that was welcome.

Pushing open the door, my eyes met my mom's first and I took in their glossy state. She'd tied her hair back, but a few tendrils had escaped and were now plastered against her face. When I turned my head, my upper body broke out in a sweat.

My mother had had many boyfriends over the years, many of them repeats—the kind of people you wouldn't close your eyes around. And sitting beside her on the sofa with a smug expression on his face as he took me in was Doug, the biggest douchebag I'd ever known.

I'd first met Doug when I was twelve and he had asked me when my boobs would grow in, sharing a laugh with my mom over it. She'd dumped him months later after a broken nose, but he'd come back a couple years later, with a bag full of gutter glitter for my mom to suck up her nose. He'd been a cocaine dealer then, and had first gotten my mom hooked on it even though she couldn't afford it. When he'd come back around when I was sixteen, he'd said selling was too risky so he just used instead. And he'd asked me then, after several lewd glances, if my boobs were real or toilet paper stuffed into a bra.

He was the kind of guy who made you want to take sandpaper to your skin, just to slough off the way his eyes slid over you like you were there for his benefit.

He stood and used both of his hands to smooth back the thinning comb-over. "There she is," he crooned. I gripped the grocery bag tighter, remembering all the times he'd brushed up against me just to intimidate me. Each time, I'd had to swallow bile. "Your mom said you were out getting us pizza."

I could do this. I could drop off the pizza and groceries and walk out of here, without a care in the whole world. Preparing to do just that, I turned into the kitchen and set the bag down.

"Whatcha got there, Sunshine?" he asked on his approach. My back tightened, like I was bracing myself to be hit by a car, but he stopped just next to me in the kitchen and peered into the grocery bag. He reeked of some kind of heavy cologne and I leaned away to keep him from suffocating me with it.

"Just some food for Mom." I dropped the pizza on the counter, ignoring the growl of my stomach over the pizza's smell. "I have to go now," I said with less conviction than I felt. Doug made me shaky, from my voice down to my tingly feet.

"Why go now? Come on," he said, lowering his voice and sliding closer next to me. I trained my eyes on the gold flecks in the cheap countertop. "I brought some snow. Wanna do a line?"

"No," I said firmly, backing away. Unfortunately, that caused me to back right up into the counter. "I'm not interested." My stomach flip-flopped when he came closer, trapping me up against the corner of the kitchen.

"Don't be such a party pooper, girl." His voice was like velvet suffocation, and I searched for a way to get away from him.

"I really have to go, Doug." I put my hand in my front pocket, feeling for the sharp grooves of my key, deciding to use it if I really needed to.

"I don't think you do." With one hand, he clamped on my wrist and yanked my arm up out of my pocket. Before I could react, he used his other hand to grab my keys from me and then immediately shoved them down the front of his pants.

The shudder rocked me to my toes. I knew what he was doing, the game he was playing. He'd put me in a difficult position and I wished, fiercely, to have the courage to punch him where the keys were, in the hopes that they'd cut his dick.

And I could, easily. He was inches from me. But I remembered the black eyes my mother had worn and poorly hidden under caked makeup. Doug wasn't afraid to hit a woman unprovoked. I didn't need to provoke him when he had the keys to my only means of escape.

So I just stood there, pinned against the counter by a man who revolted me, trying to think of a way out. I had to get my keys back. I couldn't leave my car, and all the money inside, to Doug.

"Knock it off, Doug. I want to go." I realized I'd left my backpack with my cell phone inside my locked car, and I was truly trapped then. Fear blanketed me, but I didn't want Doug to see me sweat. It would only excite him.

"After dinner, you can go."

I shoved him, to give myself space to breathe, but he remained steadfast, pressed against me. "Seriously. Let me go." I tried to force strength into my voice, but the truth was, with his hips pressed up against me, I was feeling whatever power I had slip away.

"What else do you have?" he asked in a voice that was probably meant to sound seductive, but all it sounded like to me was danger. He pressed a hand against the front pocket where my keys had been before curling his fingers into the opening of the pocket. Immediately, he shoved his hand into my pocket and felt around, coming dangerously close to the apex of my thighs. My legs jumped then, and a cold sweat prickled my back.

I fought against him, knowing his game, and shoved against him with a frenetic energy that surged through my veins. When he moved far enough to give me space, I stepped away from the counter and tried to move around him, but—once again, before I could react—he spun me around and put his hands in the back pockets of my jeans as I was bent painfully over the counter, the hard edge pressing against my rib cage. Wincing, I bit my lip to keep from hollering out. I pushed away from the counter, trying to free myself, but he had at least a hundred pounds of muscle on me and so my struggle was fruitless.

Droplets of sweat gathered along my forehead, and I bit down harder on my lip to keep from crying. I never felt as powerless as I did when someone larger and stronger than me pinned me like I was nothing.

His fingers curled in the pocket, a grope that was sexual enough to make me want to vomit. I looked over my shoulder and glared at him with all the anger I could manage to pull into my eyes.

"There it is," he said happily as he came away with money. With one hand, he squeezed my ass while he smelled the money with his other hand.

After delivering an elbow to his chest, he backed away enough for me to move away from the corner and I sucked in a breath.

I said a hundred swear words in my head, feeling so fucking stupid for letting Doug take advantage of me. "Give it back," I said, sweat dripping into my eyes.

"Nah, I don't think I will." He gave me a grin that was more violating than his hands had ever been. "You're welcome to some powder," he gestured toward the living room, like he was some game show model gesturing to the grand prize vacation in Maui.

"I'll pass," I said bitterly, wrapping my arms over my chest. Internally, I was screaming. How had I let him take such control over me so quickly? A glance at the couch showed my mom to be smiling with her head dropped back on the couch cushion. She was completely oblivious to what had happened.

I took a deep breath, swallowing the lump in my throat as I watched Doug count the bills he'd taken from my pockets. I'd put myself in this position, at the mercy of a man who was merciless, with not a single person in the world to help me, to defend me. It was a very lonely reality, and I wished—not for the first time—for Jude to be at my side.

"Come on, girl. Relax. Look at your mom—look how content she is."

I didn't believe that a child of a drug-addicted parent could easily live through the damage inflicted upon them and then decide to become a slave to the drugs themselves, too. I had not an ounce of desire to ever try anything my mother snorted up her nose or lit with her lighter. And after Ellie, well, I was in no hurry to be under the influence of any illegal substance.

"Fuck off, Doug," I said, hoping the venom would mask the fear. But I could feel the way my throat trembled.

"Ah, sweetheart. You wish." He grabbed his crotch and made a lewd gesture before I looked away, clenching my jaw. I didn't want him to see how he affected me—he got off on that sort of thing.

"Give me my money back."

"No can do. Your mom owes me money."

I curled my lip. "Take it from her, then."

He stepped toward me, which caused me to step back. I hated this, hated showing my vulnerability to him. "You know as well as I do that she doesn't have it. So it's take it from you or take it out on her."

I knew what he meant by that. The bruising on his knuckles was reminder enough, and I had purple-colored memories of the many times I'd heard my mother scream, and even sharper memories of all the times I'd hidden.

And so, as a repentance of my past fear, I sucked up the fact that I'd have a few hundred less in my pocket. It wasn't my fault that my mom leeched on to abusive drug pushers, but I didn't have to ignore the pain she brought on herself.

As I stared at her, eyes closed and a dreamy smile playing on her lips, I wondered how the hell she had gotten here. A man had loved her and then left her and now she eschewed meaningful personal relationships in favor of a chemical reaction with a powder. I thought of my grandparents, of their steadiness, and wondered how she had curled from that to this.

"What kind of pizza did you get us?"

I hated the connotation of the word *us* when it slithered from his mouth. As far as I was concerned, there was no us. There was my mom and me, and in the same room happened to be the scumbag who had stolen from me.

"Pepperoni," I spat, rubbing along my rib where it had been pressed against the counter. I knew I'd have a bruise soon.

"That's boring," he said mildly, lifting the lid and closing his eyes as he inhaled the scent. Everything he did made me shudder with loathing. He grabbed a slice anyway and then eyed me for a plate. "This shirt's expensive," he said with a laugh, like I knew what that was like. My clothes had holes and I hadn't purchased anything that wasn't used in years. "Don't want to get grease all over it."

I handed him a plate and then walked past him to the bathroom. I needed to prepare myself to spend time with him and my mother.

The water was ice cold as I splashed my face with it, and my hands cramped from its coldness. I flexed them into fists and squeezed even harder when I heard my mother's laugh from the living room. She was so near-sighted to her own life that she couldn't see her maybe-boyfriend/definitely-drug dealer in the kitchen groping her daughter. But with a sick twist in my stomach, I knew she wouldn't have done anything anyway.

My mother was team herself, first and foremost. And she wouldn't lift a finger to help me if it didn't benefit her.

I turned the water to warm to help the abating cramping and let my hands just relax under the running water. The sink was dirty, with hairs and dust and grime clinging to its entire surface. I thought to wipe it down, like I had done with the kitchen, but I didn't want to lift another finger for my mother, not after having just paid for the high she was experiencing.

My time in the bathroom took longer than necessary, just so I could avoid being face to face with Doug again.

I looked at myself in the mirror, at the way my hair hung lifeless on each side of my face. I didn't look like her—I had all the parts that belonged to the person she'd loved before she'd had me. Who had he been? By all accounts, my mother hadn't been such a degenerate until she'd had me. She'd been with someone who had seen who she was and loved her—what had he loved about her? And why had he left her?

For years, I'd wanted to ask my grandfather about him. But I never had, and he was probably the last person I could ask. I wasn't sure of who my mom was before me, but I got the impression that her relationship with my grandparents—her parents—had been strained. I wanted to know the history behind my brown eyes, behind my pale skin. I wanted to feel a sense of belonging, in the hopes that maybe I'd understand who I was.

I dropped a fist to the counter. I'd left Jude to find out who I was, with no plans for how to do that. I just knew I needed to do what my grandfather had told me to do, to find an adventure and chase it.

Sucking in a breath, I held it in my chest for a second before I let it go. I'd need all the patience in the world to deal with the two people who were likely devouring my pizza in the living room beyond the door.

My mother was still on the couch, her head still tipped back. Her smile was soft, her eyes dreamy, and if I hadn't seen the same look on her face at least a hundred times in the last twenty years, I might've marveled how . . . soft . . . she looked. My mother was not a soft woman.

Doug saw me before she did and patted the seat beside him on the sofa, where his arm was draped over the back of the headrest.

Ignoring him, I sat in one of the seventies-style chairs across from him. There was only enough room for me in this chair, which would prevent him from inviting himself to sit beside me.

"You know you want some," Doug said when I looked across the paraphernalia littering the coffee table.

Without looking at him, I said, "I definitely don't. All I want is my keys."

He sighed and the couch creaked under him as he settled deeper in it. "Well, that can wait. Your mom says you haven't been around in a while. Don't be an ungrateful bitch, and try to spend some time with her before you flit off again."

That got me to look at him, which I did with a burr under my skin. "I'm an ungrateful bitch?" I asked, knowing my voice sounded shrill and angry. "I bought her groceries and dinner, and you stole my money and my keys. How does that make me 'ungrateful' in your eyes?"

There was a glint in Doug's eyes. He was entertained by seeing how he successfully weaseled under my skin. "Your mother hasn't heard from you in a month. She's been worried."

"Funny." I crossed my arms and sat back in the chair. "She hasn't said any of that to me."

Doug picked up a joint off the coffee table and held it out to me. There was dirt under his nails and his cuticles were overgrown. When I shook my head, he shrugged as if to say, "Suit yourself," before he lit it and sucked on it. He had a grocery store of drugs he carried with him everywhere, so seeing the coke, pills, and marijuana didn't surprise me. But it did surprise me that he let my mom snort the coke without taking some himself.

I looked back up at him. "What did you give her?" I asked with a nod to my mom.

He smiled, the lines around his mouth deepening. But he didn't answer me, just rolled the joint in his fingers.

That was possibly the most infuriating thing about him—he kept his words to himself, knowing I wanted an answer. He was baiting me, trying to get me to talk. I was just another person to prey on, another one to torment.

"She's been talking to me the last few weeks," he said after a loud exhale. "This is some good shit. Sure you don't want some?" He held it up again and I shook my head adamantly. "And she's told me that you went chasing your boyfriend. How'd that work out for you?"

I wouldn't give in, I told myself. Not to him, not about Colin. Doug hadn't been around when I'd started dating Colin, not that it would've mattered because I'd never have brought Colin around anyway. "Can I just have my goddamn keys?"

He patted his package and smiled with the side of his mouth, revealing his yellowing teeth. "They're all yours."

No matter how many times I told myself to calm down around him, to not let him see that he was affecting me, the longer I was in the house the more I wanted to scour my skin with a copper scrubber. I knew I'd reek of smoke and dirt long after I left.

I needed to get out of this fucking house.

In a split second, I grabbed the bag of buds and held it up. "Give me my keys or I'll flush these."

Doug's mouth set in a line and fear made my resolve waver at the way his eyes darkened. "You flush those and I'll be finding other ways to get more money—" his eyes slid down my body "—or use out of you."

I was going to call his bluff. It was probably stupid. Okay, it was *definitely* stupid. But I backed up toward the bathroom anyway.

I hadn't gone more than a few feet when he was on his feet and advancing on me. Before I could turn around and run into the bathroom, he'd grabbed me and slammed me against the wall that separated the living area from the bathroom. My shoulder blades had twin bursts of pain and I exhaled from the shock of hitting the wall.

My head bounced off of a frame before it fell behind me, the sharp corner landing on my ankle bone.

"Stupid, worthless, fat bitch," he spat in my face as he wrenched the baggie from my hands. I slapped his hand away from where he held me firmly against the wall, but his hand moved up to my neck and he wrapped his calloused fingers around it. "Don't," he hissed, flecks of saliva hitting me in the face, "tempt me, girl."

The thing that made the guys my mom hung around scary was how unpredictable they were. But Doug was another story—I knew he meant what he said. I knew he could inflict pain upon me if I pushed him further.

Over Doug's shoulder, my mom was slowly moving each shoulder up and down to a silent beat, one only she heard. Her yellow, frizzy hair looked like she'd spent time shoving forks into outlets and her shirt was slipping over her shoulder.

"Let me go, Doug," I said, realizing I had to play this safe. My mom wasn't in any shape to shield me from Doug's violent side, and Doug had my means to escape shoved down his pants. I could run, sure, but then I'd leave behind my entire life in my car.

He leaned in, his face inches from me. Body odor and something sour engulfed my nostrils. "Don't fuck with me," he said, giving me a squeeze strong enough to show me he was serious about inflicting pain on me before he let go and stalked away.

20

I sunk down the wall until I was crouched and let my knees splay out in front of me. Doug poured vodka as I tried to figure out how to get my keys from him without actually touching him. My phone was locked in my car, and over and over, I cursed myself for not running sooner. For not dropping off the food and taking off. I was stuck, in this stale room with my mom and her drug pusher.

Not for the first time, I clenched my fist and thought of Jude. If I closed my eyes, I could almost imagine him holding my hand.

So I did.

CHAPTER THREE

I opened my eyes and sucked in a breath at the same moment. Something loud had woken me. The room was dark and I blinked several times, adjusting my sight. That's when I heard it.

A grunt, a slap of skin, the sound of things rolling off of the coffee table and their soft thud when they fell to the carpet. I curled my fingers into the carpet underneath me, feeling its fibers in my nails. I wanted to remain quiet, but I didn't want to be in the same room as my mother when she was having sex with Doug. I knew, without sight, that's what was happening. I could've placed those sounds anywhere.

Quietly, I rolled to my side so I could push myself off the floor. Over the coffee table, I saw them. There was low light washing across the crusty carpet, stopping when it reflected on my mom's face. Her eyelids were half open, but all you could see were the whites of her eyes and the splash of purple that circled one of them—a souvenir from Doug. The way her body moved against the carpet despite the lack of movement in her face was eerie, and a tingle prickled my skin as I moved my gaze down her body. My mother was lying on her stomach, and her pants were pulled down. Doug was slamming into her, over and over.

I blinked several times, trying to comprehend what I was seeing. I'd assumed my mom had been awake, an active participant, but she looked completely unconscious. Her mouth was open, but her face was still.

Her hands were lying, lifeless, on the carpet at her sides. She wasn't awake. She barely looked alive.

My mouth tasted of vomit when it hit me: Doug was raping my mother. Stunned, I stepped back, bumping into the loveseat so hard that I fell into it. The room bounced in my vision. My gaze shot to Doug, but he was still moving as if he hadn't seen me. I was in the dark corner of the room, a place that suddenly felt safe. I'd never felt safe in my mother's house, and right now was no exception.

Beside Doug, I saw my keys. I could grab them. I could run.

I was a coward, I knew.

It made me ill to even think it—because I was witnessing Doug violating my mother while she was unconscious. I couldn't run from this—not a chance in hell. Who did it make me, if I left my mother at his mercy?

Over and over, he slammed into her, his stringy hair stuck to his face with sweat dripping down his neck. His greasy hair was shiny from the light that shone on it from behind him. He looked like he hadn't bathed in weeks. And he was violating my mother.

If I could rewrite the dictionary, I'd put his photo next to the definition for "repulsive." Frantically, I searched for something to stop him. Words with Doug would not do. If I spoke, if I alerted him to my presence, I didn't know what he'd do. I'd have to stoop to his level.

I saw the bottle of vodka on the floor and scooted down to the other end of the couch slowly, hoping the movement wouldn't alert him to me.

Fear made my throat thick and my chest tight as I slid off the couch to the floor and crawled to the bottle directly in front of me. When my fingers curled around its neck, I let the coolness of it ground me. Fear may have made me quiet, but it wouldn't make me placid. I moved farther to the side so that Doug's back was to me before I stood, my bony knees wobbling like I was a child taking her first steps. But I took them. One, and then another, and another, until I was directly behind Doug.

I lifted the bottle, intending to hit the back of his head. But just as

I brought the bottle up, I saw the shadow I was casting over his back, spilling to my mother's. I froze in fear, felt sweat slide down my spine.

He turned just as I brought the bottle down and instinctively reached a hand up to block me.

"What the fuck?" he growled, hitting my forearm hard enough to knock me off balance and to knock the bottle from my grip. I fell forward but reached a hand out to break my fall as my knees hit the carpet.

"What the fuck, Trista?" he repeated louder as I frantically reached for the dropped bottle.

Everything from that point happened quickly.

He grabbed my hair and pulled me forward to him. Unwillingly, my hands moved quickly toward him as I crawled across the carpet, trying to relieve the sharp bite of pain in my scalp from where he pulled my hair taut. He twisted his arm, causing me to roll over to my back beneath him. His jeans were open, and he reeked of sweat and sex. My stomach rolled but I couldn't lose focus, so I fought against his grip as he was upside down in my vision.

"Let go," I yelled, clawing at his hands with my nails. I dug in, hard enough to feel the pressure in my nail beds, and his hold on me relaxed enough that I moved my head completely away from him. The bottle glinted just inches from me. I quickly turned around and crawled to it before I felt his hand wrap around my leg and pull me back.

Raw, hot desperation snaked through me as I watched the bottle get smaller in my focus. Doug was strong, much stronger than I was. And he was pissed.

"You thought you'd hit me with that?" he asked behind me as I tried in vain to shake my leg from his grip. He yanked hard and my stomach slid across the carpet with a burn as my shirt lifted beneath me, exposing my skin to the fibers. I winced from the pain but didn't give in to it.

I felt myself being flipped to my back, where I came face to face with him. I refused to look away from his face, because out of my periphery I could see his undone pants and the blur of skin that hung there. The way he pinned me scared me, and I felt the shake in my bones.

His hands clamped on my shins as he climbed over me, his weight pushing me in the ground. I watched his eyes slide over me, resting on the exposed skin of my stomach, and I quickly tugged my shirt down.

"You think I'm going to fuck you?" he asked, his voice raspy and his hands clamped on my hips. I bucked, trying to get away, but he was too strong. Saliva pooled in my mouth and my stomach revolted. His fingers were inches from the edge of my jeans. "You're too fat for me."

I wouldn't give him power, I told myself. I reached my hands out, in search of something to hit him with. My fingers clawed the carpet, my nails filling with all the gunk that had never seen the inside of a vacuum. I realized how an insect caught in a spider's web might feel, watching a predator advance upon them.

He was straddling me, his knees on either side of my thighs. He leaned over me, bringing his face close. A drop of his sweat dripped on my neck at the same time as my hands grasped something heavy and I lifted it, successfully hitting him over the head this time. Whatever it was, it was made of glass, and as it broke in my hand, pieces rained all down me. I turned my head to keep it from my eyes and mouth as I dropped the shards I held in my palm.

A grunt came from him before he slumped forward, his head landing hard on my chest. But he wasn't out cold, and his fingers dug painfully hard into my hips. I wrestled under him, trying to free myself, but he lifted his head and his hands at the same time, grabbing my shoulders even as I writhed desperately for escape. His fingers brushed my neck in my thrashing, but landed on my shoulders, pressing right into the space above my collarbone.

The entire time, I'd been fighting him away from me, but I hadn't felt true fear for my life until his thumbs pressed hard, right down onto bone. I knew it was seconds away from snapping.

Suddenly, everything started hitting me: his weight on my waist, his rancid breath as he let out shudders above me, his smell, and the way I kicked my legs in vain. The way the broken glass between us pressed against my skin from the pressure of him on top of me.

I forced myself to think, even as I considered giving up. But I'd pissed him off enough that I knew giving up would mean something devastating for me.

"Stop!" I screamed, but it came out of a voice box that felt broken. "Stop!" I screamed it over and over until my voice lost its power. I started beating on his chest, his neck, his face—anywhere I could touch. My movements were fueled by panic and frustration, hitting, scratching, pulling. I did everything I could think of in that space of just a few seconds to free myself.

Pain bloomed from my knuckles, but I kept hitting. Blow by blow, I felt the impact knock back in through my hands, the jarring of it all vibrating up my arm and into my elbows. I felt myself growing weaker, and bit down to keep from giving up.

When my fists weren't doing what I wanted, I grabbed his hands on my collarbone and used my fingers to pull his thumb back in a direction it wasn't meant to bend. It relieved a little pressure from the force he was applying and I breathed in as the pain replaced his hands on my shoulders, but then he gripped my jaw, squeezing tight enough that I saw white spots in my vision. I reached out, clawing whatever skin I came in contact with, and choked on the air that filled my lungs.

Holding my jaw, he lifted my head and then slammed it back to the floor. The white spots in my vision grew into stars, large stars, as I was completely stunned by it.

Again and again, he lifted my head and slammed it to the floor. I knew I was seconds away from blacking out. Each time he lifted my head, I could feel myself losing my grip on reality. When he delivered a punch right to my face, I heard a crack by my inner eyelid and then his weight was off of me.

I sucked in a breath, but it wasn't complete—it came out in a stutter and I choked on it. Tears pooled in the eye he'd hit, so thick that it blurred my vision entirely. Pain spread through my face and I struggled to breathe one deep breath without wanting to die from the pain in my collarbone, my jaw, and my eye. It felt like my eye was being repeatedly pricked by a needle, over and over, like the entire area had fallen asleep.

In the background, I heard him moving around and coughing. I knew I should move, but I was so frozen by the pain that I couldn't.

I was still seeing spots when my head dropped to the side, and I blinked with my good eye at what I saw. Doug was in the kitchen, leaning over the sink, splashing water onto his head. As my eyes moved down, I caught the glint of something shiny on the carpet.

My keys.

He turned off the faucet and I made my move, rolling to my stomach and crawling to the keys. I blinked over and over, realizing that I couldn't see out of one eye, and the one eye I could see out of was still registering spots all over the place.

I wrapped my fingers around the key ring just as I saw his steps meet the spot where carpet changed to vinyl. Pulling myself to standing, I kept my eye on him the whole time as he watched me.

I opened my mouth to make noise, but nothing came. Coughing seemed to produce some sound, and I held up my keys. "Don't come near me," I said, wishing my voice sounded less shaky, less raspy. I curled my fingers around the ring, feeling—for the first time since I woke up on the floor—safe.

He ignored me, taking one step forward. I looked out to my side at the door before looking back at him.

"I'm not fucking kidding," I said, spit flying out of my mouth.

"Why? So you can run to the cops?" He shook his head and stalked toward me.

His gait was fast, but freedom was within reach, so I lifted my hand and brought the sharp side of the keys down across his face when he grabbed my forearm.

And then I ran, wrenching the front door open and stumbling down the steps like I was drunk, to my car.

My hands were shaking, but I managed to shove the key into the lock and slide into the seat.

When I looked up, he was standing in the doorway of the trailer. His eyes were blazing as I slammed the car door and he staggered down the steps.

I did the only thing I could think to do: I pressed hard on the car's horn. He stopped moving and looked around.

That was the thing about my mom's trailer park—it may have been full of convicts and questionable characters, but all of them loved a good show.

I laid on the horn, over and over, knowing that people would be woken up by the noise and look out their windows or come outside. And then I started the car.

He made a move toward me again, but the car was locked. I was safe.

So I peeled out of the drive and drove out of the trailer park, not even slowing down for all the potholes.

I debated doing it, but knowing the mood I'd left Doug in, I knew I couldn't leave my mom alone. So I called the local dispatch and informed them of drug activity and violence at her address before hanging up.

And then I pulled over and screamed. A tsunami of emotion overcame me, and I pressed my hands to my head as tears flowed from my eyes and sobs wracked my throat. A ballad roared on the radio, somehow louder than my cries, and I wailed along to my own lyrics, creating a mashup with the female singer's lament about losing her lover.

CHAPTER FOUR

I drove for forty minutes before I'd pulled enough glass off my face and my hair and my neck to fill my ashtray. After stopping at a gas station near the interstate, I dropped the visor to get a good look at my face.

The first thing I saw was blood. I hadn't even realized he'd cut me when he'd punched me in the face. It was a small cut by my inner eye, but I knew from experience with my mother that head wounds bled badly, even when the damage was minimal. I reached into my backpack and grabbed wet wipes, running them just under the cut and down my face. My left eye was bloodshot, and I knew from driving that while I'd been able to keep the eyelid open, my vision was spotty at best. Gently probing the skin around the eye yielded sharp pain, and I dropped the wet wipe in reaction. There were little nicks across my skin, what I guessed to be from the glass that had shattered in my hand. I pulled a speck of glass from my eyelashes and scratched against some of the blood that had dried around my face. I couldn't go into the gas station looking like I'd walked away from a car accident, so I put my hair up in a ponytail, wincing as pieces of glass fell from my strands to my back. The skin around my jaw was tender, and my collarbone felt like someone had tried to squeeze me flat. But other than the bloodshot eye and the cut near my nose, I looked okay enough to buy a water bottle, ice, and the biggest bottle of ibuprofen they had.

As I exited my car, I felt the trembles take me over. I'd indulged in a crying and screaming fit in my car for a couple minutes before I'd gotten back on the road and continued on. Everything north of my waist was in pain, from where he'd sat on my rib cage to where he'd slammed the back of my head onto the floor. I knew I could have a concussion, so while I was in the gas station bathroom I searched on my phone for a motel nearby. I'd need to pay cash, because I didn't own a card, so a shoddy motel was it for me.

After paying for my purchases, I returned to my car and picked out the glass that had collected in my seat. I filled up the tank and then continued on, holding a cold water bottle to my neck as I drove.

The motel was tucked off the highway, with a light that blinked on and off by the entrance. A neon open sign glittered in the dark, missing a bulb behind the *n*. There were a few people hanging out in the plastic lawn furniture by the reception area, but I didn't even glance at them as I stepped inside and paid for my room.

"Can I have a room in the back?" I asked the attendant, motioning with my hand to the space around the building. "For two days?"

She pushed her headband up and back, not even looking me over once. I was grateful for her lack of curiosity at the moment, knowing I'd need to hole up and ice my hands and my face to keep my swelling at bay before I continued on.

To . . . where? I stared at the plaques on the wall above her head as she wrote my information down, the sounds of some pop station bleeding out of the radio on the counter beside her. Her fingernails were rainbow-colored and decorated with black tiger-like stripes across them. Her skin was unmarred, and every strand on her head was in its place. I couldn't help but compare myself to her, with the blood under my fingernails and the bruises I knew lay in wait under my skin.

Even the way she held on to the counter as she reached behind her for the key cards was graceful, like a dance she'd practiced a hundred times. I wanted to cry watching her slide the key card because she did everything with a smooth sense of confidence. A confidence I envied.

She handed me the room key and rattled off the pertinent information about checkout times and then I pulled my car behind the building and parked several spaces away from my room.

More than once, my mother and I had run away to a motel like this one. She'd sat at a table by the window, cigarette in one hand and the other hand on the curtain as she peeled it back, waiting for someone to find her, find us.

The room was unremarkable, standard for what little I'd paid. I yanked the old floral bedspread off the bed, and grabbed the ice bucket and the cooler I'd brought in from my car.

Once I'd returned to the room with a full cooler and full ice bucket, I turned off all the lights in the bedroom and stepped into the bathroom.

My reflection looked like me still, but it looked like a me who had fallen down a dozen flights of stairs. I hunched my shoulders and then immediately stopped when the pain in my collarbone became too much. I turned my head but realized my eye struggled to follow the line of sight. Sighing, I stepped into the shower and laid my head against the tile as water rained down my back.

I thought I'd cried my last tear on the side of the road when I'd pulled over and screamed, but I was wrong. As the water poured over me, over all the places Doug had held me, hurt me, it was like feeling his touch all over again.

Unwittingly, an image of me doing this just weeks earlier blipped into my head. After Jude had kissed me on the roof, I'd climbed into the shower and tried to wash myself of it.

And that's what caused me to cry as the water pounded my skin. Because Jude's touch had been good, and beautiful. And Doug's had been the opposite. I tried to remember the weight of Jude's hands on me, the heaviness of his gaze in my eyes. But all I saw was Doug.

And that's what caused me to cry even harder—Doug's touch had erased the good kind of touch from my skin.

I let out a growl, both to get me to stop crying and in frustration, as I dragged the rough washcloth over my skin, rubbing it raw at my shoulders.

My hands cramped from the movement, a reminder of how I'd hit Doug. I stared at them, marveling at how the same hands that Jude had cradled in his had hit with such violence.

I wasn't a violent person. It didn't run in me like it ran in those who were born to be cruel. But Doug had brought it out in me, had tainted the skin that had touched Jude and then I roared, wrapping my arms around myself to keep me safe from any more violence.

I didn't remember shampooing my hair, but I knew I'd done it because as I toweled it dry, it smelled like flowers and cigarettes. My mother's house still clung to my skin, which meant Doug's touch did too.

I wrapped myself with one towel, but it was too small. I thought of Doug's words, about me being useless, fat, as I wrapped a second towel around the side that gaped.

Rationally, I knew I shouldn't pay any mind to what he said. He was an abuser, with his words and his actions, and he was worthless to me.

But there was a part of me that had lain dormant in my soul when I'd been with Jude, a part that fed off of criticism. A benign piece of my ugliness that took what Doug said and sucked it inside of myself.

I changed into pajamas before lying down in the dark, ice wrapped in towels on my face and chest, and under my hands.

And I wished for Jude.

I smelled the juniper first—that fresh little bite. I greedily inhaled it, letting out a sigh immediately after I'd had my fill. Opening my eyes, I met his brown ones, and the corners crinkled in concern.

"Are you okay?"

I swallowed. "Yes." I wanted to touch his face, feel the prickle of his beard against my palm. But my arms were heavy with fatigue, so I could do nothing but lie there as he looked me over.

"You're a terrible liar," he said, one side of his mouth lifted in a smile that was heavier with sadness than it was with humor.

"I'm not the only one," I said, immediately regretting uttering the words. "I'm sorry."

"Don't," he hushed me, closing his eyes and shaking his head. I was mesmerized by the way his lashes lay against his lower eyelids when he closed his eyes. He opened them and looked into mine. "I'm sorry. I should've—"

"Shh." It was my turn to hush him. "I don't want to talk about should'ves."

"What about would'ves?" The half-smile was back, and I was so grateful that I felt it pull on my chest.

I shook my head but it hurt. "Not those either. Let's talk about the now."

His smile slipped away. "But you're not ready."

That word. That stupid, five-lettered word. He wasn't wrong, but I wished he were. "I will be."

His eyes closed halfway, a wrinkle forming between his brows. "I know." He reached to touch me and I strained against the invisible weight that kept me in the bed, but it was useless. His hand stopped, inches from my face.

I begged him to touch me, to erase the violence that marked my skin. I wasn't sure if one kind touch could eliminate another born of violence, but I was willing to try. Anything to feel him again.

His eyes bored into mine, their steadiness calming me and putting my heart at ease. I opened my mouth to ask him to hold me, but nothing came from my lips.

And then I realized with a start that it was all a dream. I stared at the popcorn ceiling in my motel room as the weight of everything overcame me, slowly making my body something foreign to me as the pain radiated in my knuckles and my shoulders and face. My tears came again, white hot as they slid down bruised skin and dripped into my ears, soaking my hairline.

I was alone. There was no Jude here to keep me safe. It was just me, in this cold, dark room. I rolled over in my bed and wrote something to remind me of this moment. But I knew I wouldn't forget what it felt like, to feel hate upon your skin.

The violence inflicted
upon my skin was not unlike
every negative thing
I've thought about myself.
But this time it was a manifestation;
something I could see in a mirror,
something I could touch,
something that reminded me,
with each painful step,
with each stiff lift of my head,
and with every solitary beat of my heart,
that I was a maker of mistakes
which led me to a place
where I awoke in bed,
alone,
with a body covered in blood
and bruises
and a soul
that was heavy
but somehow not full.

CHAPTER FIVE

When I woke, I wasn't sure I was even alive. Pain radiated from my center, between my spine and my rib cage, all the way up my neck, wrapping around my head like a mask. I couldn't tell what hurt worse, the pain in my shoulders or in my face.

I blinked a few times, but couldn't feel my left eye actually blinking. The skin felt taut around my eyelid and down the side of my nose, like a deep pencil-shaped ache.

I sat up and blinked again, adjusting to the sliver of light that poured in between my curtains. I turned to the green lights on my clock and waited for my vision to focus so I could make out the time: 6:07. Was that AM or PM?

Gingerly, I peeled the covers from my body, but the movement caused the deepest ache in my shoulder. The motel bed was lumpy and dipped in the middle, but I'd slept deeply regardless, only waking once to replace the ice on my hands and face.

In the bathroom mirror, I saw a kaleidoscope of color, bruises all over my hands and roaming up my arms, to collect in perfect fingerprint-sized bruises along my neck and shoulders. Bruises continued along my jaw, ending with a perfect burst of color over my left eye. The skin below my eye was swollen and when I touched it, a white spot formed against the dark, angry red. My eye was almost swollen shut and I winced when I touched it gently, just trying to see if I could open it.

For some reason, I felt very detached from what had happened to me. Almost like it had happened to someone else. I kept expecting myself to breakdown like I had right after I'd left my mom's trailer, but I'd adopted a coldness toward my injuries overnight, now that I was an hour from her house.

I washed my hands, careful not to press the sore skin around my knuckles. The shower the night before hadn't gotten rid of all the stuff under my nails, so I spent the next ten minutes scraping them with a plastic fork I found by the microwave.

After washing the sleep from my face, I grabbed my phone from my backpack and the road atlas I kept with me. I was close to the Colorado border, but I couldn't go there. As desperate as I was for Jude, I couldn't go to him so soon after leaving him. Especially not like this. I couldn't let him save me; I needed to save myself first.

I ate a granola bar and washed it down with water before I studied my atlas more seriously. My grandfather's words, telling me to go on an adventure, echoed in my head.

I looked at the west coast first, California and the Pacific Northwest. But California was too hot and both California and the Pacific Northwest weren't far enough from Colorado. I wanted to get lost, really and truly lost, so I dragged a finger along the east coast, nixing the southern states because of their heat before my finger landed on Maine. It was about as far as I could go while remaining in the contiguous United States, and it would give me a completely different setting to figure my shit out.

My eyes traced the various routes I could take, before I finally sucked up enough courage to open my phone.

Three missed calls and several missed texts.

My hand went cold as I looked at the calls first. One from Jude. One from Mila. One from a number I didn't recognize.

I opened my laptop and Googled the phone number. It was the local police number, and after checking my dialed call list, I realized it was the same number I'd called the day before when I'd left my mom's trailer. I guessed they wanted to tell me their findings or get a more formal report from me, but I was interested in neither. I ignored the other two missed calls and opened my texts.

Mila: I'm sorry it happened the way it did. But can you please call? Or call Jude? He's worried about you.

Nope. I wasn't doing that. I moved to the next text, the one from Jude, the one person who never left my thoughts.

Jude: I went up on the roof tonight. It didn't feel the same without you there. I hope you're okay.

I thought I'd been completely unaffected. But those three sentences had reached inside of me and pulled on whatever strings held my heart in its place. I felt the pain in my chest, and wrapped a hand around my midsection. I could deal with physical pain—ibuprofen and ice would get me on the mend. But pain like that, pain that hit a place inside myself I couldn't touch? I was completely powerless.

I wanted to reply. So I did.

Me: I'm okay.

It seemed like a lackluster response. So I typed again.

Me: I miss you.

Once again, I was unsatisfied with how inadequate it sounded.

Me: I'll look up at the sky tonight. I hope you do, too.

I pressed send before I could talk myself out of it and then threw my phone down on the bed before I stood and paced. I couldn't believe I'd said that. Couldn't believe I'd essentially asked him to connect with me tonight, even from faraway.

When my phone beeped, I waited a full ten seconds before picking it up.

Jude: I will. Every night until you come back.

I dropped the phone again and pressed my palm to my good eye, holding in the emotion that welled up there.

After my second night in the motel, I packed up my car and set off on the road. I hadn't replied to Jude's last text, nor had I replied to Mila.

When interstate 80 met interstate 25 to Denver, I steered the car to the right to head south. I did it unconsciously, like I'd planned all along to go to Colorado. But at the last second, I veered the car left, away from the exit and back on my path. A car honked and flashed its lights at me and I gripped the wheel tighter.

Just breathe, I reminded myself.

*I hooked my finger through
the hole in my heart.
Trying to fill the places
you kept when I left.
But it's useless.
Because I don't want to
fill the void*

with more of me.
Maybe I'm learning
I'm less of me
when I'm not
with you.

CHAPTER SIX

JUNE 2013

"Trista," the voice repeated. "Are you there?"

It couldn't be him, I thought. I couldn't be talking to Jude.

I collapsed to my knees on the hot asphalt. "No," I said, but my blood was so loud in my ears that I wasn't sure it'd been even audible to him through the phone.

"Mila called you," Jude said. He sighed, a sound so long and solid that I dug the fingers of one hand into the hot stones on the roof, needing to feel tied to the earth, to reality.

I coughed his name, feeling the clench in my gut. It was him. He was alive.

My eyes closed as I remembered Mila's call. I'd ignored the first one, but when the second had come through seconds after the first ended, I picked it up.

"Mila," I said, prepared to launch into a reminder of why I didn't want her calling me. But her sobs thundered through the phone, so I froze in place. "What's wrong?" I tried to keep myself from panicking, but there was only one reason Mila would be calling me.

It sounded like she was gasping for air. "Oh my god!" she cried from the other end, her voice in a state of agony. I'd never heard anyone in grief like that, like she was sucking up all the air she could, but her grief was so great that it was compressing her chest. Her sobs were immediately followed by a loud suck of breath, followed again by a sob that vibrated through the phone. And then she cried harder, and tears pricked the insides of my eyes. I imagined her doubled over in emotional pain as she tried to tell me what was wrong. The very thought made the first tear slide slowly down my cheek; it was impossible to hear someone grieving that desperately and not feel a single thing.

"What?" I asked, breathless as I felt my own chest constrict. Suddenly, it felt like my heart was too heavy to beat. I could feel each movement of breath, arching my chest and painfully pressing against my rib cage. I gripped the bedspread as tight in my fist as I could, until my hand began to shake. "Tell me."

But she only kept sobbing, and I wanted to vomit. I knew. I knew, I just knew. My life was about to be decimated.

I pressed a hand to my mouth, to keep myself from crying with her. Her grieving continued, and before I knew it, more tears slipped down my cheeks. "Mila," I cried, my hands shaking so much that I couldn't hold the phone. "Tell me," I pleaded. "What's wrong?" I couldn't believe I could even get the words out.

"He was okay. He was!" She sounded so adamant about that, like she was trying to convince herself. A sound of something falling came through before she hiccupped, the sound rough and gasping. "And then, oh my god." The last words were spoken in time with a wail.

It was then that my legs crumpled to nothing under my body weight. I registered a tinge of pain from where my knees scraped on the wood floor, but it was nothing compared to the rolling of my heart in my chest.

"His face, it wasn't his face. It was someone else's face." She was still sobbing, and it was all I could do to clutch the phone in my fist as my body slowly curled up in a ball on the floor, as knives dug in the spaces between my ribs, in search of what made me mortal. "I watched him struggling to

breathe, Trista. Oh my g—" She couldn't finish the sentence, choking on her sobs.

I swallowed and whispered, "Is he okay?"

"No!" she screamed through the phone. "He went into cardiac arrest. Fuck." I heard a loud banging on the other end, and bit down on my lip to contain what was coming. It was like a wave of knives, the tide pulling back and rising above me.

"His heart fucking stopped. His heart! His heart stopped. His heart stopped! Trista," she screamed, as if I couldn't hear the echo of her words like a bullet to my chest. "I watched him, I was with him, when his heart stopped beating." Her sob after that was so gut-wrenchingly awful that I turned my face into the floor and let out my own, feeling the reverberation of the wood against my lips as I let it loose from my chest.

Jude was dead.

I couldn't stop it, I rolled over and vomited right there on the wooden floor, and dropped my phone as I pressed my hands to my face to catch the flow of tears as they flooded my eyes. My mouth was open, but no sound came. It was hard to speak, to wail, when I felt like I couldn't even breathe.

From that point on, I'd sobbed until one of my neighbors had banged on the wall that separated our apartments. In an effort to grieve in a way I needed, loudly and without reproach, I had found myself on the roof of that shitty apartment building. Being up high like that was how I always felt closest to Jude, with the sky the only thing above me.

Jude was dead, I'd told myself over and over, until the sounds of me saying it mixed with the echo of the words themselves, so it was a discombobulated chant in my head, and it lasted so long that the words became something else when I said them, sounds I didn't even understand.

I'd hated myself while I was up on that roof. That I was breathing the air Jude wasn't. That I was living a life I was destroying when Jude had lost his, after already giving so much of himself to me.

After Ellie had died, I'd found myself on a roof once too. I hadn't known if I would jump, but I had looked over the edge, felt the nothingness kiss my face as I peered down. In the end, I'd chickened out. But standing on the roof as I had been the moment I'd heard Jude's voice, I hadn't chickened out yet.

As if realizing just how close I was still to the edge, I crawled back away from it. I still held the phone in my hands.

"But you—" I pressed my face to my free hand, the overwhelming urge to sob my way through this conversation more powerful than anything I'd ever known. But nothing came, even as my eyes burned and my bottom lip trembled against my hand.

"Colin," Jude said, but his voice sounded harsh when he said it like that, like he was breathing through a cotton ball. "He went into cardiac arrest while he was at the gym. With Mila."

I shook my head, trying to accept the fact that Jude was alive. I was talking to him, but I had convinced myself he was dead. "Colin?"

"He was lucky, God." Again, his voice didn't sound like the voice I knew well. I knew it was him, but there was no mistaking the grief in his voice. "Someone started CPR and the gym had a defibrillator, so his heart started working again." I heard him swallow, and while I knew it was a terrible thing to think, to feel, I was so grateful for each breath I heard him breathe into the phone. Even though I knew something was wrong with Colin, I couldn't yet let go of the fact that Jude was okay.

Jude was okay.

"But it's not good, Trista. Damn it. It's not good." I could hear noise in the background, but I still felt like I was slowly waking up—my brain wasn't processing things as quickly as I knew it could. "He's in heart failure. After his hospitalization two years ago, they determined he was in advanced cardiomyopathy. He had valve replacement surgery, but his heart is beyond help at this point. He's severe enough to need a transplant."

I didn't know what to say. It felt like a new grief was carving a hole into my chest, like an ice cream scoop-sized swoop, and I was already so weakened from when I'd thought Jude had died. I pressed a hand to my rib cage, wishing I could reach in and loosen my ribs one by one, just so I could breathe.

"Where is he now?"

"At the hospital. That's where I am, too. He's been assigned high priority on a wait list, but I'm going to be frank—" he let out a big breath "—chances are he'll pass away before that can happen."

I didn't trust my legs yet to stand, so I stayed there on the hot roof even though I could feel it burning the skin of my knees. "That bad?" I asked, my breathing slowing but my eyes still leaking.

"Yes. You should come, Trista."

I was already nodding, trying to think of how much money I had in savings to buy a ticket.

"I can buy you a ticket on the next flight out," he said, as if he was reading my mind.

My stomach hurt from this conversation. I felt like I couldn't digest the fact that I was talking to Jude, but not talking to him about all the things I wanted to. And my ex-boyfriend was lying in a hospital bed, on the edge of losing his life, and I had just been on the edge of a building, thinking Jude had lost his.

The fact that I had considered a very *Romeo and Juliet* way to end everything suddenly hit me and I sucked in a breath. I wasn't going to jump. I'd gone up on the roof to be closer to Jude. "Okay," I found myself agreeing. I couldn't say no. I couldn't not go to Colorado. I wasn't poor, but I certainly didn't have enough money to purchase a plane ticket and sustain me while I was out of work.

"When can you leave?"

"Today," I said, not convinced by the conviction of my own words. "Tomorrow," I added. "Just . . . you tell me when and I'll be there."

"Okay. Can I reach you on this number?"

Closing my eyes, I said, "Yes."

I stared at the skyline, the noise of my surroundings rushing back. After Ellie had died, I'd walked onto a roof, too, like I couldn't get enough air in my living space.

I wasn't going to jump, I reminded myself.

Seventeen hours later, I boarded a flight to Denver.

CHAPTER SEVEN

2011

A week after leaving Wyoming, with significantly less cash, I walked into a beach hotel on the rocky Maine coast and dropped cash onto the counter.

"A room, please."

The woman wore a muumuu that crinkled when she leaned against the worn counter, bringing with her the scent of fish. "We don't take cash for rooms." The light under her head brought her more into focus, and I put her around fifty to sixty years old. She looked hearty enough to weather many decades still.

But I didn't own credit cards. I'd emptied my only bank account before I'd moved to Colorado, so I didn't even have a debit card at my disposal. "I can pay more."

Her rubber-gloved hands came to the counter, the source of her fish smell evident from the fish guts I saw around the fingertips. "Don't matter," she said, but it sounded like "mattah" from her accent.

I shifted weight from one foot to the other. "Maybe I could speak to the owner or something? I don't have a credit card."

"You could, but it won't make no difference."

"Please," I pleaded. It was near midnight and I was ready to fall into a bed for a week.

"Okay." She snapped off the gloves and wiped off the fish guts from the counter with a disinfectant wipe. After rubbing hand sanitizer over her hands, she flipped her head back and forth so the frizzy gray strands flicked over her shoulder. "I'm the owner."

My heart sank. "Of course." I stared at the wrinkled bills, one of only a handful left in the cigar box. "Is there another place that would take cash, do you happen to know?"

She grabbed a binder beside her and flipped it open, loudly moving through the pages. Once every few seconds, she looked up at me, taking me in. "Are you looking for a room for an hour?"

I scrunched up my nose. "An hour? No, more like a week or so. Maybe longer?"

"Are you a hooker?" It sounded like "hookah" and took me a second to get her meaning.

"What?" I laughed. "God, no."

"Runnin' drugs?"

I shook my head. "I just got here, from Pennsylvania. I just want a place to stay while I figure out what I'm doing."

"What's in Pennsylvania?"

"Nothing."

"Hmm." Her lips moved like she was chewing something. "Why here?"

Shrugging, I said, "Why not? My car needs some work done. I've been on the road for a while."

"Running from an abusive husband? Boyfriend?"

It gave me pause as I thought of Doug. "No. I don't have a boyfriend." *Do not indulge, Trista. Put it in the back of your mind.*

"If you don't gotta abusive boyfriend, what are those bruises about?" She motioned with one chubby finger at my face, but her eyes looked calm. "You make a habit of walkin' into doors?"

I shook my head. "It was an accident." It was my first lie to her.

"Well, you're going to have to give me more. Tell me what you are, since I know what you aren't."

I curled my fingers on the countertop. "I'm just looking for a place to rest my head while I figure my life out." It was heavier when I said it like that, and I regretted not stating it in simple terms instead.

She pursed her lips, her gray eyes crinkled and tired. "It's against policy to rent without a credit card for incidentals. If you take off and leave with a TV or something, I wouldn't have a way to find you."

"I don't know what to tell you. My car has been ticking and having little hiccups as I drive. It needs work, so it's not like I'll be able to take off anytime soon."

"Uh huh." She picked up a pen and then turned her head to holler over her shoulder. "Chuck!"

Her voice when she yelled was all power. She may have seemed older, but she was still a powerhouse. The way a man poked his head into the front office from a room in the back, looking like he was worried he'd done something wrong, showed her dominance over him. He looked about twenty years younger than she was. I guessed it was her son by the way she jerked her head to get him to come to her.

"You got keys?"

I blinked. "To my car?"

"Well, yeah. You don't got keys to anything else, do ya?"

She looked impatient and I felt bad for taking a minute to get on the same page. "Why do you want my keys?"

"You give me your keys, Chuck'll take a look at your car and then I'll know I can trust that you're not going to take off with my TV."

Chuck glanced over me before pulling his Red Sox cap off his head and running a hand over the long blond strands. "What's wrong with it?"

"It's been ticking since I left Pennsylvania and sometimes it doesn't want to start," I said as I handed my keys to him. "Are you a mechanic?"

"He is. Boats, bikes, cars—he can fix it all."

Chuck seemed to blush under his mom's praise. "I mean, I can sure try."

"Uh, can you let me know what the damage is before you fix anything?" I couldn't believe I was handing over my keys after a quick five-minute conversation. "I just want to make sure I can afford it."

The woman leaned on the counter. "And if you can't afford it, what's your other option?"

I shifted on my feet again. "Well, I don't suppose I have another option."

"Uh huh." She looked over the pile of money on the counter and took out a few bills. "A week, you say?"

I nodded.

"Can you work, too?"

"What kind of work?"

"Let's say dishwashing and room cleaning and picking up trash?"

"Sounds easy enough."

"Uh huh." She said that a lot, I was beginning to learn. "I'll charge you half for the week. You can make up the rest by doing some housekeeping and dishes work. And if you can't afford the car repairs, we can work something out."

I shook my head. "Are you serious?"

"Do I look like I'm yanking your chain?" Her eyes were hard, her mouth in a line.

"No." It intimidated me, the way she stared at me like she didn't expect her kindness to be questioned. "Thank you. That's very generous of you."

"Don't look too grateful; I'm giving you one of the rooms we haven't renovated since the nineties."

"That's okay. As long as it has a bed, I'm happy."

And I meant it. Hard to be picky when your car had served as a bed for the last two nights, parked in an empty rest area on the side of a highway. So when the woman, Maura, unlocked the door and gave me the spiel about the air conditioner not always working, I nodded gratefully. "This is great, really."

She looked me over dubiously, like she'd wait to see how I pulled my own weight in the morning, but she made sure to tell me, "That's what windows are for, you know. No need to rack up the air conditioning bill."

After she left, I dropped my suitcase on the floor and peeled the clothes off my body. I hadn't had air conditioning for most of the drive, since my air conditioner had gone out a thousand miles earlier, so a cool shower was like a blessing from above.

After leaving my mom's, I'd called my grandpa to check in and to tell him, in as few words as possible, that mom was as close to all right as she'd ever been. When I mentioned Maine, his voice warmed in a way I hadn't heard in years.

"You should see the ocean," he'd said, and told me he'd spent many summers as a kid on the beaches of Maine, particularly Kennebunkport. "Great seafood. Great old city."

My aim had been for Kennebunkport, but shortly after I passed Portsmouth, in New Hampshire, my car had given me a warning that its end was imminent. The last sign on the highway I'd seen had been for York Harbor, and I'd followed directions from the services just off the interstate for the inn I was now at.

After washing my body of three days of driving dust, I collapsed onto the bed. It wasn't overly soft, but it also was not lumpy. The comforter was years past its prime in style, but it was too hot to use it anyway. I stripped to just the sheet and climbed into the bed before letting out a sigh.

The room was small, with just the bed, a low white dresser with an older television and VCR, a mini fridge, and a worn oak table with two chairs. Beside the bed was one nightstand with an old but dust-free dandelion-yellow lamp. The room was older; Maura hadn't been lying about that. But it was clean. Next to the lamp was a telephone and I remembered my own, in my pocket.

When I'd left Wyoming, I'd picked up a new phone—a burner phone—and had passed my number along to my grandfather and the staff at his assisted living facility.

It hadn't rung once in four days.

I tried to feel peace about that. The only ones with my new number were my grandfather and his assisted living facility. That was what I wanted, was the reason I changed my number. But all it did was reinforce my complete and utter loneliness. I had no one in the world with me.

It could be argued that I did have people. But I'd left them with every intention of a fresh start, a time to grow and become who I was meant to be, without their influence.

And as I rolled onto my side in the bed, I told myself this again, repeated the thing I'd said to myself a hundred times.

You chose this.

It was one of the first decisions I'd made for myself in years.

That didn't stop me from rolling to my stomach and burying my face into my pillow, the ache for Jude so deep and so profound that I could scarcely breathe and not feel the hollow.

I woke up at five in the morning thanks to the sounds outside my window. Bleary-eyed, I pulled on a tee and walked to the window, peering out in the distance as the morning sky just kissed the harbor. Maura was surveying some goods in a truck and it was then that I realized my room was situated right over the side entrance, where the kitchen was.

"Come on, Tommy," she said, putting her hands on her hips. "Did your ma feed you this morning?" she asked with a clap on his back. "I've got some cream pies on the cooling rack and coffee on the burner." She looked softer in the early morning light, like the weight of the day was still light upon her shoulders.

I dressed quickly, made my room up to look as neat as it had been the night before, and took the stairs to the ground floor.

Maura was just in the kitchen doorway when she saw me. "Ah, there you are. Your name again?"

"Trista."

"Trista, this is Tommy. He brings me seafood and hooch."

Tommy was young, no more than nineteen, and looked like he was wearing clothes three sizes too large as he awkwardly stuck out a hand for me to shake. In his other hand was an oval donut covered in a chocolate ganache. "Hey," he said simply, before shoving the donut in his mouth. "I gotta go, Maura. I'll be 'round tomorrow."

Maura handed him a bag and then waved him off before she wiped her hands on her apron. "Come along then, Trista. Gotta get this fish on ice."

I spent the next hour helping Maura pack the fish and then disinfecting the countertops before working on the dishes. Later, she showed me how to glaze the donuts, which I learned were Boston cream pies, made fresh every day in Maura's kitchen. When the hour was up, Maura poured me a glass of milk and pushed a cream pie at me. "Milk's fresh from my cousin's dairy," she stated proudly.

It tasted fresh, as fresh as any milk I'd ever tasted. It didn't have the taste of milk that had been in the refrigerator for days, and it had a richness about it that I wasn't expecting. "Wow," I said, holding the glass away from my lips. I watched as the white clung to the insides of the glass, slowly slipping back to the rest of the milk at the bottom. "Rich."

"If you're not used to it, don't drink so much. I'll be making regular breakfast in a minute, and you can help and then eat that later. You'll need the protein."

"A second breakfast?"

"You'll burn it off today, trust me."

She wasn't wrong. By the time we'd finished the scrambled eggs, bacon, sausage, oatmeal, and fruit and yogurt parfaits for the other guests, we had five minutes to eat a quick breakfast before she had me help with making a second round of everything, for the "later risers," as Maura called them, but pronounced "latah risahs." It seemed almost like another language, with how thick her accent was sometimes. While Maura set out the next batch of breakfast in the chafing dishes, I cleared the tables, took out the trash, and did three sinkfuls of dirty dishes.

Immediately after the later risers' breakfast was served, Maura had me get started shadowing one of her housekeepers, Claire. Claire was my age, but seemed to have enough energy to power the whole building if she wanted to.

She snapped bubble gum as she introduced herself to me. "I'm Maura's niece. I bring the milk."

"Ah," I said, pointing over my shoulder in the direction of the kitchen. "I had some. Very good—rich."

"Fuckin' right," she said, pushing her cart down the hallway. "How long you been here?"

Even the way they pronounced "here" was something to get used to. "Um, what time is it?"

"Ten." She blew a bubble with her gum and then popped it back in her mouth.

"Ten hours then," I said.

Claire nodded and scrunched up her nose. "The last gal, Charlotte, was here all around five minutes before she went and took off."

"Oh," I replied, not sure what to say to that.

"That girl is like the fuckin' tide, I'll tell ya." Claire rapped on the first door after referring to a notebook in her pocket. When there was no answer, she slid her keycard in and pushed the door open. "She does this all the time, comes in and out. Summer's our busiest season, of course, but that Charlotte don't care not a bit about leavin' people high and dry."

"And Maura keeps hiring her back?"

"Ah, well, Aunt Maura's got a soft spot for Charlotte. She was homeless when Maura found her a few years ago, and pretty much useless in the way of life skills. But Maura hooked her up with a job and ever since, Charlotte comes and goes throughout the summer, when she's done chasing the impossible."

"The impossible?" I asked as I followed her into the bathroom, where she began picking up the towels and emptying the trash.

"Yeah, you know. The boyfriend. The summer fling. Charlotte's a sucker for love."

"Aren't we all," I murmured, taking the towel she handed me and shoving it in the laundry bag on the cart.

"What? You got a boy who broke your heart?"

I'd made a silent vow to myself when I'd woken up that morning. *Don't talk about Colin. Definitely don't talk about Jude.*

So I shook my head, said my second lie since leaving Wyoming. "Nope."

"Maura says you're probably clumsy." At my confused look, Claire motioned at the fading bruises on my face. "But let's be real. Did some prick do that to ya?"

I shook my head. "No. I don't have a boyfriend or an ex-boyfriend, especially not one that would put his hands on me." It wasn't a lie, necessarily, but I still looked down at my feet on the thick carpet, not wanting to have her scrutinize me.

"That's good. Maura puts up with Charlotte because she saved her, but she don't do that for just anybody." She handed me the dirty glasses and showed me where the supply in the hallway was for clean glasses. "And if you expect to be kept on here, you need to focus on your shit."

"Oh, well I'm only planning on being here a week. I was heading to Kennebunkport."

"Ah. I went to Bunk."

"Bunk?"

"The high school." She held up a fist and punched it in the air. "Go Rams, rah rah, yada yada."

"Don't sound so enthusiastic." I handed her toiletries and watched the process of her placing them along the countertop.

Claire looked up and shrugged. "Too many memories. Boyfriend drama. I'd be a Charlotte if I'd stayed."

"Oh, okay."

"So I came down here. Less tourists, too. If it's tourist-shit you're after, you should go farther north, to O.O.B."

"O.O.B.?"

"You're not from around here, are you?"

I shook my head, but didn't want to talk about where I was from. "Sorry, I'm just trying to get familiar with the area. I'm looking for a place to settle for a bit."

"Ah, in that case, don't go to O.O.B." She leaned in, pushed my shoulder with hers. "Old Orchard Beach. Killer boardwalk, but packed to the fucking gills with people, man."

"Oh, well, I'm looking for more quiet. A place to think and figure out what I'm doing."

"Then you'll have better luck in one of the smaller seaside towns, if that's what you're into." I followed her as she walked into the bedroom and started stripping the bed. "Are you a surfer?"

I laughed. "No. Not a surfer."

"Good. There aren't many surfing beaches around. Long Sands is the closest, but it's usually busy." She pointed to the cart. "Grab the sheets on the bottom, won't you?"

I pulled them out and tossed them to her when she gestured for me to. "I've never even been in the ocean."

"What? You really aren't from around here, then."

"Nope," I said.

"What do you like to do then?"

I thought of Jude. His eyes, steady and sure on mine as we set up tents. His hands, strong and solid, holding me to him. "I like camping."

"You can do that just about anywhere around here. What else?"

I shrugged as I watched her make the bed. "I don't know. That's what I'm figuring out."

"Ah. Sheltered? That's cool." She looked me over for a second and pushed her black bangs away from her eyes. "Charlotte was sheltered too, I think. Explains why she's making up for it now. We're going out for drinks tonight. Wanna come?"

I struggled to keep up with her and how she changed the course of our conversation so easily. "I'm not really much of a drinker."

"That's cool. You can be our driver." She grinned at me and blew a bubble with her gum as she fluffed the pillow.

I got the feeling that Claire steamrolled people often. "I don't have a car. Chuck is working on it."

"That's okay. You can drive my car." She smoothed a hand down the bedspread and then pulled a fresh pad and pen out of her waist belt and set them on the table. "There now. Fourteen to go."

"Fourteen?" I asked as she helped me pull the cart out into the hall. It was still relatively early in the morning, but I felt a few beads of sweat lining my spine already.

"Yeah, there are twenty rooms on this floor, but only fifteen need service."

Pushing the cart to the next room, I asked, "Is this place usually full?"

"Oh, it's full now." She slid her keycard into the next door. "Welcome to summer in Maine."

CHAPTER EIGHT

Charlotte and Claire had picked a restaurant right on the water, which surprised me. I'd expected a dive, with picnic tables and citronella candles clustered around fake flower centerpieces.

Instead, we were seated at a table with cushions and cloth table coverings as we drank ten-dollar drinks. By we I meant Charlotte and Claire, because I was the designated driver, nursing my third chocolate milk.

Thousands of miles between us and I couldn't escape Jude's influence.

"So I tell him, 'Dude, if you want this you gotta work for it,'" Charlotte said after blowing a stream of smoke from her cigarette. She tucked her thick brown hair over her shoulder before leaning forward on the table, right on her elbows. "And what does he do? He comes over with fucking flowers and chocolate, like we're in middle school and it's Valentine's Day or some shit."

I sipped my chocolate milk through the straw as I observed them. Looks-wise, they were complete opposites. Claire resembled a Snow White crossed with a pin-up girl, with her thick, jet-black hair she wore over one pale shoulder. When she laughed, her bright red lips spread into her cheeks and her dark eyes sparkled. Charlotte looked almost feral—not in a homeless-kind-of-way, but a wild way. She wore minimal makeup, which I found interesting. For someone as boy-crazy as Claire had described, I'd expected excessive makeup. But Charlotte didn't need makeup because she was gorgeous—sharp angular face, deep-set eyes, dark hair and skin. Not in a girl-next-door kind of way, no. She had green eyes that cut right through you and spoke through lips that would give Angelina Jolie a run for her money.

Both of them were exaggerated in how beautiful they were, and when they were a couple drinks in and engaging in more personal conversation, I felt very sober and very plain.

After a long day of doing various jobs for Maura, she'd let me off around dinner. Chuck had told me they'd had a couple jobs come in at the shop he worked for, so they'd get to my car in the next couple of days.

I'd showered and worn my hair in its natural, frizzy state. In the humid summer weather, my hair had poofed up as soon as I'd left the inn and followed Claire to her car.

The purple that had been in my hair had faded significantly, so much that it looked almost brown, and I hadn't bothered with makeup. I wasn't looking for attention—I was looking for a time out of my life on the go.

"Oh, don't be such a snob, Charlotte," Claire admonished her, leaning back in her chair and propping her feet up on the chair beside her. "Boys are clueless; they don't know any better."

"What did you expect him to get you?" I asked, surprising myself. I hadn't contributed much to the conversation so far because I felt completely out of my element with them both.

Charlotte looked at Claire, clearly feeling the same surprise I felt. When she looked back at me, she looked like she was trying to dissect my question. "Flowers die. Never have I ever expected flowers from him."

"Okay." I looked at my drink, wishing I were back in my little hotel room, with the TV that didn't always work and the whish-whish-whish of the ceiling fan.

"Look, Joey usually buys me a gift certificate for somewhere, something he knows I can use. I can't use almost-dead flowers for obvious reasons." She sucked on the cigarette and then blew it out in the air above her head. "And chocolate? Well, I hate chocolate."

A waiter walked past us with a bright red lobster on his tray.

"You're not even a girl." Claire shook her head before reaching over and grabbing the cigarette from Charlotte's hand, catching her off guard. I watched as Claire snuffed the cigarette out in the glass ashtray. "You're supposed to be quitting and this is the third stick I've watched you light up tonight."

Charlotte rolled her eyes but leaned back in her chair. "Don't be such a killjoy, C."

"I don't have any brothers or sisters to take care of me when I'm old as fuck—you're it, buttercup. Stop smoking so you can be around to wipe my ass."

Charlotte laughed and threw an ice cube from her drink at Claire. "See what I have to put up with?" she asked me, like we were close friends already.

"Did you grow up together?" I asked.

They exchanged a look, and I remembered Claire having said something about Charlotte being homeless before Maura found her. I thought it interesting, that Claire could accuse someone who was once homeless as a snob.

"No, we just spend a lot of time at the inn. You'll see." Charlotte gave me a smile that looked like she could slice right through me.

"You will," Claire agreed.

"I don't plan to stay here long," I protested.

"We'll see," Charlotte said knowingly. She exchanged another look with Claire.

Claire clinked her glass against mine. "We've done all the talking tonight. Tell us something juicy, Trista."

Suddenly, I wished I hadn't opened my mouth to ask anything. I wished to keep my mouth firmly shut and shrink in my seat so that they didn't know I existed. "Well," I played with my straw in the glass, spinning it around. "I don't have a dad."

"Oh." Charlotte scooted closer, as if she'd be able to see my life better.

"Do you have a mom?" Charlotte asked.

Nodding, I said, "I do. But we're estranged." That seemed to be the nicest way to put it.

"So you're like Charlotte. An orphan?" Claire asked.

Charlotte reached over and slapped a hand against Claire's arm. "Don't be a dick, Claire."

"No, it's fine." I tried to think of a way to make it sound less . . . well, just less. I didn't have much in my possession except for my honesty. "She and I have differing opinions on how to live."

The table went silent for a moment and I sipped my chocolate milk before continuing. "I have my grandfather, though. He's the reason I'm not a complete waste of space."

Charlotte pursed her lips as she regarded me. "And friends? Boyfriend?"

I shook my head so fast I was surprised it didn't fly off my neck. "No. I'm starting over, figuring my shit out."

"Yeah, well what's that on your face then?" she asked with a motion of her straw at my face. I wondered if all the strangers in this small town were this intrusive, but I realized that having a bunch of colorful bruises on your face likely welcomed you to this kind of talk.

"It's nothing," I said. "Certainly not anything I want to talk about." It was as honest as I wanted to be about it. "And same with my mom."

"Sounds like you already figured out your mom shit. What other shit is there?" Charlotte peered at me and I felt that same dissection as before. But I stared back at her coolly, not entertaining her prying.

"Maybe next time, you can be DD and we can get Trista to divulge all of her secrets," Claire said.

I laughed, quickly. "Probably not."

"Some drunken oversharing is always a good decision," Charlotte said before shrugging. She waved down the waiter and ordered a basket full of biscuits. "I'm starving."

I looked her over then, surprised she could eat a basketful of biscuits and look all lithe and airy, like fat had never passed her tongue. We were silent when the waiter dropped off the biscuits and walked away.

"So, how do you know Claire?" Charlotte asked, pinning me with her green gaze.

"Trista worked at the inn today, since you were MIA again." Claire popped three bites into her mouth and then spoke, "Who got a hold of you this time?"

Charlotte was watching me, holding the bread like I would judge her for eating it. "Jake," she said, not tearing her eyes away from me for even a moment.

Claire made an "ugh" noise.

"Jake?" Claire asked. "He's such a prick."

Charlotte shrugged and looked at Claire. "He's changed."

"Oh, dear baby Jesus in a wicker basket," Claire groaned. "He's used that line so much, he's ruined it for every other guy who claims they've changed." She waved her hand to the beach. "I saw him just yesterday, in the water with what's-her-face from the ice cream joint down on the boardwalk."

"Which ice cream place?" Charlotte asked, her chewing halted as she watched Claire intently.

"The one that has the cotton candy on top."

"No way," Charlotte said, "she doesn't work there."

Claire shook her head. "She sure as shit does, I saw her there two days ago."

"No, she works at the taco place, by the arcade," Charlotte argued.

"She doesn't. She was up to her elbows in cookie dough, so her name tag was all I could see."

"If that's the case, then what's her name?" Charlotte asked, "Not where she works."

"What *is* her name?" Claire asked herself out loud. "R-something. Rachel?"

"No, I think it's Rachelle."

"That's right—Rachelle. The one who always gets the heart sticker when she gets tanned, so she's got that white heart peeking out of her bikini bottoms."

"Oooh," Charlotte said, understanding coming to her. "Didn't Chuck work on her car a couple weeks ago?"

"You both are exhausting," I said, because they were. The back and forth reminded me of a tennis match, watching them lobbying words with hardly a breath.

Charlotte laughed and Claire joined in a second later, and then they both exchanged looks that spoke to their deep camaraderie. "Sorry, Char. Anyway, Jake the fake was all up in Rachelle's goods on the beach. It was like watching the soft porn that's on those movie channels late at night." Claire mimicked dramatic hands and a tossing of her head.

"Gross," Charlotte said, making a face. But the hurt was there, even as she tucked it away and focused her attention on a biscuit. Her mouth dipped down and I watched, slowly, as her good humor left her.

But Claire continued. "I swear, he carries at least four STDs. Sorry, Char," she added as an afterthought. "He didn't have any two years ago," she said before immediately sipping her drink. It suddenly felt awkward among the girls, like I was privy to a secret drama between the two of them. "But seriously, Charlotte. You can do *so* much better." She exaggerated the *so* with a slap to the glass table, which startled Charlotte and me.

"I like him," Charlotte said with a shrug of her shoulders. I could hear the defensiveness in her tone and realized how quickly her confidence had faltered when Claire had told her about Rachelle from the ice cream place. "Obviously you liked something about him too, once."

"Yeah, the fact that he told me he was different from everyone else." Claire sipped loudly before waving for the waiter to bring her another drink. "Spoiler alert—he tells every flavor of the month the same stupid shit."

Charlotte looked offended and for some strange reason I felt for Charlotte, so I changed the subject. "What else is there to do around here besides drink and flirt?" Two things I wasn't remotely interested in. I didn't know how long my car would be out of commission, but if it was long enough that I'd be here a while, I wanted to get familiar with the area.

"Depends on how outdoorsy you are," Claire said, shaking off Charlotte's offer of buying her another drink. "There's bowling, the zoo, the Wiggly Bridge if you want to walk across the world's shortest suspension bridge and follow some of the trails. Hmm. . ." She tapped her chin as she thought. "You can ascend Mount Agamenticus if you're into hiking—it has a few trails. I think the longest trail is less than an hour."

It didn't surprise me that the first thing I wanted to do was hike Mount Agamenticus, but it did surprise me that I was a bit disappointed by the shortness of the hike.

"Why do you look like someone pissed in your cereal?" Charlotte had her head tipped to the side, and one dark lock fell over her shoulder. Her hair was so dark that the white Christmas lights around the patio blinked against the strands, distracting me momentarily.

"I like hiking," I said. "And I'm still a novice, but all the hiking I've done in the past has been several miles, minimum."

Charlotte blinked at me, like she couldn't believe I'd said as much as I had. "So, you're a tree hugger?" She looked at Claire and then back at me. "That's interesting. Where'd you say you came from?"

"I didn't say." I squared off with her, seeing through her suddenly. She wasn't a threat or anything, but I could tell she liked to collect information from those she spent time with, as if she would then use that information to benefit herself somehow. I felt like I'd had a taste of that with Charlotte.

"I'm getting tired," I said pointedly, when Claire was sipping the remnants of her drink. Claire and Charlotte exchanged another look and then they both shrugged.

"Sure, let's go. Char, you need a ride?" Claire asked as she grabbed her purse.

"I've got my bike," Charlotte said, abruptly standing and leaving the patio through the side gate. Her back was straight, but her head was bent down and I wondered if she was eager to lick her wounds.

We watched her leave, like she couldn't wait to get away from both of us. Not that I blamed her; I was looking forward to locking myself in my little room at the inn, away from their questions. Away from anything that would bring my past to light.

As I was tucked away in my room, all I could think about was how much watching Claire and Charlotte had made me ache for the friendship I'd had with Ellie.

CHAPTER NINE
OCTOBER 2011

My life was eclipsed by a shadow, hiding from a truth I was afraid of.

There was no denying that I loved Jude. It slipped into me like warm molasses, coating me with its stickiness, telling me no, it wasn't going to slide off like it had with Colin. Those feelings clung to my bones, even as the miles between Jude and me grew. I couldn't shake them, shake him.

And months later, still I found myself closing my eyes and visualizing him in front of me, his easy calm and quiet introspection providing a meditation-like tranquility. I wondered all the time what he was doing, who he thought of as his eyelashes brushed against his cheeks at night.

After my car had been fixed, I'd stayed on with Maura at the inn. I didn't have any other prospects as it was, and I'd been slowly getting familiar with the little beach city I lived in, and the people I worked with, day in and day out. Breathing in and out, writing up my poems and publishing them on an online journaling account after I'd closed the last one.

And through it all, he'd had a hold over me.

Which was why I found myself texting Mila, late one night after I lay in a recliner by the now covered pool, watching the stars. It wasn't the roof, and it wasn't the mountains, but it was outside—which was the closest I'd been to Jude since I'd left Colorado.

Is he okay? I asked her, not bothering to say who I meant.

I stared at my phone until my eyes crossed and the words bled into each other. I was two hours ahead of her, and I knew she would still be awake, probably practicing lines.

Finally, my phone beeped and pulled me from the silence I'd surrounded myself with.

Mila: Who the hell is this?

It caused a smile to curl my lips.

I debated what to say for a while, but worried Mila would show the number to Jude and ask him the same question, so I replied as quickly as I could.

Me: It's Trista, please don't tell him.

I sent it immediately as I formulated my next words.

Me: I am trusting you to keep my new number to yourself.

Her reply came right away.

Mila: Roger that. Can I call you?

I shook my head over and over, but typed: *Yes.*

It felt like hours before my phone beeped the generic incoming ring tone and my thumb hovered over ANSWER for far longer than it should have, considering that I'd invited her to call me.

"Hello?" It came out like a squeak, as if I hadn't used my voice in a long time.

"It *is* you." Her reply came breathlessly. "I thought it might've been a prank or something."

I sucked in a breath and let it out. "No, it's me. I'm sorry. . ." I faltered. Pressing a hand to my forehead and closing my eyes, I said, "I just, I know when I left things were. . ." I stopped. I didn't know what to say.

I heard a heavy sigh on the other end of the line and used my other hand to hold the bottom of my phone, waiting with bated breath for her to speak.

"I don't even know what to say. Except that I'm sorry. It was a real shit thing that happened in that hospital room. I shouldn't have befriended you with everything that was going on behind your back." I heard a noise and then she said, "Sorry, had to close my door. I don't know who might be listening."

"I hope no one is listening," I said. "I don't want anyone to know I'm calling you. I know I'm asking you to lie, but—"

"But it's the fucking least I can do for you," she interrupted. "What do you need? Money? I can send you some."

I shook my head before realizing she couldn't see me. "No. I just worry about Jude. Is he okay?"

"He's fine. I mean, given the circumstances, he's okay." She lowered her voice for the next thing she said. "He moved out. He's living on his own in a studio apartment. It's for the best. Things were tense after you left. Colin had surgery and I stayed in the apartment to help him and. . ." Then she paused. "I don't even know what to say, honestly. This is so fucking weird."

"I agree." I was talking to my ex-boyfriend's girlfriend, the one he cheated on me with. She also happened to be the twin sister of the man I was in love with. There was nothing not awkward about our conversation. "Listen, I just wanted to make sure he was okay. I keep thinking about when we went to Yellowstone and he struggled during one of the hikes. I worry, that's all."

"The good thing is that winter is coming soon and Jude isn't a winter climber. So he's spent most of his time traveling places warmer, with fewer strenuous hikes." There was silence for a moment, but I sensed she had more to say. "He wasn't great, after you left. He looked for you. Went to Wyoming."

My breath caught and I pressed a hand to my chest to hold it still.

I always thought that my life was separated into a before and an after. Before Ellie's death, and after. But I hadn't even known who I was then, so how could her death define my life so sharply? Now it felt like my relationship with Colin and its conclusion had caused the fault line that separated my life. Who I was before and who I was in that moment. I was still figuring it out, but I knew, solidly, that I wasn't the girl I'd been before.

I was the girl who'd caused Jude to follow me to Wyoming.

"He did?" I asked when I'd caught my breath again.

"Yes. He met with your grandfather I guess."

"How did he find him?"

"Colin told him. It's really weird since you've been gone. I know you were here only a few weeks, but nothing is like how it was before. I don't know how to explain it."

I took a strange kind of delight knowing that my absence had affected the three of them in a way that made Mila uncomfortable. But I needed to ask about Colin, because despite how he'd hurt me, he'd been such a big part of my life when I'd loved him. "Is Colin okay?"

"Yeah. New medication. He'll have another surgery in the spring. He's fine." Her voice was strange when she said that, but I didn't press her. I felt lighter for knowing Jude was okay, but the scale tipped back to sadness too, knowing I wasn't there for him. "Where are you?"

I wouldn't tell her. My phone number was Wyoming, thankfully, so she wouldn't be able to figure it out. "Not in Wyoming."

She snorted. "No shit, Sherlock. But if you don't want to tell me, I get it."

"You have my number regardless. Could you let me know if things change for Jude? I . . . that's why I called."

Her sigh was loud and long. "Yep. Look, I know that what I did was unforgivable, so I'm really sorry. I don't know what to tell you. I didn't want to like you when I met you. But I couldn't help it. I wanted to tell you immediately, but Colin was waiting and—"

"Don't worry about it," I cut her off, not wanting to go into that tonight, if ever. "Just text me if there's something I should know. Or call me."

"Will do. Trista?"

"Yeah?"

"Take care of yourself. Jude has me to take care of him. But you don't have anyone."

I rubbed my lips together and closed my eyes, taking it in—the fact that I was still alone. "Goodnight, Mila."

After hanging up, I dropped my phone beside me on the recliner and slouched farther down in the chair before tilting my face up to the night sky. I tried to find the constellations Jude had shown me one night, but the Maine autumn sky was so much different than the Colorado summer sky.

I wanted to be back on the roof with Jude. But I wasn't ready.

More than once I'd put my things in a suitcase with every intent to drive back to Colorado. But then I'd remembered that it was just three months since I'd ended a six-year relationship, one that I'd sort of lost myself in. I could run to Jude, but I couldn't burden him with making me happy. I couldn't let him be the sole reason for my happiness.

"Let's get drinks," Charlotte suggested as we ate lunch on the patio the next day.

"I'm not a big drinker," I said, though she knew this about me. Charlotte and I had struck up a friendship after the night of drinks, when she'd dumped the dirtbag she'd been dating and had returned to Maura's doorstep, much to her own chagrin.

"Duh. But I don't want to drink alone and Jesse dumped me."

Jesse had been her most recent flavor of the month. He was six-foot-six with dimples and curly blond hair that poofed into a lazy fro after he'd been in the ocean. He said all the right things and charm practically oozed from his pores, but I hadn't liked him. He had a look in his eyes that reminded me of my mom's many exes, like he was a man who used and abused, but as long as he was providing for you, you should accept his behavior with a grateful smile.

"You're better off," I said, squinting against the sunlight that poured across the patio.

Charlotte sucked on her straw until the noise of an empty drink caused me to give her a look. She knew I hated that sound. She sat back against the metal chair and grunted. "I'm just sick of riding the same rollercoaster, you know?"

"Then get off of it." I shrugged and wiped my mouth with my napkin. "You don't have to have a boyfriend. Especially not the same kind of boyfriend, over and over."

"I don't want to be lonely," she said with a hint of sadness in her voice that had echoed my mother's. I think half the reason I had been pulled to Charlotte was because of how much she reminded me of my mother. She had similar quirks, similar taste in men, and a fondness for heartache that was completely foreign to me. Who wanted that? To continually feel like their heart had been wrung out like a sponge, by the hands of someone who didn't care how deeply you hurt.

"Then find something else that makes you happy. So you don't seek out happiness in a penis."

Charlotte snorted, tossing her head back as she did. She was so pretty; it was obvious what attracted men to her immediately. But she was self-destructive and would seek out people who would only wind up hurting her in the end. "But Trista, penises can be a huge—" she waggled her eyebrows "—source of happiness."

Rolling my eyes, I turned my head to look out over the pool. "Sometimes they're more trouble than they're worth." But I wasn't thinking about Jude when I said that. Jude made it easy—like love for him had always been inside of me, dormant but waiting for the right person to nurture it.

"That sounds like the grumbles of a chick who needs to get laid."

I had to resist rolling my eyes again. "Just because I'm a little soured to men doesn't mean I need one to stick it into me."

"It's your vagina's funeral," Charlotte said, holding her hands up in surrender. "I'm just saying, you'd probably feel a lot better if you had that particular muscle massaged a little bit."

"I can assure you, I wouldn't." I wasn't normally so uptight, but the idea of a random hookup didn't appeal to me. What was the point? I couldn't do something casual like that, when I'd only been with two men—both of whom I'd cared deeply for. I didn't judge anyone who engaged in regular one-night stands—as long as they were being careful. But for me, it was so much more than just sex. I didn't want just sex. I wanted more.

I wanted Jude.

I also wanted to drop my face into my hands. Just a few months had passed since I'd last seen him, and I couldn't get him out of my head. That didn't bode well for the next few months while I figured my life out.

Jude was a forever kind of guy. He wasn't the guy you hooked up with on your quest for the last guy. He *was* the last guy. And in many ways, he was the first guy for me.

But that didn't mean I wanted any other kinds of relations during the in-between.

"Where'd you wander off to?" Charlotte asked me, waving a hand in front of my face.

I blinked quickly. "Just thinking."

"About tonight? And the hangover you'll have tomorrow morning after spending the night drinking my woes away?"

"I don't think there's enough alcohol in the world to drink your woes away." I twirled the paper straw Charlotte had put in our drinks. The pink faded into blue as it spun in my fingers. "But fine, I'll have some wine or something with you. Nothing hard."

"Okay," Charlotte said, her cheeks pink and her eyes glittery. She'd changed from the meek, quiet, almost-feral woman at the beginning of the summer. "I'll even graciously supply the booze."

"I expected you to," I said, brushing crumbs from my lap as I stood. "Come help me with the suite that was booked on the fourth floor."

Charlotte groaned. "Is that the one that had the group of dudes?"

I nodded, picking up my plate and cup. "Yeah, and the blow-up doll they brought in with them. I'm sure the room is something else."

Charlotte followed me, albeit reluctantly. "Do you think I should text Jesse?"

I wrinkled my nose as I turned to her. "Are you kidding? No."

She loaded our dishes in the dishwasher. "Why not?"

I had a feeling I'd need to find a way to steal her phone away from her that night and make sure she didn't drunk text him. "Because he dumped you. Why would you text him?"

Charlotte snapped a rubber glove on her hand before we boarded the elevator to the fourth floor. "To see if he misses me?"

I watched the numbers climb from lobby to four before I spoke. "If he missed you, he would tell you. Don't give him the satisfaction of knowing you miss him by asking him if he misses you." In a way, it felt like I was talking to my mother, someone lovesick and insecure in the aftermath of a broken relationship.

Charlotte fit her fingers through the other glove and looked up at me from under her long lashes. "You're kind of smart, you know?"

I didn't think it was very smart—more like common sense. But

Charlotte's tender heart didn't need me to say that. "My mom is a lot like you," I said, which was the first time I had mentioned any bit of my past to Charlotte. "So I'm well-versed in this kind of thing."

"I'd like to meet your mom."

I shook my head at her as I unlocked the supply room and wheeled out the cart. "I think you and my mom together would be completely destructive." I didn't want anyone to meet my mother, least of all someone as mentally fragile as Charlotte.

After giving the room a thorough wipe down, Charlotte told me to come to her room around nine that night with an extra tumbler for the wine and left me to clean the rest of the floor by myself. I didn't mind cleaning alone. As much as I enjoyed Charlotte's company, she was completely distracting. I found myself needing more time to think, to reminisce about Jude, ever since talking to Mila.

Part of me expected Mila to text me in the morning, just because she had an opportunity to. But it was for the best that we kept our contact to a minimum. I didn't want to run off to Colorado when the wounds of what happened were still so fresh. I'd never had a healthy relationship in my life. My relationship with Colin had started out with me grateful and star-struck that he liked me. And I'd stayed with him after Ellie died as a way to somehow hold on to her.

I had to remind myself that I left Jude because I didn't want a relationship with someone who lied to me, who'd lied along with my ex-boyfriend and his sister about their relationship. But even more—I didn't want to jump from one relationship to the next, without taking some time off in between to see what I wanted. Loneliness was my most loyal companion, and I didn't want to drown it in a relationship just for the sake of not being alone.

But in truth, it was getting harder and harder to remind myself of why I left him, when all I wanted was some of the steadiness he'd given me. The peace I'd felt on the many nights we'd spent lying on the roof and watching the stars move across the sky.

But I tucked all that away in the corner of my heart as I finished the rooms I had to do and grabbed dinner after. The kitchen where I ate was blessedly quiet, so I retreated to my room to write a poem with a brain at peace.

All that
is holding me
together
is some foreign skin
and fragile bones.
Around my waist
is a tether to you
and I'm afraid
it's longer than
I am strong enough
to carry
this sack of skin
and pile of bones
back to you.

When I showed up to Charlotte's room, she was in her pajamas and I breathed a sigh of relief. I wasn't sure if Charlotte wanted to pre-game with a bottle of wine in her room before we went out. But her pajamas told me she planned on staying in, which made it easier for me to agree to drinking more than I probably would have otherwise.

"I bought the three-dollar wine," she said, gesturing to the bottles on top of her mini fridge. "But I bought a ten-dollar one to start with. Start with the best because the other stuff will taste good once we get a little buzzed."

I shrugged and handed her my tumbler. Wine was wine to me. I couldn't taste the extra dollars in a more expensive wine, so it made no difference how much a bottle had cost. I looked around her room, which was much more updated than mine, boasting a flat-screen TV on the wall opposite the bed and a table that looked like it had barely been used.

"Nice room," I said as my gaze moved over the white comforter that just screamed to be jumped on.

"Yeah, it's been 'my' room ever since I first stayed here." She kicked the fridge door gently closed before sauntering over to me with one wine-filled tumbler in hand. "I put a little brandy in it and some lemon-lime soda, too."

"Fancy," I said with a raised eyebrow.

"I figured we could hang out and drink with a movie on?"

"Of course." I moved to the other side of her bed and sighed as I settled into it. "I think I need a room upgrade."

"You do," Charlotte said with a contented sigh. She pressed the power button on the remote and then tossed it to me. "Find something to watch."

I flipped through the channels absentmindedly, watching Charlotte as she disappeared into the bathroom for a minute. I settled on a documentary on the Discovery Channel and my heart pinched, thinking of Jude. A part of me resented the hole inside of me that suckled on anything Jude-related, never letting me forget the fact that I was here and he wasn't with me. But, in a small way, I understood why my mother was always seeking love. I was better with it than without it, I was learning.

"What's this?" Charlotte asked as she walked back to the bed.

"A documentary on land mines."

"That sounds uplifting." She raised an eyebrow. "I guess I thought we'd be watching something girly, you know—like a romantic comedy."

Tossing the remote to her, I said, "Then find one. I'm still not very familiar with the TV channels."

"You're not?" she asked incredulously. "What do you do to entertain yourself then in that old-ass room?"

It was on the tip of my tongue to reply, "I write poetry." But that would only invite questions and, most likely, her insistence to see said poetry.

"I read a lot."

"Huh." She scrunched up her nose like the idea offended her, and sniffed. It was then that I noticed her eyes were red.

"Are you okay?"

She side-eyed me before turning up the volume on the remote. "I'm great."

But she wasn't. Her pallor wasn't right, and the skin around her lips was reddened. "What's wrong?"

She dropped her head back against the headboard and I knew she had rolled her eyes. "Why are you even worried about it?"

"I might not know you all that well, but I do know something's up."

"I'm going through a breakup." Her voice was flat and she sipped from her tumbler. "I'm practically in mourning."

But she wasn't in mourning. Something wasn't right with her, but I couldn't put my finger on it. "I know we don't know each other all that well, but you can talk to me if you need to."

"Oh, is that a two-way street?" She raised an eyebrow and pursed her lips as she studied me. "Because I think you have more secrets than even I do."

I thought of the night on the roof with Jude. "Tell me something honest. And I'll tell you something in return. A secret, maybe."

"What if I tell you something deep and you tell me something stupid in exchange?"

I hadn't ever had this thought with Jude because I'd trusted him. Instinctively. In all our exchanges of secrets and our open honesty, I'd never once worried that I'd tell him something deeply personal and he'd reply with something shallow. "I will tell you a secret that no one here knows," I promised, hoping she'd confide in me. I wasn't sure why I wanted her to, except that I was in short supply of friends at the moment and she looked like she could use one herself.

"Fine." She sat up in the bed and put the tumbler on her nightstand before turning to face me. "I'm bulimic."

It shouldn't have surprised me, and I don't think the surprise itself had anything to do with what she said but rather how she delivered it, like she was telling me her favorite color was blue. "Oh," I said, fumbling for words. "Why?"

She blew her bangs away from her face with her hand and I found myself examining her more closely than before. The lines around her mouth suddenly seemed deeper, and the dark circles that wrapped her eyes were louder than I remembered them being.

"Because it's the easiest way to lose weight. Because I don't like feeling full. Because, why not?" She wore nonchalance around her shoulders and candor at her lips. It was a side of her I'd never seen—this brutally honest side.

"But it's dangerous," I said, feeling stupid for saying something so obvious. "Why don't you try dieting or exercise?"

Once again she rolled her eyes, acting as if she had expected me to say exactly what I was saying. "I tried those things, Trista. But after I got on birth control a few years ago, I gained fifty pounds that year. Do you know what that does to someone's self-worth?" She tucked her hair behind her ears and glanced at the television. But she wasn't really watching. She was thinking. "I went to the movies with this guy once and he took me for frozen yogurt after. As we sat on the promenade, eating ice cream, he placed a hand on the one I had wrapped around the spoon and said, 'That's about enough for you, isn't it?'" She turned her head to face me, and the light from the television played with the shadows on her face. "I asked him what he meant and his hand slid up my arm. I thought he was making a move and I leaned into it, but then his fingers flicked against my neck and he said, 'Your second chin is showing.'" I watched as she swallowed and looked down at her fingers. "I threw away the frozen yogurt and went home and cried so hard I vomited. And then I felt better, knowing I wouldn't digest all that garbage."

I didn't know what to say to that. I'd also had feelings of self-disgust, feelings that I was too overweight for anyone to find me pretty. When Jude had touched my collarbone and made me feel like I wasn't as disgustingly large as I felt I was, it was the first time I'd believed him. Middle school teachers had cautioned us against eating disorders, but I'd never truly thought I'd meet someone affected by them. I'd never entertained the thought of shoving my fingers down my throat, but Charlotte's casual demeanor made me wonder more about it.

"How long have you been doing it?"

She looked over at me, searching my face as if she was deciding how to tell me. "Well, after my date I didn't do it all that often. Just once in a while, when I was getting a little chubby. But then. . ." She paused. "I was pregnant once." She looked down at her stomach before flicking her eyes away. "I didn't know I was pregnant until one day, I was brushing my teeth and once I'd gotten to my molars, I felt bile come up. That had never happened before—puking from brushing my teeth. One of the girls I was with at the time told me to take a piss test, so I did." She brushed strands of hair from her face. "But after I miscarried, I had a pooch below my belly button I couldn't get rid of, so I started brushing my teeth just a little too far back until I puked. And now I just use my fingers."

I tried to take it all in without a look of shock on my face. "Do you do it all the time?"

She tilted her head. "Only once a day, usually. So I'm still getting calories. It's not as bad then." She sounded convincing, but I didn't believe even doing it once a day was 'okay,' so I just rubbed my lips together as I considered. She pulled her brown locks into a bun and in doing so, I noticed a thick strand was wet.

She must have seen my attention zero in on that piece, because she tugged on it, saying, "I got puke on this, but don't worry, I washed it." She said it so calmly, it was hard to imagine her bent over the toilet, letting the contents of her stomach empty themselves into the bowl. "But I had to, since we're drinking. It was vomit my food or vomit my wine, and wine hurts when it comes back up."

I scratched along my forearm, just wanting to feel like this was a dream, like my friend wasn't telling me that she puked regularly and it wasn't a big deal to her. "Does Maura know?"

Charlotte rolled her eyes and leaned back against the pillows. "Yeah, right. No one does. But you, and now you owe me a secret." She sipped her drink and her eyes glittered in the low light of the room. "It better be a good one."

I turned to the television, which she had turned back on and changed to a channel with cheesy B-movies. I settled on the easiest thing to say. "I had a boyfriend in Colorado," I said softly, the colors on the television blurring as I thought. "And I had a someone else, someone who I didn't expect."

"Oh?"

I could tell from the shift on the bed that she was sitting up straighter, but I was still staring off into the distance. "Yeah. I'd been with my boyfriend for a long time, but we were growing apart. Had been, for at least half of our relationship." Saying it aloud made me feel silly, knowing that 'half of my relationship' was actually three years. Not just a handful of months. "His roommate was the someone else."

"What happened?"

I debated unloading it onto her, telling her the whole story of my move to Colorado, of my breakup with Colin and my budding relationship with Jude. But the end of the truth always made me sad, and I didn't feel close enough to Charlotte to trust her with something of that nature just yet. If I'd told Claire, I'd have this—probably irrational, but still—worry that she'd always look at me differently. That was the problem with divulging secrets—it changed how you looked to someone else.

"That's another secret, for another time."

Charlotte groaned. "But you were just getting to the juicy part."

And that, that was precisely why I didn't want to tell Charlotte any more, especially not now. My heartache was not a spectator sport.

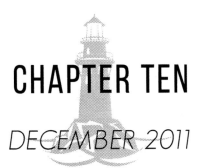

CHAPTER TEN

DECEMBER 2011

Months had passed uneventfully. I spent my days doing normal tasks around the inn, but since leaf peeper season—when all the tourists came to watch the leaves change color—was over, business at the inn had slowed considerably. Luckily, Maura had planned her renovations around the slow months, so the remaining un-renovated rooms were getting an overhaul, including mine.

"You going home for Christmas?" Maura asked after I'd emptied the dishwasher one day, a few days from Christmas.

"No," I replied, as I closed the door to the dishwasher. I didn't even know what constituted as *home* for me anyway. It certainly wasn't my mom's house. And with my grandfather in an assisted living facility, it would be the first holiday I didn't spend with him in his trailer. Most holidays for the last few years, Colin had come up a few days after Christmas, staying for about a week before he returned to Colorado. But there would be no Grandpa, no Colin, no family. It didn't make me sad, to think about it, but when Mila had texted me around Thanksgiving to give me an update, I realized how far away I was from everyone and everything I knew.

"You should," she said. "I was fine with you bumming around for

Thanksgiving, but we've waited too long to start on your room."

"I can just move to one of the others while I wait." I dipped my hand into the sink and pulled out the dishes that remained, running my finger over one of the chipped bowls.

"We're getting a wedding right before New Year's," Maura told me. "They rented out the entire inn for their wedding party."

"Wow," I said, realizing that I would have no place to stay for a few days. "Okay, I'll figure something out."

"I don't want you to feel like I'm booting you out. But, I s'pose that's exactly how it feels."

I waved her off. "It's not a big deal. It's just a little while. I'll be fine."

And that was how I found myself agreeing to Charlotte's offer to stay with her and her boyfriend's family, even though I didn't really want to.

"It'll be totally cool," Charlotte assured me as we did laundry in the basement. "Brendan's parents don't want me staying in his room with him anyway," she said with a mild look of annoyance across her face. "So I'll have a room all to myself." She shook out a towel with a snap. "Brendan's family is super cool, you'll like them."

I regarded her with a look of skepticism. "I'll like them? I like three people in Maine. Three."

"That's because you're prickly."

I'd been pulling a towel out of the dryer when she said it and, hunched over, I paused. Jude had said something similar once, likening me to a cactus. It had been five months since I'd last seen him, and I still felt the weight of his impact on me.

Part of me expected the wanting to fade, and another part of me wanted it to. It would be easier not living with all this regret. Because that's how I felt now, like I regretted leaving Colorado. But I didn't have the courage to return now, months after leaving and still no closer to figuring my life out.

"Maybe I am," I said softly, running my hand down the fibers of the towel. Looking at Charlotte, I said, "Or maybe I'm just not a nice person."

Charlotte laughed, which was such an opposite image of how she'd appeared when I first met her that I was taken aback a bit. I could hardly reconcile the Charlotte I met, with feral eyes and a hunger she couldn't satisfy, with the Charlotte I knew now, someone with her heart on her sleeve and arms ever-reaching for the next thing. I envied her a little, envied her confidence in her decision-making. And I'd be lying if I said I didn't envy her trim figure. After two seasons working for Maura, I'd begun to pack on a little bit of weight around Thanksgiving.

"Because you're an emotional eater," Charlotte had explained to me then, but I'd never seen myself as one. I was an emotional writer, sure. But I didn't eat to soothe the places I couldn't touch. "I am too, which is why," she'd continued, looking to see if Maura was listening in on our conversation, "I, you know." She held two fingers up to her mouth, gesturing like I'd forgotten what she'd told me on her bed two months before.

"Yo!" Charlotte snapped, holding a washcloth in front of my face. "You still there?"

I shook my head. "Yeah. Sorry."

"So as I was saying, Brendan has this sick house—including a pool house with a heated pool. You'll have so much fun."

But it wasn't fun I was seeking; it was a place to crash until I could return to my safe, cozy room at the inn.

"See?" Charlotte said as we pulled up the gravel driveway to Brendan's family home. It was a two-story monstrosity, with at least two dozen long windows across the front of it. The front porch appeared to wrap around the entire thing, and I saw at least four additional buildings on the property.

"It's a mansion," I said as I leaned down to take it all in. "Are his parents rich?"

"They're old money. They've had this house in their family for like a hundred years or something."

But the house didn't look a hundred years old. Maybe it had begun as a smaller building and had expanded. What sat before me looked like a cross between a southern plantation home and a New England cape home. But bigger—the biggest house I'd ever seen

"Is it a bed and breakfast or something?" I asked. We stepped out of the car and grabbed our luggage from the back seat.

"Don't be ridiculous," Charlotte said, stepping around the car to join me as we stared up at it. "It's just their house."

"Hey, babe!" We both turned at the sound of Brendan's voice. He stood in the doorway, arms spread wide.

Charlotte skipped ahead of me, practically bouncing into his arms. I'd only met Brendan once, but he was the first of Charlotte's boyfriends I'd met that didn't give me that skeevy feeling, which I'd become accustomed to with her other boyfriends.

His blond hair was buzzed so short, he nearly looked bald. But he had a nice face, a face that I realized then fit with his wealthier background. I think it was his skin that had tipped me off—how perfectly flawless he looked. Not a single blemish. Even his eyebrows were perfectly groomed. He was tall, lean, and his clothes looked like he'd put them on fresh for the occasion—not a wrinkle in sight.

I looked down at my jeans, at the hole in one of the knees. I'd worn high socks to help battle the cold that filtered through it, so yellow and black stripes peeked through it. At least I'd worn one of my nicer shirts, but because of the cold I was bundled up in an over-sized sweater and scarf that didn't match any of my outfit.

Brendan smiled at me as he hugged Charlotte. "Trista, right?"

Nodding, I climbed the steps up to the front porch as he let Charlotte go. "Thanks for letting me tag along."

"No big deal," he said with a purse of his lips. He ran a hand over his hair, but there was no hair to push back into place. "All my cousins are coming up from Vermont, so it'll soon be like *Home Alone* in here." Wrapping an arm around Charlotte, he added, "But I chose the best room for you two, so don't worry."

I wasn't worried about there being a lot of people, because I'd had plans to bunk in the room the entire time I was here, until I was able to go back to the inn. "Sounds great," I said, forcing a smile as we followed him into the house and down a quiet hallway that was lined with photos of Brendan and, who I assumed to be, his brother; Brendan holding trophies for academic tournaments and sport tournaments; Brendan's high school graduation with a thick gold sash around his neck; his college graduation, and several more that highlighted his many accomplishments. His success was intimidating. What did I have to compare it to?

I grew up in a decrepit trailer park with my druggie mom, dropped out of college when my best friend died, stayed in a relationship with a guy who didn't really love me, and then got myself beat up by said druggie mom's boyfriend before I drove to Maine with a car that ticked for nearly a thousand miles. It was a far cry from the successful life Brendan had lived, and it was another reason I didn't tell anyone much about my background, and my family history.

"Here we are," he said as he pushed open one of the many doors in the hallway.

The room was bright thanks to the large windows that faced the front and the yellow paint that covered every wall. Two identical twin beds were lined up against the wall opposite the windows, their fluffy white comforters looking inviting enough for me to face plant in the first one I saw.

"This is great." I gave him a grateful smile as I set my bag on the floor.

Charlotte echoed me but in her Charlotte way, with much more enthusiasm. "I love it!"

"Why don't you two freshen up and then come meet the fam." He pointed down the hallway, the way we'd come in. "Just go past the stairs and follow the noise.

"Fantastic," Charlotte beamed, closing the door when he retreated back down the hall. She turned and leaned her back against the door as she faced me. "This place is great, isn't it?"

It was hard not to agree with her when she was smiling at me like that. But I still felt a little weird crashing on my friend's boyfriend's holiday weekend and I tried not to let it show on my face. "But freshen up? It was only an hour drive."

"Well, I know that." Charlotte flopped onto the nearest bed and sighed contentedly. "But I'm guessing he means our current clothes. You've seen how he dresses."

"Like a mannequin in the mall," I said, but it wasn't an insult. He did dress nice, from the ironed black shirt he'd tucked into dark jeans to the matte black belt and fancy penny loafers. It was certainly different from the lazy holidays I was used to.

I opened my suitcase and thumbed through the offerings. I'd counted on spending most of the time in my room, with my face in a book or my fingers smudged with ink, but thankfully, Charlotte had convinced me to pack a couple nicer outfits.

I dressed in black slacks and a white sweater. It was simple, but Charlotte had smiled approvingly as she changed into a knee-length, long-sleeved red dress with black nylons and black ankle boots. She always dressed with such thought, something I'd noticed about Claire too. I brushed my hair, which was now past my shoulders and bleached blonde again, while Charlotte reapplied her eyeshadow and lip gloss.

"Have you met his parents before?"

She rubbed her lips together and then made a kissy face in the mirror. "Yep. They're great." But Charlotte said that about nearly everyone. Even people who weren't great. It made me a little anxious, to be the sidekick in this situation, but Charlotte and Brendan had both acted like it wasn't weird for a stranger to spend time with an unfamiliar family on Christmas.

I followed Charlotte down the hall and around the curved staircase, following the noise that seemed to echo off the wooden floors and up to the high ceilings. The family room was large, with a wall of windows that faced the backyard and a ceiling that stretched so high that Charlotte could've stood on my shoulders and still been several feet from touching it. Candles were lit across a white brick fireplace where over a dozen stockings hung. A large evergreen tree was tucked into a corner, white lights blinking all around it. Brendan, spotting us from the recliner he was stretched out on, stood up and joined us by the entryway. "Hey, everyone," he said, stopping the chatter of the ten or so people around the room. "This is Charlotte—I know you've met her, Mom and Dad—and Trista, Charlotte's best friend."

The best friend part prickled me a little, not because I was unhappy with being called her best friend but because it surprised me. I didn't have a best friend, but if I did Charlotte wouldn't be it. And I realized how ungracious that was, but it wasn't because I didn't like Charlotte. It was because a best friend, to me, was someone you shared deep things with. Not someone who skimmed across the surface of your life.

"Hello." A woman I assumed to be Brendan's mom approached us and smiled at me before giving Charlotte a hug. "So glad you two could join us." She had a calmness about her, and I instantly felt at ease around her. She tucked a long blonde strand behind her ear. "It's going to get wild in here pretty soon, so I'm pleased you arrived early before the chaos."

Charlotte hooked her arm around mine and pulled me tight, as if she was trying to illustrate our sudden best friend status. "That's what Brendan said," she said with a smile in her voice. Charlotte seemed a little different around her, like she was more subdued and yet more affectionate at the same time.

"I can't wait, Mrs. Waterhouse," I said with more excitement than I felt at the prospect of being surrounded by even more strangers.

Brendan's mom put her hand out to me. "Call me Elizabeth," she said. "There will be more than one Mrs. Waterhouse here soon, so no need to address me so formally." She nodded toward the dining table. "Help yourself. There's a mimosa station and some hors d'oeuvres."

Brendan steered us toward the table where there was a whole station for mimosas. Different bottles of champagne, schnapps, and four different kinds of orange juice in glass pitchers were surrounded by tall glasses with orange slices on the rims. "My mom likes her mimosas." Brendan laughed as he handed me an empty glass. "How would you like it?"

"Uh. . ." I held my glass and stared at all the options, not even sure how to begin. My Christmases had never included mimosas, so they weren't exactly something I was used to.

"I got this," Charlotte said, taking my glass and beginning to assemble mimosas for both of us. As she did, I looked back at all the people in the family room, sitting along a fluffy-looking sectional, on the floor with mimosas in hand, or peering out the windows as they chattered. Christmas music was playing on a low volume; from speakers I couldn't see. Above the fireplace was a large portrait of Brendan, his mom, and who I assumed to be his dad and his brother. I couldn't tell for sure from this far away, but it looked like it was a painting, not a photograph.

I'd only been there for ten minutes, but already I was so far out of my element that I looked at Charlotte a little desperately. "I feel weird," I whispered as I stood beside her.

"Don't feel weird," she said in a voice that was *not* a whisper. I elbowed her in the arm that wasn't holding a mimosa.

"Thanks," I hissed.

"Just relax." She handed me a mimosa. "Drink, because if this many people make you nervous already, it's only going to get harder when this room actually fills up.

She wasn't wrong. Just a couple hours later, the house was packed to the gills. The hallway with many doors, where Charlotte and I were staying, was suddenly so loud that even sitting in my room wasn't peaceful. If anything, it only made me more anxious, keeping a watchful eye on the door every time I heard footsteps thunder down the hallway.

I wondered if I'd have felt more comfortable if I'd grown up with siblings or with larger family get-togethers during the holidays. But for the last ten years, my holidays had been spent with my grandpa, sometimes my grandma, and sometimes my boyfriend. I was used to opening presents and then spending the rest of the day lumped on the couch, watching every holiday movie on cable television. There hadn't been socializing, no mingling around with groups of strangers, wearing a plastic smile the whole time, even when you were repeatedly bumped into from behind so hard that you nearly lost balance.

The first day, Charlotte had left me to sit in our room with my ear buds in my ears the whole time while she got to know Brendan's family. I wasn't upset by that, in fact I relished the alone time, even if the noise from the younger kids was enough to have my eyes darting to the bedroom door every few minutes. I couldn't write, not with music in my ears and all that noise interrupting any deep thoughts I may have tried to consider.

The second day, Christmas Eve, the entire family did a white elephant Christmas. I sat on the side, watching how they all laughed until the point of crying with some of the gifts. Charlotte had participated, receiving a lightsaber, which she used to poke at Brendan playfully. Brendan had told us that they did this every year, because summers were too busy to spend any considerable amount of time together, so winter was the only time they got together.

After the older adults had retreated to the family room, Brendan and his brother Chris took Charlotte and me to the pool house. It was separated from the house by a stone walkway, set off at one corner of their massive backyard. Three sides of the building itself were completely glass, and on our approach I could see all the lights that cast different colors over the pool water through the windows.

Chris stepped up beside me, bumping into me companionably. "Did Brendan tell you about the time I shot one of those windows out with my BB gun?"

The windows looked to be at least five feet in height, three feet in width, and I couldn't even guess what they must have cost. "No," I said, glancing at Charlotte and Brendan as they huddled together just ahead of us. "How'd you manage that?"

Chris looked over his shoulder back to the house. "Don't tell Mom," he said on a laugh, "but the story I told her is that I tripped and the gun went off." He shoved his hands into his pockets.

"What's the truth?" I shivered on the walk across the stone pavers, but there was only about six inches of snow around them. I was glad I'd insisted on wearing sweats over my swimsuit, especially when I saw how freezing cold Charlotte was in just her bikini a few feet ahead of me.

"The truth was that I wanted to be wicked cool. Brendan is a little older than me, and he's always succeeded in everything he set his mind to. But me?" He pointed to his chest. "I've always had to work for everything. So when I saw this bird fly by, I thought, 'How bad ass would it be if I brought this bird to Mom for dinner?'"

I laughed, trying to imagine how anything Chris could kill with a BB gun would make a sufficient dinner. "How old were you?"

"Oh, this was just last summer." But then he flashed a grin, nearly identical to Brendan's. "Just kidding."

"Thank god. I was about to feel bad for laughing."

"I was nine years old. Total bad-ass age. So when the bird flew by the pool house, I didn't even think—I just lifted my gun and aimed."

"Did you get the bird?"

"Hell no. It flew off without a care in the world, while I watched the glass split and then shatter all over the grass."

"Did it shatter in the pool, too?"

"No, see," he put his hands on my shoulder to turn me when we reached the pool house in a gesture that I knew was innocuous, but it still made me freeze up. No man had touched me since Doug, and before that, Jude. If Chris sensed the way I bristled at his touch, he didn't show it. "Look." He pointed at the window. "It's double-paned. So I only destroyed the outside pane."

I could see the separation between the two windows as I followed him through the French door entrance. "That's lucky, I guess."

"I guess. Mom didn't see anything lucky about it though."

"No, I imagine not." I gave him a smile. "I bet that was expensive to replace."

Chris shrugged like it was no big deal, and I realized that was one of the comforts of having money—expense wasn't a worry. I'd never had that luxury, and still didn't. Maura didn't treat me like a peasant, but after providing room and board, I didn't exactly receive a large paycheck. I made just enough to float me until next payday, but with no backup plan if there was a problem. I envied Chris a little for that—not for the fact that he had money, but for the fact that he wasn't weighed down by the burden of money.

The pool was one of those above-ground pools, but there was flooring built around it so that it felt in-ground. Against the only wall that was without windows were a few doors to what I assumed were bathrooms. Between two of the doors was a bar built into the wall, which was where we found Charlotte and Brendan, already mixing drinks.

"What'll you have?" Brendan asked as I took a seat beside Charlotte.

"Just water is fine, thanks."

"Get me a beer, will you?" Chris asked from behind me.

Brendan tossed him a bottle and Chris popped the top off of it on the edge of the bar counter. I felt like maybe he was trying to impress me a little, but I had zero romantic interest in him. Not that he wasn't attractive; he was. He looked like his brother, but a little broader, like he played football or something of that nature. But I wasn't interested because I wasn't looking for anything. If I couldn't be with Jude because I didn't know who I was, I certainly couldn't casually date anyone else.

I watched as Brendan tapped a few buttons on the wall and the pool house transformed from a brightly lit room to being dimmed, with the lights in the pool the brightest and lights under the bar top being the only light to guide us around the pool house. Music poured from three wall-mounted speakers above the bar and Charlotte clapped gleefully. In a different circumstance, I might've found it exciting too, but I had the feeling that I was on a double date of sorts with Brendan's brother, and that made me itchy.

"There is a bathroom through here," Brendan said, patting on the middle door. "Down there is a towel room, and it's a bit warmer than in here, so you dry off quickly.

"What's that room?" Charlotte asked, pointing to the third door at the other end.

"Storage and the water heater."

"This is so nice, you guys." I was glad Charlotte was doing all of the talking, because I definitely felt like I was on uneven ground around Chris.

"We know how to party," Chris said behind me, and Brendan smiled at him. The look they exchanged made me feel a little uncomfortable, or at least more uncomfortable than I had already been feeling. "Help yourselves to whatever. I'm getting in the pool."

And not three seconds later, he was jumping into the pool, sending water all over us and the windows.

"Come on," Charlotte said, grabbing my hand and pulling me with her through the door to the bathroom. Once we were safely on the other side, Charlotte pulled her hair up into a high pony in the mirror. "Chris is cool, right?"

I narrowed my eyes, but not in annoyance. "Chris seems nice, sure." I glanced back at the door for a second before turning to her again. "But I hope he's not under the impression this is a date or something."

"Don't be silly," Charlotte said, pushing loose strands of hair back and pinning them with bobby pins. "It's not a date at all. We're in their house, swimming at their pool."

Her nonchalance didn't ease me even the slightest, but she did have a point. "Okay. I just wanted to make sure he wasn't expecting anything."

"Even if he was, all you'd have to do was say no."

She made it sound easy, like words had that much power. But I knew from experience that sometimes saying no wasn't enough in the ears of someone else. "Okay," was all I said to her instead.

"Take off your sweats and let's go."

Charlotte was thin, with the faintest trace of muscle definition in her stomach. Standing next to her really made me feel like a whale, which was why I was glad I'd opted for a tankini suit with shorts.

"What is this, the nineteen-twenties?" Charlotte asked as she tugged on the fabric that covered my stomach.

"Some of us aren't as comfortable with ourselves," I said, the bite of bitterness sharp even to my ears.

"It's not like you're chunky," she replied. She poked my stomach and I winced. "You have a little belly fat, but it's not bad or anything."

"Gee, thanks, Char." She ignored my sarcasm and shrugged.

"You could always try to lose the weight, like I do."

But what she did wasn't healthy, I reminded myself when I felt the faintest hint of temptation. I couldn't do it.

I wasn't sure why I needed to remind myself of these things.

When we finally left the bathroom, the guys were in the pool along with four beach balls. They didn't notice us at first and I was thankful for that. Even though I wasn't romantically interested in Chris, I still didn't want him to look at me and see the fat that clung to my figure stubbornly.

The moment they lifted their heads in our direction, I jumped into the water.

It was like bath water, warm and soothing over my limbs. I treaded water on one end even though I could easily touch the bottom, as Chris and Brendan tossed a ball back and forth to one another. Charlotte climbed down the ladder into the pool, and I found it an interesting contradiction to how she approached life. She'd been single for two weeks before she'd latched on to Brendan, and her relationship with him was longer than any of the ones I'd been around for.

I watched her arms circle his neck and his hands went to her waist as he spun her around. The lights in the water changed from blue to green and the music could barely be heard over our splashing and swimming. "Catch!" Chris called just as he lobbed a beach ball my way. I barely had a second to register its approach, but lifted my hand just before it hit me in the face, hitting it back in his direction. The pool was only about four feet deep the whole way around, so we were able to move around with ease.

"Let's play chicken!" Charlotte shouted before Brendan dove under the water between her legs and lifted her in the air on his shoulders. He shook his face and then wiped the water that poured over his eyes.

I started shaking my head, but before I could say anything, I felt myself being lifted off of my feet and I yelped, grabbing hold of Chris's body as he emerged from the water. "I've never played chicken," I said weakly, feeling even more self-conscious of the fact that I was on Chris's shoulders, his neck in line with my crotch. But his arms crossed over my shins, holding me firmly to him.

"All you have to do is knock me off of Brendan's shoulders," Charlotte said as Brendan stepped toward us and Charlotte put her hands out to grab me. I let her hold on for a second before I pushed her a little. Brendan barely stepped back a step before coming forward again. Chris stepped left and right as I reached for Charlotte, keeping us moving so that we were a harder target for them. Once I'd grabbed hold of Charlotte's forearms, she grabbed mine and we struggled back and forth, twisting one another as the guys laughed at the noises we were making. Slowly, I lost what had made me self-conscious and began to enjoy myself. I knew my thoughts were exhausting, which was why I often kept them to myself, but I hadn't realized how much they hindered me.

We struggled for a few more minutes until I grabbed Charlotte's hands and then pushed, sending her sliding backward off of Brendan's shoulders. Immediately, Chris went under the water and I slid from his shoulders. The water felt shockingly warm on the backs of my thighs after being on Chris's shoulders for so long.

When Charlotte emerged, she shouted, "I call a rematch!"

"Come on, brother," Brendan said to Chris as he pulled Charlotte to him.

"No way, I'm whooped." Chris swam to one side of the pool and then leaned back against it, his arms up on the side as his legs kicked out.

"Oh, you really put the 'baby' in the label 'baby brother.'" Brendan picked Charlotte up and tossed her in the air as she squealed.

"Well, you had it easy," Chris said with a nod to where Charlotte had landed in the water. "She weighs less than a beer."

I wanted to curl into myself then; make myself so small that not only would they be unable to see me, but their comments couldn't touch me.

"Ouch, dude," Brendan admonished him with a look at me.

It didn't matter, I told myself, at the same time as Doug's haunting words filtered through my thoughts.

Fat. Worthless.

I rubbed a hand over my stomach under the water and turned my face away from them. Why should I have been so affected by what Chris said? It was amazing to me that we could hurt so deeply over the things said by inconsequential people.

"I didn't mean it like that," Chris said as Charlotte's head popped up from under water.

"What did you mean?" Brendan asked, and I wanted to tell him to shut up so that I didn't have to listen to them having a conversation about my weight while I was within hearing distance.

"I meant that Charlotte," Chris said, with clear and defined frustration in his voice, "weighs practically nothing."

"What did I miss?" Charlotte asked, but I had turned away from the lot of them to look out of the window, at the stars that blinked up in the sky.

"Chris won't go again because Trista is too heavy for him."

I closed my eyes and curled my toes into the smooth bottom of the pool. *Shut up, shut up, shut up,* I thought.

But somehow, the silence that ensued after that comment was even worse—like everyone was looking at me, or thinking about me, and the way I was too heavy for another guy to carry on his shoulders.

I didn't last long in the pool after that, and went back to my room alone. Charlotte was splashing around when I left, so I knew she hadn't noticed me leaving. Which was fine. It was. I didn't need her taking pity on me.

As I brushed my teeth for bed, I stared at my reflection in the mirror. My cheeks were rounder than I remembered them being and my pointed chin wasn't so pointed, not with the flesh that surrounded it. I was wearing pajamas, but my shirt was tight enough on me that I could see the roundness in my belly protruding against the fabric.

I gripped my hand around the toothbrush handle a bit tighter, sliding over the back of my teeth more rigorously.

Remembering the story Charlotte had told me, about being pregnant and puking, I paused in brushing my teeth.

I wish I could say I wasn't fully aware of what I was doing, that the toothbrush moved back, farther and farther until I felt my stomach clench down, that I wasn't controlling it all. But I was—I was the one in control. I was the one that pushed the toothbrush all the way to the back of my mouth until I felt that hot vomit rise up my throat and pour out of my mouth into the sink.

Gagging, I dropped my toothbrush and gripped the sides of the sink. Their coolness seemed to have an immediate effect, calming my stomach and my nerves, and my breathing became less shallow as the water pulled my vomit down the drain.

Looking into the mirror, I saw the blood that had rushed to the skin around my mouth, the tears in my eyes, and I found myself hating that person in the mirror a little less than I had when I'd left the pool house. Even though most of my vomit had just been the water I'd drank in the pool house, there had been a little bit of food. My stomach whined from being empty, so I filled my hand with water from the faucet and drank it, clearing my mouth of the acid taste.

And then, with more calm than I knew I possessed, I squirted another glob of toothpaste on my brush and brushed my teeth again.

I felt like my thoughts were swarming me, trying to get me to sort out how I felt about puking.

Relief was the biggest sensation, but close behind was disgust. I was weak. I'd followed a crooked path, made a decision I couldn't take back. I had given in. I was weak. And I was still fat. Still worthless.

But I was empty—a feeling I knew all too well, a feeling that was comfortable, in a way.

And overwhelming all of this was knowing that it wouldn't be my last time forcing myself to vomit. I was weak. Fat. Worthless.

I'd already admitted defeat in doing it the first time. Why shouldn't I do it again?

Just then, my phone buzzed. It took me a second to register what the sound was, because I so rarely received texts or calls, but there it was. Buzzing.

I looked down at the name that flashed across the screen: Mila.

There were few reasons she could be calling me, but I found myself pressing answer anyway.

"Hello?"

The silence on the other end was punctuated with the sound of one breath being exhaled. "Trista."

It wasn't Mila on the other end. It was Jude.

I didn't know what to say. My fight or flight response kicked in and I wanted to drop my phone. Instead I cradled it, not saying a single word.

"Are you okay?"

I nodded, but the vomit smell that remained in the bathroom with me was pungent all of a sudden. "I'm fine." I was glad he couldn't look at me, call me the liar I was.

"Where are you?"

"I'm somewhere safe," I told him, but it felt false somehow.

"It's Christmas. Are you alone?"

"No." It was a whisper.

"I'm worried about you."

"Don't be."

"I miss you," he said, and I felt it slither in between my ribs, racking against my heart.

"I miss you too." And then I hung up.

CHAPTER ELEVEN
MAY 2012

Tuesdays were my favorite, because I had the day off. I worked half days on Wednesdays and Thursdays and full days every other day of the week.

Except Tuesdays. Often, I spent them in a coffee shop, reading books on poetry so that I could learn more. I didn't need more inspiration, necessarily.

But that Tuesday, something in the air felt different, so I took my books and a roll-out towel mat to the beach. The weather was much cooler than what was typical desirable beach weather, but I wasn't going to go in the water, so the cooler air didn't bother me.

On my way out the door, Maura stopped me as she dried her hands on a dish towel.

"It's my day off," I told her, like she wasn't the person who made the schedule and knew when my days off were.

"I know," she said plainly, looking me up and down with an eagle eye. "What's wrong with you?"

"Huh?" I asked, slipping my bag up higher on my shoulder with one hand while I wrapped my fingers around the strap.

She pointed with one hand at my face. "You've lost weight. I'm not sure as to how much, but something's different with your face."

Ever since Christmas, I had found myself more comfortable with vomiting after eating. Not all my meals. Not even every day. Just a few times a week. I'd noticed a negligible difference in the way my pants fell from my hips, but then, I wouldn't notice a difference in myself. I wore this skin day in and day out, my feet carried this weight every single day. I wouldn't notice any change over a period of five months. "I've been more active since I started on here."

"Uh huh." It was Maura's favorite thing to say. "For someone who claims to be active, I sure see you sitting in the sunroom a lot, tapping that pen to your mouth."

I blinked at her, surprised she'd noticed. In my off hours, which were blessedly few, I often found myself in the sun porch Maura had installed at the back of the inn, curled up in the window seat if it was free, staring at a notebook as I contemplated what to write. "It's the nicest spot in the house."

With a lift of her eyebrow, she said, "I know that, girl. But what I'm saying is that I don't see you walking around," she lifted her hands in air quotes, "being 'more active' and such." She tucked the dish towel in her apron and cocked her head to the side. "I've noticed you've been hanging around Charlotte more."

I'd been growing closer to Claire before Christmas had hit, but ever since Christmas at Charlotte's boyfriend's house, I'd felt more drawn to her. She understood what it was like, to walk around in a sleeve of flesh that you didn't understand. To live with heartbreak and find solace in other things.

"I've been walking a lot, on Tuesdays," I explained, which wasn't a total lie but not the reason I left the inn on Tuesdays. "Do you need me today?"

Maura peered at me, and I had the feeling that she didn't believe me. "You taking the laxatives?"

With a laugh, I gave her a raised eyebrow. "The laxatives? Is that code for something?"

Maura pointed above us at the ceiling. "Claire, when she was in school, got into the laxatives."

"Do you mean actual laxatives?"

She narrowed her eyes. "'Course I do. Do I look like someone who would one, know street names for drugs and two, use code words? I'm talking plain English, straight up laxatives, girl. Follow what I'm sayin' here."

She had a point, so I nodded. "But why would Claire take laxatives?"

"Psh," Maura said with a roll of her eyes. "Girl thought she was fat or something. So I told her if she was worried about it to lay off the midnight ice cream. But does she listen to me? 'Course not." Maura seemed to fire up the more she spoke. "But then my brother calls me and tells me she's taking laxatives to lose weight. Couldn't have been comfortable, being on the shitter all the time, but what do I know?" But Maura, with one hand on her hip and the shake of her head, was keenly aware that she knew better than a teenager taking laxatives to lose weight.

"I've never heard of that."

"Well, that's because it's stupid." If Maura could spit in her own home, she would've. But she tossed her head back and shook her hair away from her face. "Anyways, she's not on them anymore, but I wouldn't be surprised if you did something like that too."

I laughed, because it was Maura, someone who did better with insults than compliments. "Thanks for the vote of confidence, Maura." All this talk was making me more anxious, so I hiked my bag up higher and gave her a raise of my eyebrows. "But I'm going to go down to the beach for the day, if you need me."

She wagged a finger at me as she shuffled some papers along her desk. "Can you help me with the site later? I'm getting double bookings for some reason when people try to reserve a room."

I nodded, my hand on the door. "Sure. I can do that tonight."

She nodded but then tilted her head. She looked me over like she saw something in me, but wasn't sure what it was. "You got a coat in there?

It's breezed up out there," she said with a tilt of her head to the window.

I was getting used to some of the Maine colloquialisms, but they still set me back for a pause as I looked out the window—seeing the wind sending a stray bit of trash down the drive. "Come on, Maura," I said with a light laugh. "It's the warmest day we've had in ages."

She waved a hand at me. "Then get off with you, if you know so much."

"I'll be back before dinner. I'll look at the website then."

"Good." She nodded like I'd satisfied whatever worries she had for me. I said one last goodbye before I left the house.

I was halfway down the planked walkway to the beach when I felt my phone vibrate in my pocket.

In the months since I'd first texted Mila from my new phone, we'd exchanged very few texts. In fact, I could count on two hands the number of times she'd initiated conversations with me, whereas I hadn't reached out to her even once. But the text that came through made me pause my steps.

Mila: I'm really sorry.

I stared at that for a minute before I scrolled up through our previous messages, wondering what her meaning was. Our last text exchange had been a week earlier and had gone simply:

Mila: Just checking in. You okay?
Me: Peachy. You?
Mila: Fine. Just bored, waiting at a casting call.
Me: Jude?
Mila: Everything is good here. I'd tell you if it wasn't.
Me: Thanks, Mila.

And that was it. That was how our conversations generally went. She often extended the olive branch to talk to me about things going on in her life, but part of me still hadn't forgiven her for what had happened before I'd left Colorado. I was still angrier with Colin, but that anger felt abstract—like I wasn't that upset because I hadn't felt much for him in so long. But the apology text confused me. So I replied simply.

Me: ?

She didn't respond immediately, so I spread my towel mat onto the sand and wrapped myself in the sweater I'd packed before I laid out my pens and notebook.

Maine was such a different landscape than Wyoming or Colorado. And even though I'd lived in Maine far longer than I had ever lived in Colorado, Maine didn't feel like home. I had a job, I had people counting on me. But it wasn't a place that felt permanent. It was just a place that I was in for the time being. I likened it to a grocery store, a place I visited to get what I needed. I just hadn't figured out yet what I needed.

But when I said that to myself, my mind always, always went to Jude. I needed to change my way of thinking, because I shouldn't *need* anyone to be myself. That's how I differed from Charlotte. She chased heartache so much that it was a part of who she was. But I'd had enough sadness to last me for a long while. I just didn't know who I was outside of the pain.

I opened my green notebook, and thought of who always crossed my mind the moment I put pen to paper.

Jude. My muse.

I never realized
my silence
was tied to
my suffering.

I never realized
how lonely
my heart was.
Until your voice
filled my ears
and your love
filled my heart.
And now
it's always silent
and I'm always empty.
But it was my choice,
and, very likely,
my mistake.

I no longer cried when I wrote words like these ones, the ones admitting that leaving Colorado had likely been a mistake. But it'd been ten months, and I was still gone. In my head, I wanted to know he was happy—even if it was with someone else. But if I let myself think about it too much, my heart, my undeserving, selfish heart, wanted him to be waiting for me.

I'd been so lost in the space I occupied in my head when I wrote for Jude that I didn't hear my phone go off with a new notification.

Mila: I'll call you later.

For some reason, that was more alarming than the apology text from earlier.

Me: Is something wrong? Is Jude okay?

Thankfully, her reply to that was quick.

Mila: He's great.

But that didn't soothe me like it should've, because I did that thing I didn't want to do; I overanalyzed. What did 'great' mean? Had he moved on? Found his hands filled by someone who wasn't me?

I dipped my hand into the sand, embraced the cold that hit my bones. I let my palm fill with granules and just watched them cave into my hand. Each tiny fleck, white or brown or black or green, was important. Each one. As I lifted my hand, those granules slipped from the crevices that had held them, sliding back to the ground in a new pattern. A few flecks clung to my skin, stubbornly, before I brushed my hand across my kneecap.

My kneecap was bonier than it had been. I tried not to take too much pleasure in that, in feeling of the hard bone pushing against the sliver of skin. But pleasure slithered in nonetheless, even though I knew, deep in my gut, that what I was doing was wrong.

Fat and worthless.

I could pretend the words had no effect on me, that they were colorless and tasteless, but in reality, they were louder than a neon sign and more bitter than my feelings for the person who spoke the words in the first place.

Ache lived within me, so deep that I could disembowel myself and still it would remain. I couldn't clean myself of this ache, this need for Jude. For love.

I fell back on the towel so that I faced the sky. It wasn't a roof and it wasn't a mountain. It was something else.

But it wasn't enough.

I held up my phone and watched the numbers change from 10:54 to 10:55 and then my vision blurred and the next thing I knew, it was 11:04 and I was still thinking of Jude.

Slowly, I felt the sand beneath my towel shifting, spreading, allowing me to better sink into it. I felt the weight of my decisions pushing me deeper into the earth and I waited for it to swallow me whole.

A hundred times, I told myself that I could be with Jude and figure myself out. But each time, I told myself that my identity could not be defined by a man, but by myself. And if I drowned inside of the life Jude could give me, I'd never fight my way through it.

Dropping my phone felt like I was dropping a little bit of the weight I carried.

The waves rolled up to the shore, and a wind picked up around me, whistling and singing its song.

And I gathered the words in my head and said them aloud instead of writing them down.

Because if I wrote them, they'd live longer than they would in the breezy air.

It was unseasonably warm for May, or so I'd heard from the locals when they breezed in for Maura's Boston cream pies. But it made the slow walk back to the inn a little bit better, helping to warm the coldness that had seeped in through the towel to my skin. I waved to Claire's dad, who gave me a polite smile but then turned away, on his cell phone. It'd been a while since I'd spent time with Claire outside of the inn, and I felt like I probably should message her, set something up for that weekend.

At the foot of Maura's driveway, I got a rock stuck in the bottom of my flip-flop. The sharp edge cut into my heel, giving me an ache that radiated up my leg. I paused, sitting on one of the rocks that adorned the landscape as I picked it back out. It was probably too cold for most people to wear flip-flops, but I loved kicking them off once I was on the beach, letting the sand fill all the spaces between my toes before I could shake it all off.

After successfully dislodging the rock, I looked up at the house to see if Charlotte was working yet—knowing that she'd recently picked up a new boyfriend, which meant she'd probably take off for a week here soon.

But her bike wasn't parked up against the side. The only vehicles up by the entrance were Maura's pickup and a small, sleeker car I didn't recognize.

I made my way up the driveway, stopping to kick more rocks that had gotten in between my foot and the foamy part of my flip-flop before I let myself in the back door, into the kitchen. It was distinctly cooler in the house, so I slipped a Maine sweatshirt over my head before stepping into the kitchen.

"Oh, good, you're back." Maura came huffing from the dining area, her arms laden with plates. "Charlotte didn't show up," she said, with a roll of her eyes. But I knew, whatever Maura's feelings for Charlotte, she felt sort of responsible for her, like she was the fuck-up of a daughter she never had. "And we've got a guest." She lifted her left shoulder and turned briefly, to indicate the guest was waiting in the foyer.

I looked down at myself, my sweat shorts and the oversized Maine sweatshirt hanging off my shoulder. "Let me get changed first."

Maura fluttered a hand at me. "Don't bother. It's some flatlander." She dropped the dishes onto the counter. "I've got to go up the road apiece, Chuck's car broke down and he's got my heating element for the stove." Maura smacked the stove as she passed, grabbing her raincoat that hung by the door on her way. "We've got a few rooms on the second floor that weren't used, give 'em one of them." And then she grabbed her key and was out the door a second later, the screen slamming and bouncing against the frame on her way out.

"Ugh," I said, looking down at the dirt caked under my nails and flecks of sand embedded in my nail beds. After quickly washing my hands, I ventured out into the reception area, rubbing them dry on my shorts and hoping to sneak behind the front desk without the tourist noticing my dirty shorts. But there was no one waiting in the reception area. All I smelled was the lemony cleaner Maura favored for polishing the wood up front.

After checking out front, I was assured the car was still there. I leaned against the window for a minute, watching the dark clouds coming in from the west. Maura's choice of raincoat made sense, but she hadn't even looked outside. It didn't surprise me, knowing Maura relied on a lot of old-fashioned things to tell her the impending weather.

I tapped on the glass, gently as I leaned against its wood frame. And then I heard a noise to my left and turned around.

I was still alone in the front reception area, but off to the side of it was the sunroom I favored so much.

After brushing my hair back from my shoulders, I stepped into the sunroom and, instantly, my knees locked me to keep my motions at a standstill.

My hands, which had been tugging my sweatshirt down, stilled. My blood suddenly poured hot, through all my limbs.

Broad shoulders were clothed in black-and-white checkered flannel, and worn jeans were all I could see from the back of him. But one arm was reaching up on a shelf above the wall opposite me, and the flannel was rolled to the elbows, revealing tree tattoos that climbed from his wrist to the crook of his elbow.

Every artery and every vein that held my heart in its place shuddered. A thousand bricks fell into my stomach and I gripped the back of one armchair to keep me standing, facing the back of a man I loved and hadn't seen in ten months.

I waited, holding a pocket of breath in my chest, for him to turn.

And when he did, his eyes met mine immediately. Like he was waiting, biding his time for me to see him.

For ten months, I'd wondered if I had loved him more than he'd cared for me. But the look in his eyes, that exultant shine that spread to his lips, made me wonder how I ever could have thought myself alone when someone looked at me like that—like I was the whole world wrapped up in skin and tissue and a heart that ached constantly.

"Trista," he said, saying the two syllables as if they were his favorite. And just like that, the ache in my gut was satisfied and my arms, of their own volition, reached for him as he stepped across the room to me.

"Jude," I breathed, just as his solid arms wrapped around me.

CHAPTER TWELVE
ONE YEAR LATER
JUNE 2013

Walking into baggage claim, I felt a hundred pounds heavier. I'd spent the past twelve hours of travel thinking about everything I never said.

I stared at the baggage claim screen, waiting for my flight to pop up so I'd know where to collect my bag. The green letters blurred in my vision and I blinked, feeling like my sandpaper eyelids had scraped off the top layer of my eyeballs.

There were dozens of people milling around me as children climbed on luggage carts, pushed by other children, their mothers travel-weary and staring at bag after bag as it fell from the luggage chute. I watched lovers embrace, some with tears and others with whoops of joy, and then he said my name.

It had been one year since he'd held me. One year since he'd looked at me and said my name. And in total, two years of waiting to be enough, to be ready. But when I felt his presence at my back, I squeezed my eyes tight and sucked in a breath.

"Jude," I said on my exhale.

His warm hand touched my shoulder tentatively, squeezing gently before he let go. "Hey."

Opening my eyes, I turned around. Good god, seeing him was like seeing the sun after being underground for so long. I memorized his long lashes, the warm whiskey-colored irises and the way his eyes squinted as he searched me over. "How are you?" I could inhale his voice and hold it close—it was that familiar, homey feeling I'd been looking for, for so long. His voice. I had nearly convinced myself that I'd imagined it, and him, that everything had been a lie I'd told myself, to pretend that I was worth someone loving.

The hair along his jaw moved when I watched him clench his teeth together. His full lips were set in a line, but his eyes were warm despite the fact that he seemed to want to keep me at a distance.

My lips cracked when I opened them. "I'm okay," I said, but hated it the moment it left my lips. What an inadequate word.

"You're. . ." His voice faltered as his eyes glided over me. "Are you hungry?"

I heard what he wanted to ask, but was too afraid to. It was something others had asked me with less tact, with a sneer or judgment in their voice. But Jude didn't want to split me in two in the noisy baggage terminal and I was grateful. I nodded. *Yes, I'm hungry.* But it wasn't for food. I was hungry, I was famished, to feel something.

He reached for my hand, but at the last second he didn't make contact. I squeezed my fingers into a fist to keep from reaching back for him, but a sliver of me was surprised by the ache I felt that he'd stopped. "Your baggage carousel is over here, number four." He tilted his head left, his eyes still squinted with concern. "Can I take your backpack?"

I shook my head. "I've got this," I said before leading the way to carousel four.

Knowing he stared at me as I walked away from him, I made a conscious effort to not look like my legs were about to disintegrate underneath me. I imagined myself falling to a million pieces, tumbling across the floor, just to know if he'd pick me up, piece by piece.

But I held as steady as I could, walking to the carousel with more strength in me than I knew I possessed. My legs trembled when I saw him out of my periphery, standing beside me. And directly in my vision was the image of two people embracing, clutching one another's faces like they couldn't believe their blessings, to hold the one they loved so close. I closed my eyes, not wanting to see it. Not wanting to compare it.

"How was your flight?"

Opening my eyes and attempting to appear as unaffected as he was acting, I said, "Fine. How was the drive?"

"Short."

This was not the language of two people who had been in love, something I acknowledged with a deep sadness. This was how strangers talked. A chauffeur would address me more warmly than this man, this man I loved. Not that the blame was on him—it was on me. But I was allowed very little in this life, and one of the things I was allowed was my sadness—my destiny.

"How's. . ." My voice faltered at the last second when I dared a glance at him.

He looked at me like he had a hundred things to say, but all that left his lips was, "Not good."

I closed my mouth and turned forward, feeling my pulse jump right behind my ear. "Where's Mila?"

"Not here."

I assumed she was with Colin, so I didn't ask anything else about her. But my mouth, my traitorous mouth, wanted to keep going. "How are you?"

I felt more than saw him turn beside me. "Do you really want to know?"

Did I? I asked myself the same question. I didn't have to know the things I wanted to know:

Do you have a girlfriend?

115

Are you still in love with me?

Are you mad at me?

Does my absence gnaw at you, like yours does me? A slow poisoning, with no reprieve?

But most of all, *Are you still in love with me?*

I knew I didn't have a right to the answers to any of those questions. I'd lost that right when I'd left him.

And I'd lost it again when he'd left me, a year earlier.

But, oh god, did I ache just standing next to him. Dozens of strangers milled around us, smiling and laughing, but for a moment I wasn't distracted by a single one. We stood like two people who shared nothing, but—at least in my heart—we shared everything.

I tucked my chin in my chest and breathed heavily for a moment. I couldn't believe I was this close to him. I couldn't believe I was this close to him and not touching him. What was wrong with me? With him? With us?

I knew those answers without asking.

I opened my mouth to ask him something else when the buzzer for the carousel came on, and started moving. Jude looked at me with my mouth open, knowing I had things to say but suddenly wasn't saying anything. This was our existence, two people with things to say, but interrupted at the worst times. So we held a look full of silent meaning before the first bag fell from the top of the chute, clanging loudly as it hit the carousel and knocking us both away from one another.

When I saw my bag, I stepped forward with a hand out to grab it, but Jude stepped up at the same time and brushed my hand with his as he grasped the handle and yanked it from the carousel. I tried not to notice the way his arm flexed, how the trees on his forearm glowed under all the artificial light, but the fact that we were several feet apart gave me an opportunity to study him, an opportunity I didn't often have with how close we'd always been before.

"Just the one?"

I nodded as he pulled the handle up. The click made me tug my backpack on tightly over my shoulders. He looked up at me when I reached for the handle, and said, without words, that he'd pull my baggage for me.

I knew that look—it was a look he'd given me more than once, when I'd unburdened my weight onto him. That he could be steady, he could carry the weight I could not. Something he'd told me a hundred times, but something I was unwilling to give up.

An overwhelming sense of home and an equal pang of despair squeezed me to the point of breathlessness. I wanted all of it, all of him, but I couldn't ask that of him. Not after how we'd left things.

More than anything, I wanted to reach over and pull him to me, so I could hold him the way I needed him to hold me.

The car ride out of the airport was silent under the cloud of night. There was something intimate about the lights in the vehicle, the way they glittered off his glasses as he navigated us out of the parking garage.

"Do you usually wear glasses?" I asked him after he paid the parking fee and had refused my proffered money.

He sighed, like he couldn't believe this was what I finally said to him after our prolonged silence. "Just when I'm driving at night."

"Is this your car?"

He looked over at me and blinked when we had stopped at a light. "Yes."

At the back of my throat, I felt a burn—like heartburn—except it had everything to do with the fact that we were skirting around the reason I was here. Maybe he wasn't ready to talk about it. I knew I wasn't.

Streetlights washed over us as we moved down the highway. "Can you stop at a hotel first?"

"Why?" He looked over at me like I'd asked him to throw me out of the car.

"So I can check in and brush my teeth." I placed a hand over my mouth. "I've been traveling for twelve hours. I need to freshen up a bit."

"That's fine." But he had a tick in his jaw. His beautiful, sculpted jaw. He slid a glance at me. "But you don't need to stay at a hotel. You can stay at my place."

Alarm bells went off in my head. I could *not* stay at his house. No fucking way. I could barely stand to be in the car with him; no way could I be in his home. Sleeping in all the places that smelled like him. "No, really. A hotel is fine."

"I'm not trying to be an asshole," he said carefully, switching lanes to pass a slow-moving car. "But we both know you don't have the kind of dough for a hotel for several nights."

He wasn't wrong, but it dug under my skin that I'd have to rely on him. Again. "I can't crash on your couch, Jude."

"Then you can sleep in my bed if you have an aversion to couches. But I know you can't afford a hotel, and not for how long you'll probably be here."

"You don't know how long I'll be here." My words had a bite to them, because I resented the fact that I was losing control now that I was within his reach. The truth was, neither of us knew how long I'd be here.

"All the better for you to stay with me. There aren't any reasonably priced hotels that don't require taxis. Don't be stubborn about this." The firmness of his voice surprised me enough for me to keep my mouth snapped shut. "Just stay at my place. We'll hardly see one another anyway."

I chewed on my bottom lip as I considered his logic and looked at him sideways. He was just so goddamn beautiful. With the hard line of his jaw and the brown hair that had grown since I'd last seen him—making my hands itchy to touch. "Fine. But I don't want to be in your way."

"You couldn't possibly be in my way," he said softly, even though the car was silent aside from the gentle roar of the engine. He looked at me for less than half a second, but it was long enough for me to see the look in his eyes. "I'm glad you're here, Trista."

But that was what was wrong with this situation. The reason I was in Colorado wasn't because I was ready, or because we were trying to find ourselves. And for that reason, I wished I was anywhere else.

Jude pulled his car into a carport and turned off the engine. He waited a second or two, sliding his fingers over the steering wheel. "I think we should go tomorrow."

"Tomorrow?" I echoed.

"It'll be a long night, and he'll be in a better mood tomorrow."

I couldn't argue with him. He knew Colin better than I did. And given the circumstances, he knew what Colin would prefer. "All right," I agreed. I opened my door first, not wanting to wait another second inside the car with all the tension thickening our words.

The air was cool and I sucked it in. It was so much drier here than in Maine, I realized. I'd been gone so long that everything was different— the landscapes, the air, the people.

Jude climbed out of the car and looked at me over the roof. "Are you hungry?"

Sliding my backpack over my shoulders, I studied him. He was wearing a flannel shirt, rolled up to the elbows. I thought it was part of his uniform, I'd seen similar flannel shirts on him more than anything else. I realized how awkward it was, with us looking at each other over the roof of the car as the dark swallowed us whole, completely silent.

I debated my answer for only a minute before my stomach churned. "Yes."

He looked at his watch. "I can order a pizza or make something." He looked up at the building before us. "I'm pretty sure I have eggs."

"Eggs are fine."

"Great." He popped the trunk and yanked out my suitcase. "Follow me," he said as if I had another choice.

He climbed two flights until he stopped at a nondescript door. The doors on the way up had had some kind of wreath or sign on them, warning against ringing the bell due to sleeping babies or not being accepting of soliciting. But Jude's was plain, a white metal door with just a small peephole. He unlocked the door and opened it, allowing me to go first.

I stepped into the darkness and grabbed at the straps around my shoulders, squeezing them, because I didn't know what to do, or where to move.

I felt him come in behind me and turn on the light. White lights lit up the place and I glanced around, taking in the black leather couch, coffee table, tiny two-person table in the tiny dining area and the galley kitchen that adjoined it. Despite the simplicity of his decorations and furniture, the place itself looked updated with its dark wood floors, light gray walls, and white and black kitchen. It was clean, neat, and definitely suggested that a male had decorated it.

"The bedroom's just down here," he said, hauling my suitcase down a hallway that his shoulders filled up.

Following him, I said, "I can sleep on the couch."

"I'd already planned on you sleeping in here. It's better if I'm in the living room, because I wake up so early and will need to move around anyway."

I couldn't argue with that as I stepped into the lit up room. Like the rest of the apartment, it was sparsely decorated and furnished, with the large bed taking up most of the space. There was one nightstand with just a clock and a lamp on it, and I stared at that far longer than I should have.

One of the many things I'd wondered over the last two years was whether Jude had a girlfriend. He deserved a girlfriend. He deserved more than I could give him. But the one nightstand told me he likely spent his time alone. A fact that both made me strangely happy and also sad, for his loneliness. I dropped my backpack by the bed before I sat on the edge of it.

"I just changed the sheets," he threw out as he flipped a light on in the adjoining bathroom. "There are towels under the sink, if you want to shower."

I did, which had been the main reason I'd wanted a hotel room. But I nodded at him and he tucked his hands in his front pockets. "I'll make you some eggs and we can talk for a bit before we go to bed." At my look of apprehension, he quickly added, "Or we can eat and go to bed. Either way, it's best if we get a good night's rest before tomorrow."

"Okay." I met his eyes, only for a moment, but I saw in that brief second just how much he wanted to talk. Probably so he could ask all the things that had been lingering on his tongue since we'd last seen one another. "I'll be quick," I said with a cock of my head toward the bathroom.

"Right." He left the room and closed the door behind him and finally, blessedly, I was alone.

Fifteen minutes later, I was freshly showered and clothed in my flannel pajamas when I stepped out into the kitchen where he was sitting, staring at his phone.

He must have sensed me near him because he clicked his phone off and slid the seat out beside him. "I made them scrambled, if that's okay."

I tucked hair behind my ear as I approached. Wet strands clung to my neck, but I didn't pull them away. I didn't want to draw any more attention to myself.

"That's great. Thank you." I dropped to the seat and scooted in, taking in his plate—still full. He'd waited for me.

For some reason, that little gesture made me hurt more than anything else—in a good way, but even the good way wasn't enough.

We ate in silence, with him sneaking little looks at me that I returned. It wasn't awkward or even strange, as we quietly chewed our food and contemplated how we'd ended up here, two years after I'd left Colorado and one year after he'd left Maine.

When we were finished, I started scrubbing the pan he used for the eggs and when he reached around me to grab the pan from me as I finished rinsing it, I tensed up, expecting—unrightfully so—that he'd touch me. And when his hand brushed mine in a way that I knew was not accidental, my knees wobbled against the wooden cabinet.

"Tired?"

I nodded, not trusting my voice. His juniper smell surrounded me— reminding me of the trees and our camping trips and everything I'd been trying not to remember so vividly in the last two years.

"There are extra blankets in the closet in my room," he said as I dried my hands on the towel.

I nodded. "What time should I set my alarm?"

"I was thinking we'd head up there at eight. It's about ten minutes from here."

"So I'll set it for seven forty-five."

We were on opposite sides of the kitchen, leaning against the countertops as we studied one another. I kept waiting for one of us to make the step forward, to envelope the other in a hug that was long overdue. But his hands clenched and unclenched before he shoved them in his pockets.

"You have to eat breakfast." He said it with more than a little guilt for me to bear. He wasn't stupid. He knew about me.

I shrugged noncommittally. "I'll be fine."

"You have to eat breakfast," he repeated, his voice flat. He turned around so his back was to me. "Set it for seven thirty."

I didn't like being told what to do, but I couldn't tell him no. He'd had the look in his eyes like he would've grabbed me by the ankles and forced me out of bed. From anyone else, I wouldn't have put up with it. But I had to oblige him. So I nodded even though he couldn't see me and dropped the dish towel on the counter. I stared so long at his back, waiting for him to turn around, waiting to have enough courage to carry myself across the three tiles that separated us and into his arms.

But because that courage never came, and because he stayed with his back to me, I turned and went into his bedroom.

I closed the door at first, but on second thought I opened it again. I'd become so used to sleeping in the inn before I'd moved to my apartment, and closing the door because it was the one space that was all mine, that I had closed Jude's door on instinct. But I wasn't in Maine. I was in Colorado, in the same place as Jude. I was safe. I was home.

CHAPTER THIRTEEN
MAY 2012

I didn't want to let go of him for a while. Holding him had been the most peaceful I'd felt in months—it practically radiated from him. "You're actually here," I said into his flannel shirt.

"Mhm," he said into my hair.

"Don't let go just yet," I whispered, rubbing my face over his shirt.

"I won't."

I'm not sure how long we stood there, just holding one another. His breath was warm on the top of my head and I could hear each beat of his heart against my ear, where it was pressed against his chest.

I was the first to pull back, because I wanted to look up into his face. His beautiful, tranquil face. The smile on it caused one to reflect on mine too. He was perfect. A word I didn't like, because of the expectations it required. But that's what he was.

"You look so different," he said, brushing a thumb along my cheek. I took a quiet delight in that, hoping he'd notice how much weight I'd lost since he had seen me last.

"I've lost weight."

But he didn't look pleased. In fact, he looked concerned. "Are you okay?"

I pulled away from him just a little, feeling disappointment. "Of course, I'm great. And you're here."

"I am." But something had changed in his expression as he searched me over.

"Let me show you around," I said, changing the subject.

We hadn't kissed.

I tugged him by the hand through the entry, pointing to the reception desk, which he had already seen. I pulled him back to the kitchen, and he looked around as I showed him everything I did throughout a typical day at the inn.

"Let's go upstairs," I said, tugging him along the back staircase. In my excitement, I got a bit winded when I reached the landing, and braced a hand against the wall as I smiled at him.

"Are you sure you're okay?"

I didn't like that he kept asking me, like he didn't believe me. "I'm great. I'm just a little excited." But I noticed that he wasn't winded at all, and in our hikes together, he'd been the first one out of the two of us to feel the effects.

"Here's my room," I said when we reached the room at the end of the hall.

"You live here?"

Nodding, I slid my key through the hole and pushed the door open. "I have ever since July."

"Okay."

I let him step into my room first, hoping he'd be impressed with the renovations that had happened over the holidays. Not that he'd known how it had looked before. He stepped up to the window soon, looking out over the ocean in the distance, and then he turned around. "Are you happy here?" His eyebrows were pulled together in concern, but I didn't know why he was so worried about it.

"As happy as I can be," I answered honestly. "It's my home."

"Okay," he said again, but he seemed emotionally distant from me.

This wasn't how I'd pictured our reunion in all the times I'd tried to imagine how it would go down. "And you work here, too?"

"It's my only job, yes." I tucked my hands into my pockets as he sat on my bed. "Are *you* okay?"

He ran a hand over his hair as he stared at my desk. "I am."

But he wasn't looking at me, so I knew something wasn't okay. I wanted him to hold me, to love me the way he had months earlier.

"I think I'm just tired," he said with a sigh. I watched as he fell back onto the bed and closed his eyes, feeling helpless to fix whatever it was that was wrong with us.

So I let him nap, all the while wringing my hands.

"Hello?" a voice called from the hallway.

"Shit," I mumbled, recognizing Charlotte's voice. I strode to the door and slipped out into the hall. "Charlotte."

She was wearing short shorts, much too small for the late spring weather outside, and a tank that slipped off her shoulder. She looked like she'd slept in her clothes and hadn't brushed her hair in days.

"You showed up."

Charlotte put her hands on her hips. "Did Maura think I'd bailed or somethin'?"

I walked away from my room and hooked an arm through Charlotte's to pull her down the hall with me. I wasn't sure how many guests were checked in on this floor, but I knew it wasn't professional to have them listen to our conversation.

"Technically," I said, once we were walking down the stairs, "you did bail. You didn't show up on time."

"Well, 'scuse me," she said on an exaggerated sigh. "It's not like we're all booked up anyways."

"Doesn't matter. It was my day off and you didn't show up when you were scheduled to."

Charlotte followed me into the kitchen, the one place we seemed to be able to talk about work without a guest overhearing. "What has your panties in a twist then? It's not like you were doing my work—I saw you come out of your room."

"Because it's my day off." Honestly, sometimes trying to speak sense to Charlotte was more trouble than it was worth.

"Where's Maura?" she asked, looking around the kitchen.

"She had to go rescue Chuck." I crossed my arms over my chest. "Where were you?"

"At Brendan's. Sorry, we decided to split a bottle of wine and the next thing I knew, I was waking up on his floor an hour ago."

"I thought you had a new boyfriend," I said, remembering very distinctly that she'd told me just that.

"Yeah, and I do. But you know how ex-boyfriends are." She smiled coyly as she twirled her hair around her finger.

The funny thing was, I did know. Because I had one, a sort-of ex-boyfriend, in my room at that moment. "Well, you should've called an hour ago, let Maura know you were coming in."

She twirled a chunk of hair. "I didn't know I was going to come in. Brendan had to go to work, so I figured I might as well."

She was so exasperating sometimes.

I grabbed a dish Maura had put in the sink and held it in my clenched fingers. "Figured you might as well? It's your *job*, Charlotte." I opened the dishwasher with more force than necessary and shoved the plate into it. "Honestly, I don't know why Maura lets you work for her still."

Charlotte seemed unperturbed by my anger and jumped up so she was sitting on the counter beside the dishwasher. "Because she loves me."

"Yeah, well how do you love her in return?" Maura wouldn't have put up with this kind of shit from me, so it rose my hackles that Charlotte could get away with just about anything and nothing would affect her negatively.

"Love is a feeling, not an action."

I fully rolled my eyes then. "Don't quote bullshit on me, Char. I'm telling you—you have a good gig here, and maybe you should respect everyone else's time more than your own for a change." I slammed the door on the dishwasher just as I heard boots drop by the side door.

"Well, look who decided to show up," Maura said as she pulled her raincoat off and hung it up. "I was wondering where you were," she said to Char. She turned to me and asked, "Did you get that guest settled?"

I thought of Jude, asleep on my bed, and nodded.

"What room?" she asked, coming around and brushing down the side of Charlotte's hair.

"Mine." I swallowed when both Charlotte and Maura looked at me with twin looks of surprise on their faces.

"Why, pray tell?" Charlotte asked, a glimmer in her eyes.

"Because he's my. . ." I tried to think of how to refer to him. He wasn't exactly an ex-boyfriend, but he wasn't just an acquaintance either. "He's a friend."

"A he who's a friend, huh?" Charlotte twirled another lock of hair. "Which one is he, the spurned ex-boyfriend or the something else?"

"What are you talking about?" Maura asked, swatting at Charlotte to get her to jump off the counter. I gave Charlotte a look that I hoped was threatening enough to have her keep her mouth shut.

"Nothing," Charlotte said, rubbing her lips tightly together to keep herself from smiling. "Need help with dinner prep?"

"As a matter of fact," Maura said, spinning around. I left the kitchen a second later, annoyed that Charlotte being late was already forgiven, like usual.

When I returned to my room, Jude was sitting up on the bed, rubbing his eyes. When he looked at me, with that achingly familiar sleepy gaze, it was all I could do not to collapse to my knees.

"How'd you find me?" It was the one question I wanted an answer to. Everything else could wait.

"Mila."

"I figured that," I said, coming to sit beside him on the bed. "But how did you figure out Maine, and specifically here?"

"Your grandfather. I visited him, he gave me one of the postcards you'd mailed him." He pulled out a postcard from his back pocket and opened it. It was the lighthouse I often visited when I wanted to think. I took the postcard from his hands and ran my fingertips over the edges. "I think your grandpa likes me."

I tried to think of the last time I'd spoken to him on the phone. Grandpa wasn't big on talking on the phone, which was why I sent him postcards, or letters. But I could see my grandpa being keen on Jude, and giving him a clue. Maybe my grandpa had thought I was lonely, or needed something familiar. My adventure wasn't much of an adventure after all.

"And you decided to come all this way?"

Jude pushed a hand on his knee and dipped his head down. "I wanted to see if you were okay. And I'm not sure if you are."

When I opened my mouth to say I was fine, again, he shook his head.

"You say you're okay, but your skin is cradling your bones too close to the surface. I told you once before that you had sad eyes, but they're more than sad now." He held my hands in his. "Talk to me. Tell me how you feel, please. Tell me what's wrong."

I pulled my hands from his. I wanted to go back to an hour earlier, when we'd embraced in the sunroom, happy to see one another.

"Maybe I should leave."

"No!" I lowered my voice. "Let's go on a walk," I said. "We can talk."

I took him to the lighthouse, so maybe he could see what had drawn me to the postcard in the first place. The lighthouse was on a tiny island off the coast, so we could only view it from the opposite shore, but we sat there on a flannel blanket, watching as the waves crashed against the shore.

"This is your favorite place." It wasn't a question.

"It's my favorite place in Maine," I amended as we leaned back on the blanket. The roar of the waves on the rocks was so loud, but it soothed me in a way that I couldn't articulate. It was like the storm that bubbled up inside of me, throwing itself repeatedly against what kept it contained.

"Why?"

I knew he wasn't asking because he didn't understand; he was asking so he could get insight into who I was. "Because at night, I can watch the stars bathe the sky in a storm of light, and because the light from the lighthouse shines out into the abyss." I rolled to my side so I faced Jude. "Like it's searching for something. Waiting for something to shine its light upon."

Jude hadn't turned to face me, and I could tell by the clenching of his jaw that he was thinking about something.

"What?"

"I'm thinking I should go back home."

I was positive that he could've said anything else and not shocked me as much as when he said that. "But you just got here."

"It doesn't matter when I got here. What matters is you."

"I want you to stay," I said earnestly. "At least another day. Let me take you on a walk tomorrow. I bet the weather will be better tomorrow." I made myself sound more sure than I felt about that.

"Okay," he agreed, but turned his face back to the sky. It was still hours from pitch-black night sky, so he wouldn't see with his eyes what this place had made me feel. But he was here, at least another day.

We stayed, watching the lighthouse until the sunset painted the landscape in a kaleidoscope of pinks and yellows, highlighting the rocks as the waves continued to crash against them.

The whole time, we talked about nothing of consequence. It was as if by some silent agreement, we'd decided not to talk about Colin, Mila, or anything else that awaited us in Colorado.

At the inn, we ate dinner under Maura and Charlotte's curious gazes. My steady, warm Jude returned during the meal as he picked at his lobster like a guy who seemed to understand how to open a lobster better than I did, and he lived in a landlocked state, not on the coast like I did.

"I hate that you're always better at stuff than I am," I said, watching as he pulled meat from his lobster shell like he could've done it with his eyes closed.

"I'm just that good." He winked and I felt a little bit of myself go into a gooey puddle in my seat. "Let me help you."

I tucked my hands under the table on my lap as he took over, easily sliding meat from my crab claws and then dipping it in butter.

"Would it be inappropriate for me to feed this to you?" he asked, and I shook my head immediately, opening my mouth slightly in invitation. One large hand cradled my chin as he brought the crab to my mouth, brushing his thumb against my bottom lip.

I closed my mouth, but held his gaze. He was the Jude I remembered, who looked at me like he was burning from the inside out. He always had that effect, making me feel like I was the only person in his sights.

And as we finished dinner, he grabbed my hand and pulled me from my seat, wordlessly guiding me from the dining room to my room upstairs.

He waited until we were behind my door to push me against the wall and kiss me.

Finally, I thought, opening my mouth to greedily take his lips. He grabbed my waist and squeezed, and I rocked my body against his, wanting to feel him all over me.

We moved from the door to the bed, mouths locked and fingers entwined. I'd missed this so much that I wasn't willing to let a single part of him move away from me for some time.

His lips moved down my neck, biting and nibbling along my shoulder. It all felt sharper this time, like being away from him for so long had left my skin more sensitive to touch. His fingers trailed the path his lips had made and my eyes closed as he pressed me deeper into the mattress.

When the first tear slipped out of the corner of my eye, it was like the crack that shattered the dam.

My tears were silent as he kissed me all over, like he was imprinting everything he felt for me into my skin. It'd been so long since I'd felt beautiful.

His hands cradled my face and he lifted his face over mine. "Why are you crying?"

"I'm not crying," I said.

"Liar," he murmured, swiping a thumb over my cheekbone. "What's wrong?"

"That's just it—nothing." My breath shuddered and for the first time since he arrived in Maine, I felt like I couldn't get enough air when I was with him. "I'm so glad you're here."

He gathered me in his arms and positioned me so that I was in his lap. He rocked me slowly, pressing his lips against my hair. I wanted to believe that he could hold me enough to give me strength, but I didn't want him to be the reason for my strength.

I closed my eyes as he held me, feeling—for the first time in a long time—safe.

At some point, I must have fallen asleep in his arms because the next thing I knew, Jude was laying me down in the sheets and covering my body with the blanket.

"Don't go," I whispered, the room dark. My fingers wrapped around his wrist and squeezed.

"I'm not. I'll be here." And he curled up behind me, wrapping an arm around my waist and holding me to his body.

Sometime in the middle of the night, I woke and rolled over so that I faced him. He was completely still, the moonlight sliding in the window and highlighting just above his face onto his pillow. His breathing was even, his brow unfurrowed. He looked so completely relaxed that it was all I could do to not wake him up. I wanted to kiss him, everywhere. To glide my hands over his body, leaving a brand only he could see. He was actually here, in Maine, with me.

As if my thoughts had been too loud, his eyes slowly slid open and he blinked, meeting my gaze.

"Can't sleep?"

I pressed a hand to his cheek, marveling at the feel of his warm skin in my palm. "I don't want to." It could've been a dream, that's how amazing it had felt.

"What are you thinking?"

There was something beautifully intimate about that moment, when we laid beside each other in the dark, our voices whispers and our hands seeking one another. "I'm thinking that this is a dream. That you're not really here."

"I could pinch you," he offered.

Shaking my head, I leaned in and brushed my lips across his. It wasn't a kiss, not really. It was a nuzzle, but as I came back again the hand he cradled my head with brought me closer so he could kiss me fully.

I tilted my head, my hands going to his warm, bare shoulder. I'd missed the feel of his skin under mine—his juniper scent washing over me.

He climbed over me, pressing me deeper into the mattress. I wanted all of his weight on me, wanted him to wrap me up so deeply in him that I couldn't leave this time.

I curled my fingertips into his shoulder gently when his lips moved to suck at the skin of my neck. It all felt unbelievable, that he was here, in my bed, kissing me like this.

When his fingers grazed the skin that separated my shirt from my pants, I sat up and helped him take my shirt off. He brushed his hands over my hair as it hung down my back. I reached a hand behind myself and undid my bra clasp before tossing the scrap of fabric across the room.

His hands moved to my waist as I sat, facing him. His eyes never left mine. "You're so goddamn beautiful, Trista." He rubbed his fingers along my ribs, back and forth, and I reached to mimic the movement on his abs.

"So are you." He was. His heavy, soulful eyes were like dark marbles in the shadows of my room. I wrapped my arms around his neck and pushed him so that I was straddling him. I leaned over him, my hair creating a curtain that kept our faces concealed from everything in the room.

I felt his hand glide along my spine gently as he stared up into my face. I was overcome with the urge to kiss his entire face, starting with his jaw line. So I did.

As I kissed his face gently, his hands held my body still. I liked that he couldn't stop touching me, that his hands roamed my skin like a land unexplored. We'd had so little time to do this before, back in Yellowstone. I realized the last time I'd fallen asleep with him wrapped around me had been in a tent, before my life had imploded.

Jude gently pushed me so that I laid back on the bed and he slowly stripped my pants down my legs with one hand as his other squeezed the skin that was exposed with each inch.

When he leaned over me again, he brushed his mouth against mine like I'd done to him just as his fingers touched me between my legs. The sensation of him touching me caused me to squeeze his biceps tighter, digging my nails a little into his skin. Over and over, he grazed his fingers along my center before I whispered his name, urgency clear in my voice.

He stepped away from the bed for a moment and I watched in

the light of the moon as he slid a condom over himself. I rolled to my stomach and crawled across the bed. As soon as I was at the edge of the bed, his hands reached for mine and he squeezed as he laid me back and slid slowly inside of me. He was frozen for a moment, both of us just staring at each other, before he continued.

My body matched his in rhythm, arching with each thrust, and it'd been so long for me that I climbed quickly. I watched as Jude's breathing became more ragged with each thrust and my hand found his chest, feeling his heart beat beneath my palm when he lowered himself inches from me.

He leaned forward, and I wanted to tell him I loved him then. But heat was spreading quickly and my body was shaking right before I closed my eyes and slipped over the edge.

Jude was seconds behind me, his thrusts faster and his breathing harsher, and he made a noise in the back of his throat that made me wrap my legs around his waist as his pace faltered and he came to a rest above me.

He was bracing himself on his forearms, so that his weight wasn't putting pressure on me. But I wanted it—all his weight pressing into me. He was still inside me, and I wasn't eager for him to roll off of me.

I turned my head to the left, where his face was pressed against my neck. "You okay?" I asked, feeling his heart beating fast against my skin.

"More than," he said, but his words were muffled. Slowly he lifted his body from where he partially laid on top of me, pressing a kiss to my nose.

When he pulled out of me, I closed my eyes. I was bone-deep tired, but felt somehow fulfilled. Jude squeezed my thigh before he walked into the bathroom and shut the door.

Suddenly, my stomach felt uncomfortably full. I'd become accustomed to purging soon after a meal, but this time I'd fallen asleep. I needed to puke, and soon.

I slid one of my oversized t-shirts on over my head and stepped in the bathroom when Jude stepped out. Before I could close the door, Jude hooked an arm around my waist and leaned down, kissing me fully on the mouth. The arm around my waist squeezed and I wanted nothing more than to squeeze back, to curl up against him and live the dream I'd fantasized about for nearly a year.

Waiting until he was in the bed, far enough from the door to hear anything, I turned on the faucet to its loudest level.

And then I bent over the toilet and shoved a finger down my throat. After purging, I took a small bit of pleasure in how empty I felt. It was a welcome comfort, though it was no match to the comfort Jude had provided me just by showing up. I washed my hands and thoroughly brushed my teeth, making sure my hair was brushed and clean.

After flossing and gargling mouthwash, I returned to the bedroom where Jude was waiting for me in the bed. As I stepped closer, he reached forward with his hands and pulled me to him.

His mouth covered mine before he pulled back. "You brushed your teeth?" he asked, searching my face. I was thankful for the dark.

I nodded. "I couldn't stand the lingering taste of seafood in my mouth," I explained as I crawled into the bed.

My hand reached for his under the covers and I squeezed. I thought I might be able to drift asleep immediately, but I couldn't. I turned to look over my shoulder. "Can you cuddle with me?"

Without saying anything, he slid across the space between us and pulled me up against his front, letting his arm fall over the curve of my waist. Only then did I fall into a deep, deep sleep.

The next day, I woke early and fixed the problem with the inn's website before taking Jude on a walking tour of the town as we headed out to the rocky shore I favored. He held my hand the whole time as I pointed things out to him along the way, and I found myself leaning into him as much as possible. It was surreal, having him here with me as I showed him where I'd been living for nearly a year. When we stopped for ice cream, Jude fed me a bite of his Rocky Road flavor under a bright yellow and white striped umbrella.

"Do you like it here?" he asked, taking in the beach and the people that filtered down the sidewalk.

"I like it enough." I met his eyes briefly before turning to my own cone, a cotton candy concoction. "Why?"

He sighed and swiped a napkin over his mouth. "I just want you happy, Trista. I know we have a lot to talk about—"

"I don't want to talk about all that," I interrupted. I didn't want to ruin this moment with talk of yesterday. "We can talk about everything later."

He blinked a few times. "We can't keep putting it off," he said. "I—"

"No." My voice was firmer that time. I didn't want this, to cast a shadow over our time. "I'm serious. We can talk later."

He sighed again, and I could tell he was unhappy. "What can we talk about?"

"The beach." I lifted my head to the ocean, which roared in the distance. The air was salty today, which signaled summer coming soon.

"Do you want to come back to Colorado?"

What a loaded question. There was no question that I wanted to go back to Colorado. But I didn't think they were for the right reasons. I finished the last of my ice cream cone and then sucked down some water from the bottle Jude had bought me. "That's a complicated question."

"It's really not." He looked at me as he picked up our discarded napkins. "Yes or no questions require just one of those words in answer."

Swallowing, I tore my gaze away from him. "I do. Of course I do. But I don't think I should."

"Okay," he said, but I knew the conversation was far from over. "What have you been doing since you left? What kinds of things are you doing outside of the inn?"

Shrugging, I admitted, "Well, not a lot." I didn't meet his eyes. "It was cold, and the inn keeps me busy."

"Do you have a boyfriend?"

The question was so out of left field that it shocked me. I turned to him and said, "No!" I may have said it more dramatically than I needed to, but I wanted to make sure he knew how absurd the question was.

But not absurd enough for me not to want an answer, too. But I was too much of a coward to ask.

"Well, what are you doing with your free time then?"

I wanted to tell him about my poetry, but it was so personal to me, especially since most of the words I wrote were for him. "Not a lot."

"Trista," he began, reaching for my hands across the table. "What can I do for you? I came here, to see you. To see what's going on, what's keeping you here instead of Colorado." He shook his head and I watched as his brown eyes looked almost pleading. "I don't want to pressure you. But I want to know what you're doing. So I know what *we're* doing."

My hands went limp in his. "I don't know." It was honest, but it was flimsy. "I really don't know." I wasn't sure if it was the conversation or the fact that I'd just eaten more ice cream than I normally did in one sitting, but I suddenly had the urge to barf up my ice cream. "I'll be right back," I promised, grabbing my bag off the back of a chair and stepping into the ladies room at the back of the ice cream parlor.

I didn't feel as good this time after vomiting. Instead, I felt like I was trying to purge myself of the feelings that had nestled within me at Jude's questioning. I pressed my finger to the back of my throat over and over, until I was just a shaky mess on the bathroom floor.

Once again, I thoroughly brushed my teeth with the travel-sized toothbrush I brought with me and shoved two pieces of gum into my mouth before returning to where Jude waited for me.

"You alright?" he asked, his brow furrowed and his eyes searching.

Nodding, I hooked my arm in his and led him back in the direction of the inn. Because it wasn't my day off, I couldn't spend the whole time gallivanting with Jude around Maine.

I showed him to the main recreation room as I quickly began cleaning rooms, with Claire's help. She tried pressing me for information about Jude, but I kept my lips zipped as I tried to hurry us along so that I could join him sooner.

When I was finished, I poked my head in the rec room. He was asleep on the leather recliner, so I curled up on his lap, waking him.

"Hmm," he hummed, lifting his arms to wrap around me. "Sorry I fell asleep."

I pressed a kiss to the short beard that climbed along his jaw line. "Sorry I wasn't here to entertain you."

"It's okay; you are now." His arms tightened and I didn't want to move an inch from that recliner, but I knew I needed to. Maura wouldn't be too impressed, seeing one of her employees curled up the way I was in the rec room. He let out a sigh and said, "I'm starving. Want to get lunch?"

I wasn't hungry. In fact, ever since I'd thrown up my ice cream, I'd felt off. I wasn't sure if it was the lie I was keeping from Jude or the fact that throwing up ice cream was like throwing up any other liquid. But I forced a smile and led him to the dining room before ducking into the kitchen to make him a sandwich.

"How long's he in town for?" Maura asked from behind me, startling me enough so that I nearly jumped out of my skin.

"I don't know," I answered. I didn't think he was here for long. And suddenly, the realization that he wasn't staying here forever hit me, heavier than the ice cream had been. I held the plate in my hands so hard, I was sure it would crack.

Miraculously, it didn't. I brought the sandwich out to Jude and placed it in front of him before sliding in the seat next to him. My instinct was to slide closer to him, but I didn't. Thoughts of him leaving soon kept me from closing the few inches between us as I watched him pick up his sandwich and take a bite.

"You're not eating?"

I shook my head. "Not hungry."

He chewed slowly, as if he was thinking very hard. "Would you take a bite of this for me?"

Something about the way he asked made my eyes narrow. "Why?"

He shrugged. "I don't feel right eating when you're not." When I still didn't lean in, he did. "Please? Just one bite?"

Tentatively, I nodded and leaned forward so that he brought the sandwich to my lips. It was cheese and ham, on our thickest bread, with mayo. A lot of calories. And that was all I thought about as I chewed it, already wanting to throw it up.

"Okay?" he asked and I nodded and chewed harder, not wanting him to be suspicious. I didn't need to deal with him finding out I was bulimic.

After he finished the sandwich, he took my hand and followed me into the now-empty kitchen and then upstairs.

It felt like a repeat of the night before, as we stepped into my room and his lips crashed over mine. But something was different this time; his lips seemed almost desperate. So I met him, kiss for kiss, push for push, until he was pressing me into the wall. And that was when I remembered how uncomfortable the sandwich felt in my stomach.

"Sorry," I said as I pulled away, running my hands down the front of his shirt. "Can you give me a minute?"

He didn't answer me, just looked at me through hooded eyes as I stepped into the bathroom. The urge to vomit was powerful this time, like the bite of sandwich had tripled in size and was growing ever more. As soon as the door was shut, I leaned over the toilet and it came up immediately.

The scent of vomit was strong in my nostrils and the acid burning my nostrils made me wince as I flushed and looked at myself in the mirror. My eyes were red-rimmed, probably from the sheer force of vomiting the sandwich. Quickly, I turned on the faucet and brushed my teeth before Jude called my name from the room.

I left the bathroom and made sure the smile was on my face as I stepped into Jude's arms. He leaned down, but before his lips made contact with mine, he asked, "Did you brush your teeth?"

"Yes." I curled my fingers into his hair, dragging my nails down the back of his head.

"Why?"

"Because I ate that sandwich," I said, which wasn't an outright lie, but still an omission of truth.

"So did I." His hands came to my wrists, pulling me away from holding him. "But I didn't brush my teeth."

"I just didn't like the taste in my mouth."

There was silence between us for a beat before he spoke. "I think you're lying to me, Trista."

There it was, the soft seeking voice. The one that always made everything else come to a stop as I listened to him. "Why do you think that?"

"Because I heard you vomiting in the bathroom."

I hadn't thought about that, mostly because I was always in this room alone without anyone to hear. I held my hands to my stomach. "I got sick is all."

"Would you—" He shook his head and stood, stepping away from me. "Just—don't do that. Don't lie to me." He pinned me with a stare. "I lied to you last summer. I was wrong. But I didn't come here so we could keep doing this to one another."

I didn't know what to say. I didn't want to tell him I was bulimic, but I also didn't want to keep lying to him. So as a compromise, I kept my mouth shut.

"I had a feeling, you know." He rubbed his jaw as he stalked away from me. "When I saw you, I knew something wasn't right." He held up his hands between us, his fingers curved as he stared at them. "When I held you, I felt your ribs under my hand. I've never held you and felt like I could break you." There was a burn growing behind his eyes as he looked at me, like I was hurting him somehow.

"I just lost some weight, Jude. It's not a big deal."

"Just stop." His eyes were angry. Angry Jude I could deal with, so I did. "Don't lie to me."

"I'm not. I wanted to lose weight, so I did."

"Yeah? How'd you do that? Going to the gym? Eating salads?"

I narrowed my eyes at his tone. "What are you insinuating?"

"I saw how much you ate at dinner. Someone who is on a restrictive diet would've stopped sooner. And at the ice cream parlor, you came back with your eyes red-rimmed. You brushed your teeth then. Just like you did now. I didn't know for sure, until you just confirmed it."

I moved to step around him, ready to book him in his own hotel room, but he stopped me with a hand on the wall.

"I don't understand you. You weren't yourself before dinner yesterday. But then during dinner, you were so warm and friendly."

He vigorously rubbed at his head before slumping in a chair. I watched him trying to gather his words, his hands moving in his lap like he was handpicking each word carefully. When he raised his head, his voice was calmer than before. "Because I was watching you eat, Trista." He pointed to my body. "You look like you're starved. Remember when I told you I was pulled to you because I saw you were so hungry, and I wanted to feed you? I got to do that in the literal sense. But knowing what I know—knowing about what you're doing—makes me want to throw something."

"You don't know what I'm doing. You're just guessing."

"Is that right?" The ice was back in his voice.

"Tell me then, if you think you know."

"You're vomiting your meals. Your skin doesn't look right. Your energy is lower than it was last year. You look ill, and if you're actually bulimic, then you're definitely ill."

I ached to deny it. Even though it was true—all of it—I still wanted to feel like I had some power in this exchange. But when I opened my mouth, his eyes looked at me so sadly that I couldn't do it. I couldn't bring myself to lie to him. An angry Jude was one thing. But a sad Jude was like a punch straight to my heart.

"It was hard, after I left Colorado." It was an excuse, a pathetic one, but it was all I had. "I didn't start doing this until Christmas."

"I don't care when you started, Trista. I just want you to stop."

I'd felt a divide beginning to grow between us the moment I'd brought him that sandwich. But now, it felt like we'd stepped up to the tide, but only one of us had stopped. I was walking deeper and deeper into the water, while Jude waited on the shore. I closed my eyes and sucked in a breath before saying, "No."

"What?" he asked, leaning forward. "You're not going to stop? You're just going to keep vomiting up your meals . . . until what?"

"Until I'm happy." It was weak and foolish; rationally I knew these things. But what I was doing was the smallest way I could have control over myself. It'd been nearly a year since Doug had hit me, but the effects of his mark upon my skin were long-lasting. Jude could touch me, he could love me, but he couldn't erase the way I felt about myself. Doug hitting me had almost felt like I'd had it coming, after years of seeing myself as less than everything. My injuries at Doug's hands had felt like a physical reflection of how I'd felt about myself. I'd hated myself, but bulimia had given me some semblance of control over that self-loathing.

"Come to Colorado," he said, and I could tell in a small way it hurt him to say it. Knowing he was asking me to abandon my mission to figure myself out. "I'll take you wherever you want. I just don't want to see you doing this to yourself."

"I'm fine," I said. "I've got a handle on it."

He jumped to his feet and shook his head. I was watching him come apart at the seams. "You *don't* have a handle on it. You're wasting away. Do you remember how upset you were when you found out about my heart condition, after I'd taken you down the trail that had been too much for me? I'd put my life at risk. I'd known it. You're doing the exact same thing and you're too close to see what it's doing to you." His voice was loud again, as if he didn't think I could hear him if he spoke at a lower volume.

"I need to figure my life out," I told him even though it sounded hollow to me. We both knew I wasn't figuring my life out. But something kept holding me back from taking the leap Jude was asking of me, even though his arms were outstretched and steady.

"And I need *you*. I need you whole."

"I'm sorry," I said, and I was. I was deeply, profoundly sorry that he was disappointed in the decisions I'd made and that I was stubbornly resolute on staying in Maine even though it meant constantly yearning for him. I'd have to live with that, knowing that he'd asked me to follow him and I'd turned him down.

"I can't watch you waste away."

"I know." There were tears in my throat as I said it. I closed my eyes and wished for a stillness in the water that pooled in my eyes before I opened them again.

"I want to force you to eat, but I know I can't force anything on you. I can just. . ." He dropped his head into his hands and was quiet for a moment. "I can only hope. That you'll change your mind. That you'll find happiness in a healthy way." He lifted his head, met my eyes. "You don't know how desperate I am to carry you away from this, to stop this destructive path."

"I do know," I said calmly, my hands reaching to hold him but staying still.

"You cannot possibly know." The anger was still in his voice and he pressed his palms to his temples as he looked around. "What am I supposed to do?" he asked. But he wasn't looking at me. He closed his eyes, and the pain in his face reflected back within me. I felt horrible, watching him hurt. Knowing I was the reason. He turned to me. "How do I help you?"

"You already tried."

As soon as I said those three words, I felt their weight like all the other weights in my life, sitting heavy on my shoulders. Jude's eyes burned with hurt and anger.

"I don't know how you can stand there so calmly right now."

I didn't feel calm. I felt my blood boiling, but powerless to go along with him.

"You're tearing me apart," he said. "I don't want to walk away from you. You're sick. You need help."

"And you can't help me," I reminded him, thinking it'd be easier to say. It wasn't. "You should leave." That was even harder.

"You don't want me to leave. And I don't want to leave."

I didn't look at him, I turned to the window, feeling so cold all of a sudden. "I can get you another room if you want to stay." I closed my eyes and swallowed back the lump in my throat. "But I'm not ready, Jude. As much as you want me to be—clearly I'm not."

"So this is it? You're just done. All because I want you to get help?"

"I'm not ready," I repeated, my voice a little louder this time.

"You don't have to be ready, Trista. You just have to be. We can figure it out, you and me, together."

I needed him to leave immediately. I felt like purging again, such was the heaviness of this moment. So I turned to him and said in my loudest voice. "I'm not ready, Jude! I'm just not." I felt the emotion thunder in my heart and I hated myself for feeling weak at that moment. He stood and made his way to me but I shook my head hard. "Don't. Don't touch me. Please." My voice broke on the last word and he stopped, staring at me across the room.

"I don't want to leave," he repeated.

"Please," I repeated, it coming out more like a hiss in the hoarseness of my throat.

He debated before slowly grabbing the backpack he'd brought with him. I watched him sliding it onto his shoulders with a mixture of despair and an acknowledgment that maybe this was for the best.

Just before he walked past me out the door, he stopped and looked at me sideways. "But I'm ready for you, still. And I'll wait."

And then he was gone.

I wish I could write
the things you say about me
on my body so that
when I look in the mirror
I don't see
FAT,
WORTHLESS,
I just see your words,
the ones that come
from the purest place
I know that exists:
in your heart.

CHAPTER FOURTEEN

JUNE 2013

I often had bad dreams in Maine. I'd dream of being back in my mom's trailer, and being hit by Doug, and when I woke I swore I could still feel the blows he'd delivered to my face. But when I awoke in Jude's bed, I'd felt so safe that it was almost unnerving. I couldn't remember the last time I'd felt this safe, completely secure in where I was.

In the middle of the night, after I'd stared too long at the ceiling, I got up from the bed and stepped out into the hallway. It was pitch black, and because I was unfamiliar with the room and my surroundings, I tiptoed down the hallway to the kitchen.

As I poured myself a glass of water, I looked over to where the long leather couch sat in the middle of the room. There was light music playing from the speakers, but otherwise the room was completely silent. I saw Jude's feet hanging off one end of the sofa as I approached it and peeked over the back to see him lying down on his back, his hands folded over his chest. His eyes were closed and his chest moved gently up and down to the rhythm of his breaths. I just watched him for a moment, thinking how much I wished we were together in different circumstances, and that I could ask him to come to his bed and just hold me. But it wasn't my right to ask that of him, so I backed away slowly, my sock-covered feet silently padding along the floor.

Just before I reached the door to his bedroom, I heard him call out, "Do you need me?"

I held my breath until my chest burned. "Yes."

Wordlessly, he moved from the couch and walked toward me. The entire time, I felt that burn grow larger.

He met me in the hallway under the cloak of the dark and placed a hand on my shoulder. "I can hold you." It wasn't a question, but I nodded anyway, not sure I could say yes and stay calm. He followed me into the bedroom and I climbed into the bed, waiting for him to join me. When he climbed into the bed, I rolled onto my side away from him.

He didn't dawdle, no. He scooted right across the bed, so close that I could feel the mattress give under his weight as he came closer and closer until I felt his heat at my back. Without saying anything, he put an arm around my waist and pulled me flush against his chest. Warmth surrounded me, and I closed my eyes, feeling so suddenly sleepy just at his touch.

His head rested on the pillow beside mine, but I knew he was still very close before I could feel his warm breath against my ear. He didn't hold me in a way that was sexually intimate, but instead he held me in a way that was emotionally investing. Like he knew, deep down, that I needed this from him.

"Goodnight," he murmured into my hair, and the burn that had taken over my throat raged. I wanted to roll over and face him, to trace the lines of his face with my fingertips. But this, with him spooned up against my back and the weight of his arm keeping me close, was more than I deserved. So I let myself be grateful for small mercies as my body surrendered to sleep.

I fell asleep, for the first time in a year, with Jude holding me. And even as my heart was cracking in half, other cracks were closing.

I awoke alone, the sounds from the kitchen filtering in from the open door. It took me a second to wrap my head around what had happened. Rolling onto my back, I took in the empty space beside me in the bed. He'd made the side of the bed he'd slept in, and there was a clear indentation on the pillow where he'd laid. I dropped my palm to it, running it over the still-warm fabric, before I curled my fingers into a fist and held on to the moment a little longer.

Today was a new day, a new beginning to an end.

After changing into jeans and brushing my teeth and hair, I joined Jude in the kitchen where he was flipping bacon. It brought me back to the first time I'd seen him, in a situation so similar to this one that it made my heart hurt a little bit. Once again, he was shirtless, offering me a chance to view the ink that spread across his arms and spilled over his back. I didn't see any new pieces, so I climbed onto a stool just outside the kitchen at the little glass table.

The smell of bacon was so ingrained in me from all the times I'd smelled it at the inn, but I'd never eaten it—not in years. But smelling it then made me wish things were different. Made me wish we could go back to who we were two years earlier before it all went to shit. Even one year before, I could've fixed us, could have fixed myself.

"Want bacon?" he asked, turning around. He looked a little bit hopeful then, but I realized that could have been my own yearning, seeing that in him.

A part of me really wanted the bacon. The part of me who was still left over from the girl Jude had loved two years ago. But who I was now was someone completely different, so I shook my head and tried not to feel too much regret when his face fell.

"Well, I made eggs too," he said with a tilt of his head to the bowl on the other counter. "Help yourself."

"Where are the plates?" I asked as I opened one cupboard after another.

"Beside me."

I reached up to the cabinet beside the stove and caught him watching me. "Good morning," he said with meaning.

I was stretched up on my toes to reach the top shelf where the plates were. "Good morning," I echoed.

"How'd you sleep?"

I held the plate tightly as I came back to the heels of my feet. "Better."

"Better than what?"

"Than I've slept in a long time."

I watched as he took in a breath, and was grateful to see this kind of reaction from him. "How long."

"Since June thirtieth, two thousand and eleven."

He let out the breath and looked at the bacon, but his attention seemed elsewhere as he just moved it around the pan with his tongs. "I wish. . ."

I stayed absolutely still. "What do you wish?"

He looked from the pan to me, opened his mouth before closing it again and shaking his head. "Never mind," he said, effectively ending the conversation.

I backed away as I clutched the plate and turned to the bowl of eggs. "Thanks for breakfast," I said over my shoulder. It would be my second complete meal in a row, because I didn't feel right vomiting in Jude's toilet. It sounded strange, even to me, but purging the food he'd made for me in his own house made me feel even dirtier than I already did. So I knew I'd need to keep it down, which was why I took one spoonful and then flattened it and spread it on my plate, to make it look like I'd taken more than I had.

When he joined me at the table, I was just a few tiny bites in and he raised one eyebrow. "Want some toast?"

I swallowed the bite I'd just taken. "Eggs are fine for me," I insisted, making a big show of swallowing an invisible bite. Jude wasn't an idiot; I knew he saw right through my bullshit. But he didn't call me out on it, so I was thankful we wouldn't have to revisit the conversation we'd had a year earlier.

We were both living in the same lie, but he wasn't as comfortable as I was with it.

"Have you checked on him?" I asked when I'd finished my eggs and pushed the plate away from me.

"Yes." I'd known Jude as a pretty introspective person, but in conversations he had always had thoughtful things to say. But now he was saying very little, just few-word sentences and meaningful looks.

"How is he?"

He stared at a speck of egg on his fork. "He's been better."

My empty plate became my focus when he said that. It'd been two years, and though the wounds hadn't healed, I didn't wish Colin ill. I didn't wish anything for Colin—he'd been so far removed from my thoughts for the last two years when I'd been thinking about Jude as much as I had.

"Is Mila still there with him?"

Jude sighed, a sound that he didn't often make. It made me lift my eyes and I saw the war of conflicting emotions across his face as he gathered his words. "Mila hasn't been there for a while."

I dropped the fork I was holding as I'd scooted around tiny specks of egg on my plate. The clatter was jarring, and Jude stared at me like he was shocked I'd made so much noise. "What do you mean? Is she on a job?"

"She left him a while ago."

"But she called me—she told me he was sick." But I thought she'd been talking about Jude.

"Yeah, she did. She was . . . distraught. She didn't think. She reached out to you, I'm assuming because you both loved him." Jude swallowed, as if talking about it made him uncomfortable. "But she was blinded with grief."

"But she's not at the hospital?"

Jude pinned me with his stare. "She may have left him, but I still stay in contact with her."

"And she gave you my number?"

He nodded slowly, still holding me with his gaze. "I asked for it when she said she'd called you."

It wasn't the first time Mila had gone against me for Jude, but I understood it. She owed me nothing—but Jude was her brother. "Oh." I didn't know what else to say.

"Is she coming?"

He dropped his head into his hands, his elbows braced on the table. I saw the tension knotting his muscles and wanted, for the briefest second, to reach over and touch his arm if nothing more than to say I could be there for him. "She's not coming."

That stunned me more than Mila leaving him had. Though I hardly knew her, I never suspected that she would abandon Colin when he was as ill as he was. "I'm sorry," I finally said, because I was. I was sorry that Jude had been here alone, the only one caring for Colin despite the tension they'd undoubtedly had between themselves. "You shouldn't have been alone through all of this." I reached my hand across the table, but stopped just short of halfway. He looked at my hand for a long moment.

"He shouldn't be alone." He lifted his eyes to mine and I saw, for the first time, a bottomless sense of pure agony.

Colin may have been many things, but he was still Jude's friend, someone who had been there through the same diagnoses.

I wondered if Jude witnessing Colin's mortality was affecting him—coming face to face with what could be his destiny.

"Are you okay?"

He laughed, but it was without humor. He dropped his head and stared at his plate as I had minutes earlier. "Am I okay?" Shaking his head, he said, "No, I'm not fucking okay." He pushed away from the table hard enough that the screech of the chair across the wooden floor startled me. Jude was always so steady, and while he wasn't necessarily predictable, he wasn't prone to outbursts of anger like this. He picked up his plate and walked to the sink and I stared at his back, willing him to talk to me. But I couldn't ask that of him.

Picking up my plate, I debated what to do. It was surreal almost, being in Jude's apartment but not touching him the way I wanted to. Finally, I joined him at the sink as he worked a sponge into a lather and swiped it across his plate. "Let me do it," I said softly, reaching a hand in to take the sponge from him.

He let go of the plate and clasped my forearm as I reached into the sink. His touch was gentle as he turned my wrist over and rubbed a thumb slowly across the length of my vein, visible through my translucent skin. I could only hold my breath as he touched me like this, like he was memorizing the blue lines that ran the length of my forearm. His hands were warm, searching, and I realized that I'd been yearning for this, for the simple act of him touching my skin like it was delicate. His fingers moved down, and my closed fist opened to give him access to my palm, where he traced the lines in my hands. It was so intimate, even in its simplicity, that all I could do was watch him as he examined my hands. "I've missed you," he said in a voice that was just short of a whisper. My heart turned over as he bent my fingers gently back into my fist and rubbed his soapy fingers over the knuckles.

When he let go of my hand and turned away from me, I felt goose bumps ignite across my skin. All I wanted was for him to keep touching me, but I'd hurt him. And he'd hurt me.

We had miles of pain between the two of us, and even though we were no longer miles apart, that pain existed between us like another person, holding both of us back.

"I missed you too," I said too late, when I'd caught my breath again.

"Please," he pleaded as he rinsed the plate in his hands. "I can't hear you say that right now."

Nodding, I backed away. I understood. This wasn't the time or place, and we were little more than strangers right now. I was a new Trista, someone he had never known.

Likely, someone he didn't want to know.

The hospital was bright, but it was incongruent with the feeling that settled over my skin the moment we stepped through the revolving doors. I followed Jude down many blue tiled hallways, up an elevator and down another blue tiled hallway until we reached a room marked one-nineteen.

"Do you want to go in alone?" Jude asked. It was the first thing he'd said since we'd gotten into the car and I nodded, wanting some alone time so that however I felt would be experienced for the first time without an audience.

"I'll go get some coffee," he said before disappearing.

I knocked first on the door and heard a muffled, "Come in," before I turned the handle and stepped into the room.

He was the first thing I saw, lying inclined on the hospital bed, a hundred wires strapped to his body. His head was turned so that he was staring out the window.

"Hey," I said, but it came out weird, like a croak.

Colin turned and took me in as I did the same. His black hair was matted to his head, the curls less curly and his skin much duller than I had ever seen. "Hey."

I approached the bed and took him in as I clasped the ends of his blankets, curling the fabric into my fist.

Though he definitely looked in less-than-perfect health, his eyes were still sharp as he studied me. "You look like shit," he said.

For some reason, it made me smile. Possibly because I knew he wasn't lying. I knew I looked like shit. I'd stared at my reflection that morning with a mixture of disgust and confusion. I looked like a shadow of the woman Jude had a framed photo of in the hallway, among the many other frames of the many people who had been there for him when I had not. Including Colin.

"You do too," I said, knowing it was the absolute least kind thing to say in the situation. But, like me, Colin took it with a hint of a smile and a shrug of one shoulder, the shoulder that didn't have wires disappearing under his gown.

He lifted a hand and waved it down his body. "This is what dying looks like."

That—that indifference—made my knees buckle, falling right into the bed's footboard. The noise of my knees knocking on the plastic was loud enough that he heard it too, probably even felt it. "Don't say that," I said, not ready to talk about it even though I was faced with it.

"The sooner you accept it, the better it'll be."

"For who? You?"

"For you." His lip curled. "I'm long past accepting it, Trista. This is my life; this is my end. It is what it is."

He sounded cold, like he had the last time I'd seen him in a similar position. But he'd looked better then, with life actually brightening his cheeks. Now his skin looked like a pale sack that hung apathetically off of his bone structure. He'd lost quite a bit of weight, which was saying something for someone as fit as he had been.

"You've lost weight," he said, as if he was reading my thoughts about him.

I curled my arms around my front and shrugged. "So have you."

"Mine is a symptom of dying. What about yours?"

He sounded like he held a little bit of judgment for me in his tone, but I wasn't sure what Jude had said to him about the last time we'd seen one another. "Mine is a symptom of living."

Colin snorted and rolled his eyes. I didn't recognize him from the man I'd once loved—a man who was always happy, never cynical. "Don't be so dramatic, Trista."

"I could say the same to you, Colin."

"But you can't, because one of us gets to walk out of this hospital and the other will be leaving in a body bag." He said it flatly, reminding me of my place.

I wanted to leave, I wanted to walk right out the door the way I had two years before and never look back. But Colin was alone, and I couldn't ignore our years together even though he had been a complete asshole in the end. So I sunk down into a chair beside the bed. "I'm sorry."

"What are you sorry for?" he asked as if he was mocking me. "Do you wish to trade places with me?"

The thought of it, of being strapped in that bed as he awaited death, made me feel such sympathy for him. It was the reason I stayed, because I could see just how trapped he was. And I knew he was miserable, I could see it in his eyes and hear it in his words. So that was why I chose to stay beside his bed, even when he was doing his very best to push me away. I thought of Mila then, wondering what he had done that made her not come back even for this.

"I'm sorry you're dying this way."

He closed his eyes and it was then that I saw the flicker of pain he masked behind the cynicism and sarcasm. "What a way to go, right?" he said before opening his eyes. "I thought I'd fall off a mountain, or get eaten by a cougar, before I'd ever die in a hospital bed."

I knew in sitting beside him that I didn't love him anymore—there was no doubt in my mind. But I couldn't pretend those years hadn't existed. I couldn't wipe away all the feelings I'd had for him. And if I could have chosen for him, I'd have wished he'd have died quickly, doing what he loved the most.

A slow death while virtually chained to a bed must have been hell for him.

I looked around the room, taking in the various balloons and flowers. On the nightstand was a teddy bear, and I must have stared long enough at it for Colin to make a comment. "It's like they think I'm three years old still."

"They?"

He motioned a hand at the bear before dropping the hand back to the bed. "My mom. She's the one bringing me teddies and various other stuffed animals. It's like this. . ." he motioned to the wires and all around him ". . . has made her regress so far back that she thinks I'm still a small child, needing stuffed animals for security."

I folded my hands in my lap. "She probably doesn't know what else to do. I can't imagine it's easy for her right now."

He didn't say anything to that and I made sure not to make eye contact. I didn't want to talk about death—what was the point of that? It was waiting for all of us, but was claiming Colin before the rest of us.

"Why are you here?"

I turned my gaze to him, watching him watching me. "Because I felt like it was right."

He nodded, seemed to be taking in what I said. "Did you think I wanted you to be here?"

I hadn't thought about that, but now that he'd said it, my stomach churned and I suddenly felt like I was going to throw up. I looked around for a trash can before I stood and walked into the private bathroom and closed the door.

The vomit came up easily, like my stomach couldn't stand the heaviness of the eggs nor the bitterness of my reunion with Colin. I let it all pour from my mouth, hoping to purge everything I could so that I was empty of food and feelings.

After I'd rinsed out my mouth, I left the bathroom fully intending to leave the hospital room and find Jude.

"Wait, Trista."

I closed my eyes, not wanting him to see my face. I didn't know how to feel about this, about my ex-boyfriend's life coming to an end. And, more importantly, I didn't know what to do *for* him.

But I turned back to the bed.

"I'm happy you're here."

I waited, on that precipice of running away, but stayed still for the time being. "Are you sure about that? You're not the Colin I remember." I took a tentative step toward the bed. "The Colin I remembered would smile—he didn't have to say he was happy. He just was."

After looking out the window for a moment, he said, "I have very little to be happy about these days. I hope you come back."

"Why?" I didn't feel right asking him why he wanted me back, like I was treading on ground that wasn't solid between us.

"Because I want to tell you, the next time you visit, that I'm sorry."

"You are?"

His voice was bitter as his eagle eyes set themselves upon me. "You're sorry I'm dying this way. I'm sorry you're living the way you are. Ellie would be disappointed."

I didn't believe that only flesh could bleed, not when he looked at me like that, bringing up our mutual ghost.

As I left the room, I realized we had said very little in our first time seeing one another after two years. But I would come back, I knew. I couldn't let this be the last time we spoke.

That's what was so complicated about the situation. There should be no question that I'd be here for someone I had known for years, someone who I practically grew up with. Even though he had spoken to me with acid on his tongue, I couldn't forget the boy I'd loved years ago. Regardless of how I felt about the way we'd left each other, he was still a person, a someone, dying too soon.

When I found Jude in the waiting room, I watched him sleeping upright, arms crossed over his chest and his head tilted back so it lay against the wall behind him. He looked tired, and for the first time since I had woken up that morning, I got a good look at the circles under his eyes, and the way his facial hair was several days overgrown. It didn't look intentional; it looked like a symptom of grief.

I pulled out my notebook and wrote a poem.

We're a hundred miles apart
but in the same room.
We're two different people
but thoughts of you
have consumed
me
since I exhumed
you.
I'm not ready,
I'm not who
I'm meant to be,
but I want to find her
for you.

It was the first time in weeks I'd been able to write anything, and I curled my fingers down the words on my paper, my fingertips coming away with gray smudges. When I looked up, he was watching me. He was always watching me with a quiet sort of steadiness, like he knew what I was thinking but was letting me keep it to myself—telling me he'd be there for me, no matter what I chose. I didn't deserve him. He didn't deserve my indecisiveness or my unsteadiness.

All I could think was how much he deserved someone solid, but I was still selfish enough to want him to wait for me. Wait for what, I didn't know.

I walked toward him and he stood from the chair. "I'll go talk to him for a minute," he said, brushing past me without touching me. I sank into his seat and laid my head against the wall as he had done, and I watched him walk down the hall.

The chair had started to grow hard under my ass by the time Jude returned, holding two chocolate milks and wearing a stony look.

"Here," he said, thrusting one toward me. I remembered his penchant for chocolate milk, and accepted it gratefully.

"Where'd you get this?"

He shrugged. "One of the nurses here knows me well and grabbed them for me from the kitchen."

It was the most he'd spoken to me all day, and I think he realized it too because right away he closed down and looked at me like he wasn't sure why he had said so much to me. "Hungry?" he asked, and we were back to who we'd been last night—Jude asking if I was hungry even if he knew I wasn't, because he wanted me to eat. I thought of how I'd thrown up in the bathroom and nodded, even though I wasn't hungry. Not in the least. "There's this little taco truck around the corner this time of day—let me buy you lunch."

He didn't wait for me to answer and turned to leave. I followed him out of the waiting area, down elevators and hallways until we were in the parking lot. Everything with him was so quiet, like he was saving his words for the right moment. Street tacos sounded safe—he wouldn't bombard me with the things he wanted to say when there was an audience.

As we approached the taco truck my stomach rumbled from the smell alone. The smell of grilled onions and peppers made my mouth water. Jude bought me lunch and we sat on the curb as we ate, sauce dribbling down our chins and napkins being rumpled and tossed into the trash.

"When do you want to go back home?"

I swallowed the grilled steak and felt a pinch in my stomach from the amount of food I was digesting. "I don't know."

We both knew why. Colin was dying and it was just a waiting game at this point. I wouldn't leave before the funeral, but I wasn't planning on staying more than an hour after that.

"What do you want to do while you're here? I can take you anywhere."

"Don't you have work?" I picked at the lettuce on my taco and chewed one strip thoughtfully.

"I can work from anywhere."

I glanced sideways at him. "I wanted to visit my grandfather while I was here. I haven't seen him in two years."

"Okay. I can drive you up there tomorrow, if you'd like, depending."

I didn't need him to clarify what it depended on. I tipped my head back and let the sun warm my face. It felt cruel that Jude and I were sitting out here on a curb, eating tacos in the sunshine, while Colin wasted away in a bed that would be his last one, in a room filled by artificial light, greeted day in and day out by people whose sole job was to keep you comfortable until you met the end. I wanted to be grateful, to not take this moment for granted. "I'd like that, Jude." I smiled at him, something genuine and warm.

"Just promise me something," he said, and I knew it was heavy, what he was asking me.

"What should I promise?"

His eyes burned beneath his irises. "Don't look at me like that unless you're ready."

CHAPTER FIFTEEN

The next morning, Jude visited Colin at the hospital but shook his head at me when I was going to go in after him. "It's not a good day for him," he said with an arm holding me to stop me.

I stared at his arm for a moment, feeling a little annoyed that Jude was blocking my way. "I want to see him, just in case."

"Trista." I stopped pushing against his arm and tilted my head up so that our eyes met. His beautiful brown eyes looked at me with a depth of sadness that I couldn't echo, and I wondered what was wrong with me. "He doesn't want to see you today."

I ran my tongue over my teeth as I contemplated that. "But, what if?"

"What ifs are unfounded fears, Trista. This isn't about you—this isn't about what you want. This is about him, and what he wants. He's going to be gone soon." I watched as he swallowed that word and he placed his hands on my forearms. "And he doesn't want your last memory of him to be the him he is today. Okay?"

Dying was lonely, guilty business. That's what I'd learned in the thirty-six hours since I'd been faced with it so close to me. I wanted to see Colin, but only if he wanted to see me. So I agreed and followed Jude out of the hospital, where we then embarked on the road trip to Wyoming for the night, so that I could see my grandfather in the morning.

The ride up was mostly quiet until we reached the Wyoming border, when I just couldn't stand the silence any longer. "What have you been doing in the year since I last saw you?"

Jude seemed surprised that I'd come out and asked that, but it was the only way I could think to ask him what plagued me—did he have someone else?

The thing with Jude had caused a weakness I couldn't shake. And I knew, to some degree, he was affected by what we couldn't seem to figure out. But I'd asked him to wait for me. And I suddenly, desperately, wanted to know if he had.

"After I saw you in Maine, I took on a few sponsorship jobs." He ran a hand over the steering wheel and kept his eyes focused on the road. "So I went to Greece and the United Kingdom for a bit. Then I did a few National Park jaunts."

"Yellowstone?" It seemed important, somehow, to know the answer.

"No." It came out flat, like I shouldn't have asked. But whatever Jude's stony, silent disposition, he didn't make me feel stupid for asking. Mostly he made me feel like there were several more words that he condensed down to one. "I went to Montana and Alaska and Arizona."

"I've never been to any of those states." I'd been to a lot since leaving Wyoming years ago, but only just to pass through on my way to Maine.

"Alaska is absolutely breathtaking. I mean, you can't beat it anywhere else in this country." This was my way of getting through to Jude, to ask him about things that did not involve us and all our hurt.

"I want to go someday." I didn't mean to say it aloud, but once the words poured out I saw the tick in his jaw. I knew, because Jude was giving and selfless and too fucking good for me, that he was thinking, *I could take you,* but we couldn't make those kinds of promises to one another, not right now. There was too much left unsaid for us to keep brushing it under the rug.

"What else have you been doing?" I asked, wanting to bring back talkative Jude. "Climbed any new mountains?"

"I have. Mostly this side of the country, but I'm looking to venture east."

"Where?"

"New England, perhaps."

I wondered if he meant Maine. So I asked him.

"Depends," he answered, and once again I knew what he meant by that. "But I really want to get over to Iceland this year, maybe in the spring or so."

"Iceland?"

"I've seen most of Europe at this point; I'd like to see the parts that aren't as traveled as the others."

I understood that about Jude, his desire to see things fewer people had. He looked for the good in everyone, the good in every place, and I admired that about him because it was probably the one reason he still talked to me, despite my issues.

"Enough about me," he said, interrupting my thoughts. "What have you been doing since I last saw you."

Guilt washed over me. I knew he wanted me to be honest about the things I didn't want to tell him. "I'm still working at the inn. Still driving my piece-of-shit car."

"Chasing waves?"

I laughed. "Not quite. You seem to remember our time differently than I do. That insinuates I surf. Which I can't."

I saw the slightest curl of a smile light his lips. "Didn't know if you'd practiced in the year since I saw you."

"Well, considering the beach water temp can drop to the thirties in the winter—and since I still have all my limbs, I haven't practiced at all. The inn has been remodeling rooms left and right, so that's taken up most of my time."

"It's a nice place. Homey feeling, which is probably part of the reason it's so successful during the peak months."

It did have a homey feel. It's why I'd stayed on as long as I had. "Well," I began, hoping courage would make my voice not as shaky as it felt, "you're welcome back anytime."

I watched as his knuckles tightened on the steering wheel, but his face remained straight, facing the road so I couldn't determine how he was feeling. But I'd meant it.

"Maybe I will." And just like that, talk of what would happen for us after this slithered away. "I'm going to Louisiana in a couple weeks."

Another place I'd never been, but wanted to go. "For work?"

"For fun, actually."

It shouldn't have bothered me that he chose to go to Louisiana for fun instead of going to Maine. Rationally, I understood that I never had a say over where he spent his time. I never took vacations away from the inn, but if I did, I might go back to Colorado. Back to Jude. If nothing else but for a taste of yesterday.

We rode mostly in silence the rest of the way, exchanging only the words that were necessary when we stopped at rest areas or gas stations to fill up. The last time Jude spoke to me in the car was around dinnertime, when he asked if I was ready to stop for dinner and a room for the night. When I nodded, realizing we were just twenty minutes from grandpa's home, Jude took the first exit. By the time we pulled into the parking lot for the motel, I froze as I stared up at the sign.

It was the same motel I'd stopped at to heal from Doug's violence, before I'd moved to Maine. The blinking neon sign in the window was the same, with a bulb behind the *n* still dark. The cheap patio chairs were the same. Even the crowd hanging outside the motel by the front office seemed the same, with leering looks and cheap cigarettes. Their conversation grew louder as we exited the car and I paid for the room, even after Jude had tried to pay himself. I knew it probably sounded contradictory, but while I was okay with Jude buying me lunch the day before, I wasn't okay with him paying for our motel room for the night, especially when this trip was my idea and Jude was coming along as . . . what? Some kind of moral support?

Even the room was the same as the one I'd stayed in before. I didn't remember the number to know if it was exactly the same, but the linens and the tube TV hadn't been updated from the last time I'd stayed here.

"You all right?"

Startled, I jumped from the spot I'd stood in since putting my bag on the floor and looking around the room. "Yeah." But my tone wasn't convincing. He dropped his backpack on the bed and turned to me.

"Mind if I shower?"

I shook my head and sank to the bed closest to the window, grabbing the remote from the nightstand and turning it on. The pipes made a racket when he turned the faucet on, so I turned the volume up higher on the TV just as a text message pinged from my phone.

Charlotte: Whatcha up to?

I debated replying to her. Not because I didn't want to talk to her, but because the longer I was away from her, the more I realized how toxic her influence had been. But that didn't mean I stopped caring for her.

Me: Fine. We're in a motel in Wyoming. Going to see my gramps tomorrow.

Charlotte: Two questions. Who is we and are you seeing mommy dearest, too?

The first question was something I didn't want to address at the moment, because Charlotte might have made assumptions. It hadn't even crossed my mind to get two separate hotel rooms because we'd stayed in the same apartment the last two nights. But the second part of the question was a valid one, one I hadn't thought about until we'd pulled into the parking lot. I hadn't kept in touch with her after changing my number, only getting the occasional update from my grandpa, who got most of his information from gossip. Which meant the information wasn't often good.

Me: Maybe. Not sure.

Charlotte: If you do, kick that dipshit right in the dick.

Charlotte: Don't think I didn't notice you ignored my question of defining who -we- entailed.

I sighed and flopped on my back just as I heard the sound of something falling in the shower. From what I remembered, the shower had felt cramped to me and Jude had several inches, both horizontally and vertically, on me. Figuring I was safe to talk with her, I called her instead of talking about this over text message.

"I was waiting for you to call me," she said immediately upon answering. "What's up? I can feel your weirdness through osmosis."

I looked toward the bathroom again, but the water was still running. "I'm here with Jude—" I heard her catch her breath and quickly added, "but it's not what you think."

"Oooh—Jude, the something else," she said, and her glee practically vibrated through the phone. "What do you think I think? Because I think being in a motel with your ex-boyfriend means sex and other shenanigans."

Of course Charlotte would think that. "It's not like that though. He offered to take me, and I think he's more or less babysitting me. That's why he's with me." I shook my head, regretting my choice of wording. "He's not *with me,* with me. Just along for the ride."

"All sorts of innuendos," Charlotte said, and I could practically see her, rocking back on her bed with glee. "Have you made a move?"

Charlotte didn't get it. Her relationships were usually disposable, but sometimes they'd return for seconds. The problem was that the scraps she left were never worth a damn, but she tried anyway. "You don't understand Jude." I sighed, and in my head I added *or me.* Jude wasn't someone I could climb over and lose the last two years of sadness in. "I can't get a good read on him though; he's so stoic and quiet, which is a new side of him I haven't seen before."

"He's so yummy," she said, making the 'so' especially dramatic. "If you don't take him back, someone else will."

I pinched the bridge of my nose. Charlotte really didn't get it. I could blame that on the fact that she never saw me in a relationship before, but also her immaturity played a part in her ambivalence toward the feelings of others. "I don't think he'll have someone else just because he can't have me."

"Why can't he have you?"

Because he doesn't want me, not like this. Part of me was suddenly angry with Charlotte then, because it was Charlotte's influence that had inspired me to become a little bit like her. But then it was Doug's stupid fucking echo—and my mom's echo—that lived in my head: fat and worthless. That and my weak resolve made me someone easily influenced into making a bad decision like falling into bulimia.

"Because it's complicated," I told her instead, hearing the sharpness in my own voice as I said it.

"Everybody says that," she said on a dramatic sigh. "It's complicated," she mimicked me in a high-pitched voice. "Then uncomplicate it. Get on top of him and lose yourself for a minute. God knows you could use a lay."

"He's not just someone to fuck, Charlotte." I was so wrapped up in my anger with Charlotte reducing Jude to someone he wasn't that I didn't realize the shower had stopped and by the time I said 'fuck,' Jude had stepped out of the bathroom and into the motel room with just some sweatpants on. I couldn't tell by the look on his face whether he had heard me or not—or how much he had heard if he had at all—and I wished I'd stuck to texting her instead. "I gotta go, Char." And then I hung up on her, despite her protests.

171

"Ah," Jude said, holding the towel between his hands as he alternated between running it over his hair and then running one hand over it after. "Charlotte." He gave me a meaningful look. "Your friend from the inn."

"She was just checking in," I explained, trying to gauge his demeanor so I could figure out whether he heard much of the conversation or not. I hoped he hadn't heard my last line to her before I saw him, because I wasn't sure how I'd explain that to him. "How was your shower?" I would not objectify him, I told myself. Ex-boyfriend or not, I shouldn't have looked over the lines on his chest, the curves of muscle and the way the black ink on the left side of his chest wrapped around his body.

But then he lifted his arm, raising one of his pectorals, and I totally objectified him. He was still the most beautifully built man I'd ever seen, and after living two years in a beach town, I'd seen a lot. "Want to get dinner?"

"Sure." I stood from the bed and stretched. His eyes fell to my stomach, but he frowned slightly. I yanked my shirt down and grabbed my purse. "There's a burger place just down the road a ways." I didn't want to venture too far into town lest I saw my mom, so staying in the area was absolutely preferable.

The burger place was somewhere I'd gone with Colin many times throughout high school, a fact I didn't dwell too much on because I was here with Jude. I didn't want to compare him to Colin, but there really wasn't a comparison. It was hard to reconcile the Colin I'd come to know in the last few years with the Colin I'd met in school, but I knew they were the same living, breathing person.

Jude ordered a burger with lots of guacamole and I ordered French fries, eating each slowly and carefully. The entire time, Jude watched me chew my food. I knew he waited for me to excuse myself to the restroom.

I knew that I had a careless way of approaching bulimia. Because I knew, I truly knew, its impact upon my body and the negative effects. But I also knew that I could read a hundred articles and several books on battling bulimia and not a single one would change the feeling I held deep within myself, of my own self-loathing. There were healthier ways to lose weight. I was so rational about it that I knew saying 'healthier' wasn't even accurate because—bottom line—nothing about bulimia was remotely *healthy*. To compare it to going to a gym and working out wasn't about which was healthier but which was the *only* healthy choice.

But my carelessness meant that I didn't purge every meal, just some of them. And I didn't troll pro-thin forum boards, looking for, as they called it, *thinspiration*. I did it because it was the easiest way to lose weight, and the only way I felt in control. So much in my life had been out of my control. Deciding what I kept in my body was the littlest thing I had power over. Just because it slid past my lips didn't mean I needed to keep it.

And I'd be lying if I said that looking in the mirror and seeing the push of bone against my skin didn't appeal to me in a very shallow way.

Nonetheless, I wasn't outright talking about it with Jude, who would undoubtedly tell me I was beautiful the way I was. My confidence in knowing this wasn't because of some elevated confidence in myself but in knowing him. Jude may have been distant, almost like a stranger in the way he held his words from me, but I knew the man he was at his core. And I knew how much he wanted to take me in and fix my 'problems.'

"Is there anything else you want to do while you're here?" he asked when I was halfway through my fries.

I thought about what Charlotte had said, about my mom and Doug. Part of me did *not* want to see my mom, to hear what my call to the police had cost her. But I felt, in some strange and probably biological way, that I owed it to her to see her. Say my piece, if she was willing to listen.

"I think I want to drop by to see my mom," I finally said, sipping my water quickly so I couldn't take the words back. "It's been a couple years."

Ever since I'd left Wyoming, I'd associated my mom with what had happened with Doug. I'd tried to keep him from her and in protecting her, I'd put myself in danger. I knew that she'd been too unconscious to know this, but I imagined there would've been questions when the police arrived. I tried not to feel guilty about possibly sending her to jail, but I knew she needed help—and to be separated from Doug.

"You look like you're not sure about that."

I wondered if I was that transparent. "The last time I saw her, things didn't go so well." That was an understatement if I'd ever heard one. "But I feel like I probably should, since I'll be in the same area she's in."

"Okay." He sipped his chocolate milk and set it down. "We'll spend tomorrow visiting them and head back down tomorrow night."

I didn't have much choice—not because Jude wouldn't deviate from my choices but because I didn't want to be away from Denver so long when I knew what could happen at a moment's notice.

"Why'd Mila leave him?"

"That's between them."

"Why won't she come back?"

"That's because whatever she's dealing with, mentally, is too heavy for her to accept right now." He sighed and leaned back against the booth seat. "Do you want to talk about what happened two years ago, when you left Colorado?"

We'd never talked about it, not even when he had come to Maine the year before. And while I'd liked that, I'd wanted to know. Why he'd lied to me. Why he'd lied for Colin, especially when our feelings had become what they had. "Yes. Why did you lie to me?"

He dropped his head into his hands, elbows braced on the table, and I watched the shake of his head, back and forth, as he cradled it in his hands. "To be honest," he began.

"Honesty would be nice," I said, interrupting him.

"I didn't want to tell you the things Colin was doing behind your back. I didn't want you to leave him knowing I'd be there for you." He paused when a waitress walked past our table and stared down at his plate before meeting my eyes again. "I wanted you to leave him because it was what you wanted. Most conflicts can be resolved—but I didn't want the conflict to be your reason for leaving him. I thought, and maybe it was wrong of me, that it was best for you to decide in your heart what you wanted without influence to choose one way or another."

"It was wrong of you. I deserved to know that my boyfriend—" I lowered my voice as the waitress dropped off another chocolate milk for Jude "—was in love with your sister."

"You did. I should've found another way to tell you. But I didn't want you hung up on him. I knew that your identity wasn't your own, it was defined by those you spent time with. And I worried that if you left him because of a factor outside of your control, you'd be stuck on wondering why you weren't. . ." he rubbed his lips together as he considered ". . . good enough. Because you are. You're enough, and he was blind." He pushed his chocolate milk away from him and shook his head. "I wanted him to figure his shit out and tell you, so I didn't come to you with this information that would change your relationship before you were ready."

"There's that word again," I said, drumming my fingertips on the tabletop. "You can't decide for me what I'm ready for."

"Then what do you think you're ready for?" he asked.

"I don't know," I replied honestly, putting a hand to my forehead. "I don't know what I'm ready for. I just know that I'm not ready—" I swallowed "—to watch my ex-boyfriend, someone who knew me better than anyone else living did, to die. I'm not ready to say another permanent goodbye, when I'm still not over the last one." I hated baring myself to him like this, telling him my conflicted feelings for Colin. I knew those feelings were abstract, not because I was still in love with him or even wanted to be with him, but because I was still searching for who I was and the last person to know me so well was leaving me—forever. The truth was that I didn't know what effect Colin's death would have on me. Would I feel free? Or weighed down by how we parted? I wished I could've talked to him that morning, but I respected his wishes still.

"Have you ever thought of talking to someone?" He asked it lightly, like it was fragile ground to tiptoe across.

"I have before. But it's expensive and takes effort to find someone who is actually interested in trying to help you heal enough that you no longer need them." In my last experience, my therapist had only been prolonging my grief instead of helping me see my way through it.

I always thought that funny about therapists; if they did their job right, you wouldn't need to see them again. It couldn't have been good for business.

"Let me help you."

"No." My answer was firm; he couldn't change my mind. I still felt bad for dragging him along to Wyoming though I, one, hadn't had much other choice and two, he'd offered to take me. I couldn't accept financial help to talk to someone about my feelings, knowing many of them had to do with him. "I'll figure it out." I looked out the window to the parking lot, taking in the darkening sky and the headlights from the highway as they slashed across the window. In the distance, it was pitch black, with just the briefest bits of lights as cars drove past.

"I wish you'd just let me help." He said it so softly I almost didn't hear him.

"You're doing everything you can to help me," I said, even though to him he was doing nothing. But the fact that he was driving me around Wyoming and Colorado, reuniting me with my ex-boyfriend—it was more than enough for him to do. "I will do something."

"When?"

I sighed and rubbed a hand down my face, the weight of this conversation affecting me since we were in public. "I don't know, Jude. I really don't." I knew his impatience wasn't because he was desperate for me to return to him in the way I felt he wanted me, but more that he was worried about me.

He waved for the check when I'd finished my fries and paid it in cash before he slid from the booth. On the way out of the restaurant, he wrapped an arm around my shoulders and pulled me tightly to him. My chest clenched, my rib cage collapsing in on itself, having him holding me so familiarly. "Promise me," he said, his voice gruff against my ear.

"What am I promising?" I asked against his chest as he led me to his car.

"To try. If not for you, for me."

He opened my car door and I slid in, feeling the weight of what he was asking me drop into my stomach.

Back at the motel, Jude told me he had work to do and I ventured out for ice cubes, needing space after what had happened when we'd left the diner. I pulled out my phone at the ice machine and called Maura to check in.

"Nothing much going on here," she lamented, in between sounds of her banging pots in the kitchen. I figured she was doing dishes with me on speakerphone with the way I echoed in the room. "You doing okay?"

"Yep." Maura didn't know what was going on, why I needed to go home for a few weeks. But it was the first time I had taken any considerable time off in forever, so she knew it had to involve something serious. "I'm not sure when I'll be back yet."

"Well," she said, and sniffed loudly. I could visualize her at that moment, sniffing, one hand on her hips as she tried to figure out what to say. Maura was a hearty, headstrong woman. She might not have known all the right words to say, but if I needed to lean, I could lean on her. "I hope you'll be back soon. You've left me in a bit of a lurch."

That was the other thing about Maura—she didn't pussyfoot. "It won't be long," I said, already imagining the moment I'd need to say goodbye to Jude. I looked back at the room we were in for the night and wished I could return to the room with a different mindset than the one I had.

"I've gotta go," I told her after a few minutes of idle chitchat. I couldn't ignore Jude any longer and I couldn't keep standing out by the ice machine under the yellow light, swarmed by a billion bugs.

"Fine, fine. Just check in once in a while, all right? Don't wanna worry you're dead in a ditch or something."

That made me smile. "Are you worried about me, Maura?" I teased her.

"Nah, just about hiring your replacement. So figure out your shit and come back."

Jude was propped up on the bed with his laptop on his lap. He was wearing the sweats he'd worn after his shower and a flannel shirt that was similar to mine. He had a little frown furrowing his eyebrows and his lips were pulled down.

I debated asking him, telling myself that he didn't want or need my help. But curiosity won out. "You look confused."

He broke his concentration to look at me. "I tried to make a new page for my privacy policy, so it's no longer a pop-up when you click the hyperlink. But I've buried the page somewhere, and can't find it."

Tentatively, I asked, "Can I help?"

He was still looking at me, as if deciding whether or not getting help from me was a good choice. I hated that he looked at me like that, like he couldn't decide anything about me when just two years earlier he'd been so sure, so solid, in his feelings about me. But I let it roll off my back as he scooted over to give me room beside him on the bed. I motioned for the laptop and he handed it over, all warm from being in his hands and on his lap for the last thirty minutes.

"Let me see," I said, chewing on my bottom lip as I looked through his navigation on his live site, to see if he'd hidden the privacy policy somewhere in there. "You don't want it linked, right?"

"Right. Well, I mean, I want it to be a link but instead of a pop up on the screen they're on, I want it to take them to its own page."

"Okay." I went through his draft pages, but couldn't find anything named *Privacy Policy*. On a hunch, I started going through some of the duplicates he'd had, like *About (1), About (2), Europe Travels (3),* and *Sponsors (2)* when I finally found it buried under the sixth copy of *My Gear.* "Here it is," I said, renaming the page and its link to "Privacy Policy."

"I should've known," he said, and I could hear the relief in his voice. "I keep doing that, making dupes of the other pages so I don't have to try to figure out how to recreate the template, but then I never rename them until I need them."

I smiled at him, but it felt a little sad on my face. He'd hired me once to do website work, and the last time I'd looked at the back end of his website, it hadn't been this messy, with dozens of duplicate pages and too many fonts throughout the website. It made me wish to help him again, but I knew I couldn't—I couldn't offer it to him and I couldn't do it.

"Can you help me on the *My Gear* page for a minute?" he asked, as if he knew that I wanted to help him but not on such a large scale. "I wanted to have those things where you click on a button or text and it expands to reveal more below it. So that it's not so long and drawn out the way it is." He showed me what he was talking about and I set to work on his site.

Over the next couple hours I helped Jude with other parts of his website, even deleting a good half-dozen duplicate pages after he realized they weren't necessary.

Sometime over those hours, Jude turned on the television and a documentary about surviving in the wilderness came on. It was a husband and wife pair, and while she didn't look like she had the chops to skin a snake or chop down a tree, she did all of those things beside him without complaint.

"I've always wanted to do that," Jude said after a while.

"Go out into the middle of nowhere and survive?"

"Yeah." He reached an arm toward the TV to turn up the volume on the remote, giving me a view of the trees that climbed his forearm. "I think it'd be fun—to figure it out caveman-style."

I raised an eyebrow. "You *would* think that's fun. Having a python slither through your camp sounds like a jolly good time."

"Sounds like dinner." He grinned, that bright flash of white causing me to smile back. "And besides, if you think about it, we're all descended from someone who had to do those things. Maybe not surviving in the forest, but I'm sure they had to do something necessary for survival in such a primitive environment. If they hadn't, we wouldn't be here. Somewhere along the line, someone in our bloodline built a fire with their hands. That's amazing, when you think of it like that, isn't it?"

I found myself nodding in agreement, but it wasn't anything I had ever really thought about. "Can you build a fire with your hands?" I asked, looking over his tanned hands as he used them to illustrate what he was saying.

"With a bow drill, sure. A fire starter is easier, but if you want to be a real bad ass, you use a bow drill."

I had no clue what he was talking about and I was sure my face reflected that. "Why don't you do it then?"

He turned from the TV to look at me. "Really?"

Shrugging, I said, "Sure. Why not?"

"Well." He paused and looked down before meeting my eyes again. "The biggest problem would be . . ." He paused to tap a finger over his chest. "This little guy."

It was easy to forget that Jude wasn't able to do everything he wanted to do. He was so fit, so strong and steady, I often thought that nothing could tip him over. But the very thing that pumped life into his veins could rob him of that if he pushed himself too hard. "Have you had any problems?" I asked him, which was the first time in a long time I'd asked him directly how he was doing, without Mila telling me herself.

"I haven't had any problems. But I don't. . ." he licked his lips before continuing, ". . . over-exert myself anymore."

I thought of Yellowstone, his red face from the hike down the waterfall. How I'd chalked it up to asthma or something far less serious than it was. "That's good." It came out as a whisper and I swallowed, because suddenly he was too close. His juniper scent was washing over me, but not in an overpowering way. Our bodies were touching on the bed and his laptop was still on my lap. At some point he had put an arm behind my head, probably to stretch his limbs and afford him a little more room to lean in as I worked on his computer. But suddenly, it all felt too intimate.

He could curl his arm and I'd fall against him with only a nudge.

I knew I probably had shifty eyes then, looking all around us because his eyes were on my throat and I didn't know where to look to make this less . . . well, just less.

"What's wrong?" he asked, his voice lower than it had been.

"You're too close." I couldn't meet his gaze.

"Do you want me to move?"

"I don't know."

"Yes, you do."

I tried to think of anything else, a million other things, so that I didn't think about the fact that our faces were a whisper apart, and that all it'd take was the turn of my head for our lips to meet. A few things ran through my mind, but Jude was pushing through all of them.

"I don't know," I repeated.

"Why are you lying?"

I closed my eyes tightly, gritting my teeth to keep from turning.

Don't turn, Trista.

It was a mantra I repeated over and over in my head.

But then I felt the warmth of his arm at the back of my neck and I couldn't wait anymore, not for another second.

I turned my head and met his lips immediately, as if they'd been there all along, waiting for me to be ready for them.

Instantly, it felt like I was warming from the inside out. A molten core that spread through all my limbs as my arms reached for him and wrapped around his neck. He pulled me over easily onto his lap so that I straddled him.

I remembered, suddenly, how good this felt. To be in his arms, to be held by him, to be kissed and touched by him. There was a lightness in my heart that I hadn't experienced in so long that I could scarcely believe it lived in me, amongst the heaviness and the self-loathing.

His fingers snaked through my hair, and his palms held my skull tightly. Even if I wanted to slip from his hold, I couldn't.

His lips were warm on mine, and when his tongue slipped into my mouth, I felt myself dissolve a little bit in his hands. I ran my hands everywhere, over his chest and up his arms that held me so firmly. His fingers curled where they held my skull, pulling my hair tight. And when he sighed against my mouth, my skin erupted in a billion goose bumps.

I curled more into him when his hands traveled down my spine, coming to rest right over my tailbone. He broke from my lips to search my eyes. The room was dark, but I saw the reflection of the TV in his eyes, the only light I could see. "I've been wanting to do that for an entire year."

Dropping my forehead to rest against his, I said, "Then don't stop."

"Are you sure?"

In answer, I squeezed my thighs that were straddled on either side of him before I recaptured his mouth.

I'd missed this. The feeling of belonging. And I was too selfish to tell him no.

He leaned forward, causing me to gently fall backward on the bed as he climbed over me. His hands fanned my hair out around me as he looked down at me. There was a vein in his forehead that throbbed, and I reached a hand up so I could rub my thumb over it.

"Trista," he said before pressing his lips against mine. "I've missed," he said, moving his lips to my jaw and up to my ear. "You," he breathed against my earlobe before he nuzzled his face into my neck and kissed a line down to my collarbone.

I couldn't speak. He was leaving a trail of goose bumps in the wake of his kisses, making my whole body itch to grab every single part of him, just to feel his skin under my hands so that I wouldn't forget this, forget him.

His fingers slid down the column of my throat and I tilted my head back to give him more room as his lips followed his fingers' trail. Slowly, he began unbuttoning the flannel shirt I wore. With each passing second, more of my skin was being revealed and I fought the urge to shiver—not from the cold, but from the anticipation of being with Jude again this way. With one hand, he unbuttoned the shirt and the other dragged down my chest with each new inch of skin that was exposed. I sucked in a breath, feeling it fill my lungs, when he had the last button undone and pushed the sides of my shirt away from my chest. All I wore under the shirt was a bra, but Jude climbed over me and kissed me again instead of unclasping the bra.

His lips just rested against mine for a minute, a touch that was more intimate than a kiss, as we breathed one another's air. My hands went to his shirt and, with my eyes closed and Jude nibbling my lower lip gently, I began to undo each button as he had done to me. I wanted his skin on mine, I wanted to expose him the way he'd exposed me. When the last button was undone, Jude wrapped his arms under me and pulled me up so that my ass was on his upper thighs, straddling him, and we were upright on the bed.

I met his eyes when my hands slid up his torso, feeling all that hard muscle under my fingertips. I stopped at his shoulders, my fingers curling over his muscles underneath the shirt. Slowly, I drew my hands down so that the opened shirt began to slide down his shoulders and off of his arms.

The room was dark, but my hands saw everything my eyes couldn't see. Skin met ink and met skin again, all across his chest and arms, and part of me wished to have the patience to lay him down and explore every inch, a luxury I hadn't afforded myself in the last year.

Interrupting my perusal, Jude cupped my jaw and kissed me firmly on the mouth. My nails dug into his shoulders, holding him as firmly as he held me. When he pulled back, he was breathing heavily and that rush of warmth washed over my neck, making me want to writhe in his arms. My shirt hung open, covering just my arms and back. With one hand, he pulled my hair so that it tugged my face back, once again exposing my neck to him. His lips turned hungry, with a nip here and there as they followed the curve of my neck to my shoulder. I was burning from the inside, the heat spreading to all my appendages. How strange it was, to feel that burning and want to chase it for as long as you could.

"Kiss me," he said, cradling my head to lift it again, because I felt so weak from sensation that I wasn't sure I could hold it up myself.

I slid my hands into his hair and dragged my nails down his scalp as my lips met his. Over and over, we licked, we teased, we nibbled until I was sure one of us would combust.

He climbed off the bed, but yanked me gently to him so that my arms wrapped around his neck and my legs around his waist. He carried me over to the low dresser where the TV sat and set me on it gently before he switched on the lamp light.

"No," I quickly protested, searching for the power button.

"Yes," he said, clasping my searching hand in his and bringing it to his mouth. "I don't want to be in the dark," he said between kissing each of my knuckles.

His eyes were heavy-lidded, and that vein in his forehead had softened a little, so I agreed—because I didn't want him to stop touching me, self-consciousness be damned.

After kissing my last knuckle, he yanked on the sleeve of my shirt and pulled it off of one arm before repeating the process on the other one. The flannel fell, leaving me in only my bra and my lounge pants.

He pressed a hand to my torso, just over the curve of my breast, and I looked down to see his one hand spanning most of me. And then he leaned down and kissed me again. It was like he couldn't stop kissing me, and I didn't want him to.

My body rocked into his as he leaned over me and I pushed against him so I could stand in front of him. Slowly, I tucked my thumbs into my lounge pants and tugged them down. My impatient hands reached for his sweats, but he stopped me, turning me back around so that I lay back on the bed, my legs hanging over the side. I propped up on my elbows, watching him watch me. His back was now to the lamp, so it illuminated the space around him, like a shadow looming in front of me. I reached for his pants again, but he stopped me by leaning over me and sliding his hands behind my back to my bra. Before I could think, he had it unclasped and pushed me gently down so he could slide the straps off my arms. I breathed heavily underneath him and knew my breasts were rising and falling in time with my breaths.

"Trista. You're so beautiful. Always." He looked down at me with such tenderness on his face that I couldn't believe someone could admire me that much—just thinking it made me hurt deeper than I knew he could touch.

Leaning over me, he slid a hand along the curve of my waist until it stopped just below the curve of one breast. With his eyes locked on mine, he slid his thumb gently along the underside of that curve, and then brushed his fingers over my pebbled nipple. I arched under him from the lightning bolt of heat that speared through me from such a simple touch. When he repeated the motion on the other side, I had to stop myself from pulling him down. I was trying to go slow, at his pace, but my body was impatient to be touched, to be filled, by him.

He pressed a kiss to the center of my chest and then rubbed his face over my nipple, so the bite of his stubble sent me into sensation overload. I propped up on my elbows again, just so I could watch him. He took my breast into his mouth and I felt the flat part of his tongue run along it.

"Jude," I said, knowing my voice sounded a little desperate.

But he didn't say anything, didn't even seem to acknowledge his name as he moved to my other nipple, laving it with his tongue and then sucking it into his mouth as he met my eyes. His hands were braced on either side of me on the bed and, needing a place to touch, I reached my hands up and clawed at his arms—not roughly—but enough so he would feel my impatience.

His mouth moved down my chest and his palms covered my breasts, squeezing gently, as he nibbled on the skin just below my belly button. Sparks of pleasure made stars dance behind my eyelids as I dropped from my elbows to the bed. When I felt his warm breath hit my center, I wanted to buck under him. It was like my legs were operated by some unseen being, because they wrapped around him before dropping when his finger slid under the elastic of my panties and rubbed gently along me.

It was a slow kind of torture, the way his fingers traced my opening but didn't dip into it. One of his hands gripped my inner thigh while his other explored. It was almost painful, the way he circled around me, but didn't completely touch me.

"Jude," I said again, this time while panting. "Please." I wasn't sure what I was asking for, but when I had the strength to open my eyes, I met his right between my legs. It was so deliciously intimate, having him looking up at me from that angle while I was basically a slave to his hands. I opened my mouth to say his name again, but it came out garbled when he slid one finger in and pumped me twice.

I could've bucked off the bed high enough to hit the ceiling. It was the first time a man had touched me since the last time the same man had touched me—one year before. He was reawakening all my pleasure sensors, and even though his pace was slow, it felt like an overload of sensory input. He pumped me a couple more times before I practically cried his name.

He stood and pushed his sweats down, revealing that he wore no underwear. I don't know why that was so sexy to me, the fact that he'd been commando this whole time. He walked around, completely naked, to his backpack and retrieved a condom. Watching him stand there as he slid it on only made me want to launch up off the bed and onto him.

So I did. "Now," I said against his mouth as his hands lifted my ass so that I was in line with him.

"Are you ready?" he asked against my mouth.

"God, yes," I said as our teeth clashed and he slid right into me.

He held me there for a second and I opened my eyes, meeting his heavy-lidded, almost sleepy ones. But then he began to move and I felt myself being laid back onto the bed as he thrust into me, over and over, the pace slow but climbing faster. With each push, I slid a little bit further across the bed. Finally, his chest met mine and I got to experience his full weight on me—something I'd wanted for so long. I felt myself climbing with each inch I slid across the bed, but when he put his hand between us and touched me, it was suddenly too much, too strong, and my legs jerked under his.

"It's okay," he whispered as he moved faster. I opened my eyes, seeing his concentration on mine. It was so deeply intimate, the way he was looking right through all my bullshit, deep down to who I was, that when I felt his arms at my sides clench, I closed my eyes to ride out my high, biting down on my lip to keep from yelling.

He tugged my lip from my teeth just as a groan wrenched itself from the back of my throat and he grunted from above me, his pace quickening right at the end of our highs.

I couldn't move for several long seconds. The only place that seemed to move was my chest, rising and falling in time with his breaths. But we remained silent, the two of us, just clinging to each other as we gathered our energy.

His face was tucked in my neck and I felt him press a gentle kiss there before he stood. I winced when he pulled completely away from me, but otherwise I stayed still.

He stood over me, looking down at me. There were few things etched in my memory, but this was one: his hair a mess; his warm, sleepy eyes focused; his bare chest heaving heavy breaths. "Hi," he said, causing me to curve my lips.

"Hi," I said back. I felt sated, and in a strange way, whole. I'd been in Jude's company for a couple days, but it wasn't until then that I'd felt it so deeply. Like the gouge in my heart was being filled up again.

"I'm going to get dressed, and then I'm going to grab us some ice cream from the vending machines."

I nodded, smiling when his lips spread. "'Kay."

After he left, making sure to drop a kiss to my lips before he stepped out the door, I rubbed a fist over my chest. So much had changed. But so much was still the same.

CHAPTER SIXTEEN

The next morning, I awoke curled up in Jude's embrace, the weight of his arm around my waist. It was a welcome weight, something I'd missed.

I felt him breathing against the nape of my neck and I closed my eyes once again. I was safe. I felt whole.

I hadn't puked in more than twenty-four hours.

"I feel like I'm going to break you," he whispered against my neck.

"You can't," I whispered back.

"I worry I might, from holding you tightly." He kissed my skin and then nuzzled against me. "So tight you can't leave this time."

I nuzzled against him. "How can you break me?" I asked, running my fingers over his, "When I finally feel whole?"

He squeezed me tighter then, as if he was no longer worried about breaking me as much as he worried about me slipping from his grasp. "We should get going," he finally said, after we'd stayed in the silence for long enough. "We have to hit up your grandfather and then, your mom?"

"Yeah," I said, but my heart wasn't up for the second visit I'd need to make.

"It'll be okay. I'll be with you the whole time."

I nodded and then slipped out of the bed, grabbing a pair of jeans from my bag. "Might as well get it over with before we go back to Colorado."

Jude watched me get dressed for a moment, and this time I didn't feel the same anguish I'd felt when he'd visited me in Maine. "I'll just check in on Colin and then I'll be ready to go."

Thirty minutes later, we had checked out of the motel and started back up on the road. Grandpa's assisted living facility was set back a bit in a wooded area, a large brick building that looked out of place among all the log cabins and vinyl-sided manufactured homes in the neighborhood.

Grandpa's room was clean, which was something I was grateful for. I knew he must have had help with that, because his mobility was so limited. "Trista," he said, his eyes crinkling in the corners when he saw me. "You brought a friend."

"Nice to see you again," Jude said, crouching down so he was eye level with my grandpa at the table. "It's Jude."

"I remember," Grandpa said, inviting him to take a seat. "I take it you found my girl?"

I thought about the postcard the year before. "He did," I said as I bent down and wrapped my arms around him. He was thinner than he'd been when I'd last seen him, but his color was good and high in his cheeks. He looked healthy, happy, and I wished I'd come sooner. "Are you okay, Trista?" he asked as his hands held mine and he looked me up and down.

I rubbed a thumb over his paper-thin skin and gave him a reassuring smile. "I'm better," I said, knowing that was really all he needed to know.

"Well, take a seat. Tell me what you've been up to."

I sat in the chair next to Jude and felt fractionally stronger when he laid his arm over the back of my chair. "Well, as you know, I ended up at this inn in Maine, when my car was on its last leg."

"Where in Maine?"

"Southern. Near the New Hampshire border."

Grandpa rubbed his chin, where he had a very trim beard coming in. "Interesting. How do you like it?"

"It's great," I said without forcing it. "My boss is like a protective mom, and I'm a few-minutes walk from the beach."

"What else have you been doing?" Grandpa asked.

I tried to think of what I'd done since I'd gone to Maine, but couldn't come up with anything outside of my day-to-day work at the inn and my walks around the town.

"We're going to hike up a mountain next week," Jude said.

I stared at him for a moment, not aware of the plans he was making.

"Oh yeah? Where at?"

"Not sure yet. I figured we'd open a map and close our eyes before we picked it out. It's more exciting that way." I still continued to stare at Jude, until I felt his hand on my thigh, giving me a reassuring squeeze.

"That sounds great, Trista. Oh, to be young enough to do all of those things." Grandpa patted his chest and sighed. "I used to do things like that as a youngin'. Been a long time since I held that mountain air in my lungs."

"We'll bottle some up for you and bring it back," Jude said with a soft smile. I covered the hand he held on my thigh with my own and squeezed, grateful for his support.

"What else do you have going on?"

"Outside of the inn, I'm not sure what else I have going on, Grandpa."

"That's okay. As long as you're doing the things that make you happy, that's all I really want for you. It's good to see you so content, Trista."

I felt Jude's eyes boring into my face, but I just kept my eyes on my grandpa. The fact that this was the happiest I'd been in two years wasn't something I wanted to dissect right now.

"And it's good to just see you, Gramps. I wish I had come back sooner, I really do."

He waved a hand at me. "I don't need to see you in the flesh to feel that you still miss me, dear granddaughter of mine. I just need you to call once in a while, maybe send me more snail mail." He pointed a thumb to the wall that separated his little apartment from the one next door. "Over there's Ted, and if you beg my pardon, he's kind of a wet blanket. So when I get those letters, he thinks I've got some long distance love and it makes him a little bit jealous."

191

I laughed. "If only he knew they were only from your granddaughter."

"Only?" he barked. "Don't say that about yourself, dear girl." He reached a hand across the table and patted mine. "I am glad you've come though. And I guess you'll be off to see your mom after I let you go?"

A knot formed in my stomach. I wish it was easy to shake my mom from my life, but I felt like I wanted to at least see how she was doing. If she was getting better. If for nothing else but my grandfather's sake. "Yeah, we'll stop by on our way out of the city."

"Good, good. I don't like knowing my two favorite girls are at odds, but I can't say I blame you, Trista. She was never easy on you."

Jude was still watching me, like he was watching for the moment that the prospect of seeing my mom would register. Like I would crack under the weight of it. But I kept my smile plastered on my face the rest of the visit with Grandpa and hugged him hard when I left.

"Don't forget to call me once in a while. And him," he said, pointing a finger out where Jude waited in the hallway. "He loves you. Don't take it for granted."

We both knew what love had done to my mother, turning her into a whole other person when the love had walked out of her life.

"I love him too, but it's complicated."

"Who said love was uncomplicated?" He huffed. "All that matters is that you're good to each other, and good for one another. It's really that simple. And if it's worth it, it's worth holding on to." He patted my hand and said, "I'd hate to see you suffer alone when you don't need to." "I don't want to suffer," I said. Sadness made me heavy, my voice strained.

"Then don't. Suffering is a choice. If you don't want it, lose it."

He made it sound so easy, which I told him.

He laughed. "It's not supposed to be easy. Do you think it was easy watching your mother lose herself? She was our baby. Our only child. And she lost herself when she had you. But," he said, and patted my hand, "we had you. We've loved you, for years—you were worth losing her."

My heart heaving, I looked down at where his wrinkled hand covered mine.

"And that fella out there, he thinks you're worth it too."

By the time I joined Jude in the hallway, I felt the weight of my visit with Grandpa bearing on my shoulders.

And then Jude placed his arm right around me, where I felt the burden the most, and it suddenly wasn't that unbearable after all.

My mom's trailer remained unchanged, which was how I knew she still lived there. Some rust bucket sat in the driveway, and her porch light was on, which told me she was probably home.

"I'd offer to stay in the car to give you and your mom some space, but to be honest I don't feel that comfortable with the idea." Jude looked around the neighborhood as he turned the engine off. "So, I'm telling you now that I'm coming whether you want me to or not."

I smiled at him, knowing he was fully supportive of me. "I'm not going to try to stop you, but I do want to warn you—my mom isn't all together in the head. There's a good chance she'll be at least partially nude, high, or drunk. Or maybe a combination of those things."

"I think I can handle it," he replied with a grim smile.

"Let's get this over with." I climbed out of the car and waited until Jude had locked the doors before I ascended the steps to her front door.

My knock caused the conversation inside to halt and the radio to turn down. Her face appeared in the tiny window to the left of the door and then she scowled.

"What do you want?" she asked the second she opened the door. Her eyes slid over me to Jude, who she greeted much more kindly, with a smile and a cock of her head. "Who's the tall drink of water?"

"Jude," he said, reaching a hand for her to shake.

"I'm just coming to check in," I explained, wringing my hands together in a nervous tick. "For Grandpa. Make sure you're not doing anything stupid."

"By all means, come in and be a spy." She pushed the door open and stepped aside as Jude and I walked into the trailer.

I didn't think it was possible for the trailer to be even more dingy than it had been before, but I was proven wrong. There were several patches in the carpet completely burned, and the couches and chairs she had looked like they'd been rolled down a rocky hill before being placed in the living room.

And right in the center of one of the couches sat the man I'd hoped not to see again for a long time.

I felt my breath catch and my hands begin to shake. I glanced over the carpet, where he'd hit me, and I turned my head reflexively. That spot was stained with the memory, and my body began to cower just thinking of it. My breath became tighter and my eyes filmed over. And then I saw Jude, standing at the door of my mom's trailer, watching me. Steady. He was no doubt watching my reaction to this exchange and, because of him, I pulled my fingers into fists and turned to face the man whose touch had had a lasting, rippling effect.

"Well, hello," Doug said, one arm over the back of the couch and his other hand wrapped around a bong. "Didn't get enough the last time?"

The connotation of his question had me putting my back up. It would've been so easy to walk out now, to run away. But I was really great at running away and not standing my ground. I straightened my spine and held my head up high, exuding a strength I hadn't known I'd possessed all this time. "You can fuck off, Doug."

He stood, his eyes narrowing as he looked at me from my ankles to my face. "You called the cops that night, didn't you?"

"That was you?" my mom asked, coming around and sitting where Doug had been sitting.

Doug took a step toward me and I backed up, right against Jude. His hands closed over my upper arms, holding me steady, keeping me safe. "Don't even come one step closer," I warned him.

"Of course it was her. Bitch scratched up my face and called the cops on us as she left."

I swallowed my fear. "You could've killed me," I said, looking right at my mom after, waiting to see her reaction.

Nothing. Not a single muscle moved on her face. It shouldn't have hurt me, her indifference to how I'd suffered at her boyfriend's hands. But knowing I'd been trying to protect her when it happened made me want to fall apart. I didn't have her support. I didn't have unconditional love from the person who'd created me.

"I wasn't going to kill you," Doug said, ignoring my warning and taking another step toward us. The closer he came, the more I remembered about the way he'd beat me so severely that even a raised hand in my vicinity caused me to wince.

"You came too close," I said, rubbing my elbows in my hands. "I had a black eye for a week, my knuckles were so swollen that I couldn't grip anything in my hands and I had glass lodged all over my chest for a month."

"Wait." Jude placed his hands on my shoulder. "He hit you?"

He wasn't looking at me, but I knew he was talking to me. "Yes," I said. "But I'm okay now." I wondered how many times I could say that before I believed it. Jude stared back at me, and I watched as anger and sadness intermingled, turning his brown eyes almost black.

"You owe me," Doug said, stepping closer still. "You got me in some serious shit with my supplier, and I can't forget that."

I watched as Jude turned to face Doug like it was all in slow motion. "She owes you nothing," Jude said, his voice calm but his body tightening in anger. I wished I'd told him all that had happened, but in the lone day we'd spent together last year, there just hadn't been enough time. "And we're leaving."

"Who are you, her master? She can talk," Doug spat, and I turned my face like he'd hit me again. Fear was an incredible thing, especially when ignited by memory.

But Jude squeezed my hand, reminding me that I could do this. "I can talk," I said, before leaning in so I was closer to his face. I felt safer just knowing that Jude was there to protect me, from Doug or from hurting myself in the process. "And I'll repeat what I said, go fuck yourself." I felt power in my words, a power that made me stronger than I knew I was.

Doug made the mistake of stepping forward again as anger burned in his eyes. Before he could get too close, Jude pulled his arm back and punched it forward, knocking Doug right off his feet so that he landed on the coffee table on his back. We all froze for a second, Doug included. But Jude stood solid, his presence alone intimidating for my mom, who curled up in a ball on the couch and didn't try to defend Doug once.

"Come on," Jude said, gently pushing me out the door while he kept his front to Doug. It said something about Jude, that he could go from using his hands in anger against my attacker to touching me so gently immediately after. "Touch her again," he said with a finger pointed at Doug, "and you will fucking regret it."

Jude rarely swore, so hearing the F-bomb drop out of his mouth and feeling the anger emanating from him as he held my hand made me realize just how serious he was. "Get in the car, Trista," he said, tossing me the keys and keeping his body between Doug and me as we walked back out to the car.

I didn't need to be told twice.

I was breathless as I drove down the road out of the trailer park. Jude buckled his seat belt before rubbing his fingers over his knuckles. I'd had an adrenaline rush inside of my mom's trailer, and as it was slowly leaving my body, I felt my hands begin to shake on the steering wheel. I turned on the radio, anything to drown out the roar in my head, and then when

I took a wrong turn out of the trailer park, I erupted in nervous giggles. The expelling of all that energy had made me a shaky, uncontrollable mess.

"I want to vomit," I admitted aloud. I could always regain control after vomiting.

"No," Jude said. "Pull over up here and let me drive."

I did, waiting in the driver's seat as Jude left his seat and walked around the side of the car. All the anger that he'd carried out of the trailer seemed to be leaving him, so I unbuckled and quickly slid out of the car and wrapped my arms around him. I felt a call to comfort him, after seeing how he'd defended me.

Jude's arms came around me easily, solidly. That's who he was. Solid, steady, so sure of his place in the world. It was both enviable and admirable, the way he carried himself without wearing his insecurities on his face.

"Thank you," I whispered into his neck. His arms tightened briefly before he pulled me back only far enough so that he could look in my face. "Tell me what happened."

I knew it was coming, but it still made my stomach hurt to think about letting it out. It'd be the first time I'd told anyone all the details of what had happened. Charlotte had known a little bit, that my mom's boyfriend was abusive had seemed like enough to tell her. "Okay," I said on a nod.

So I told him everything—including what Doug had said about me. Jude listened as we sat on the hood of his car, holding my hand in both of his. More than once, I had an overwhelming desire to crawl up into the smallest space I could, but as if he sensed that, he just held my hand and assured me it would be okay.

"Why didn't you come back to Colorado?" he asked, but he wasn't judging my decision to leave entirely.

I ran my thumb along the inside of his palm. "Because I felt broken." It wasn't the first time I'd thought it, but it was the first time I'd told someone else. "Everything seemed to be out of my control."

"Is that why you started purging?"

"It's part of it." I told him about going to Brendan's house at Christmas a year and a half earlier. "In some ways, I feel like vomiting can help me disappear. I'd rather not be noticed than have people staring at my flaws." Jude let go of my hand to put his arm around me and pull me against his side. "And after I'd been in Maine for five months, I was still no closer to figuring out who I was and suddenly the burden of being alone was too much."

I could feel the tremble that moved through Jude's arm as he wrapped it around me. "I wish I'd known. I would have come for you sooner."

"I was glad you'd came," I said. "But when you were disappointed in me, I just shut down. I had no one but myself to blame for what I'd been doing. But hearing from you—the one person I cared about most in the world—that you were unhappy with what I was doing made me feel empty all over again."

"I wish I could go back to that moment, to sit and listen to you longer."

The feelings churning up inside me were almost too much to bear and I looked at the ground before me, thinking about how wonderful it would be to be able to vomit. "I wish I could vomit, Jude. I really, really want to."

"I know." He pressed his lips against my hair and held me tighter still. For a brief moment, I believed that he could keep me safe, cocooned in his arms. "But I really, really don't want you to. So please, for me, don't."

"I wish I knew how to shake all of this, Jude," I confessed. "It's so hard to walk around in this sheet of self-loathing."

"If you can't love yourself," he said, tucking a strand of hair behind my ear, "let me love you enough for the both of us."

I didn't know why it felt like my heart was breaking, but it was. "I can't."

His eyes searched mine, but I didn't say why I couldn't. It wasn't fair, to him, to burden him with how very broken I was. When he opened his mouth to ask, I slid off the hood of the car. "I guess we need to go back to Colorado."

"We do. I didn't want to tell you before. But it's not looking good for Colin."

I felt my chest restrict. "Why didn't you tell me sooner?"

"We're hours away. I took a chance that seeing your grandpa wouldn't halt us from seeing Colin." He swallowed and his eyes turned sad. "One last time."

But I wasn't ready to accept that I'd only see Colin one last time.

CHAPTER SEVENTEEN

By the time we made it back to Colorado, Jude got a call from Colin's mom that Colin wasn't keeping food down. Jude's demeanor was stoic as we drove to the hospital, and he was rigid as we walked to the waiting room.

"Trista," he said as we sat in the waiting room outside of his room. "This is it. He's not going to get better. We need to say goodbye."

But I shook my head, even as the tears welled up in my eyes. "I can't, Jude. I can't say goodbye to him." I was shaking my head so hard that I thought it would twist right off of my body. "No, I cannot."

"You have to. I know he wasn't always kind to you—"

"It's not that," I interrupted as I felt the cool pool of tears in my eyes. "It's that I can't. I physically can't." I thought of Ellie, of how I'd been holding her hand when she'd gone unconscious. To lose the last person who knew Ellie the way I did was like reliving her death all over again. I stood up and walked to the water fountain, cupping my hand under the flow and splashing it on my face. Every bit of skin from my forehead to my chin was white hot, the pressure of tears so heavy that it felt like it was exuding from every pore. Jude stood next to me and ran a hand down my back.

"I can't," I said again, but the words felt like twin masses of grief, stuck in my throat. *I can't, I can't, I can't.*

Carefully, he closed his fingers around my wrists, holding me firmly to him. "You can and you will. Say goodbye—for you and for him." His voice was rough, his eyes swimming. I couldn't look into them; I was too weak. I could hardly carry my own grief for what was happening, I couldn't carry Jude's too. And that's how I knew I couldn't do it. I couldn't say goodbye.

Colin's mom stepped outside of the room and watched us for a moment.

"Go, Trista." He squeezed me tight and I felt the tremble in his touch, like my pain was a tangible thing, something he felt to his bones and echoed back at me. Pain for our loss, pain for the man we both loved in different ways, complicated ways.

"I can't, I can't." My lip trembled and I sucked it into my mouth, chewing over it, tasting blood. I said the words I knew would affect Jude, would get him to listen to me, to understand, "I'm not ready."

Jude exhaled then, hard and fast, and I felt that shift between us from a friend pleading to another friend. It became something else, lover to lover, so that our grief was intertwined with our love and loss with one another. He moved his hands to my face, so that I was forced to look him in the eyes. He cradled me so gently, but I felt the power behind his words. "I need you to be ready. God, I need you to be ready, Trista." His eyes blurred as tears coated mine. "Please." His voice cracked and so did my heart.

I swallowed the lump of emotion in my throat. I didn't know what he was asking me to be ready for, but I desperately wanted to be ready. For him. For Colin, so I could say goodbye. So he could be at peace.

"Okay," I managed, but it sounded warbled. I clenched my teeth together, sucked in a breath through my nose. As I blinked, the first tear fell from my eyes and Jude's hands on my face squeezed gently before they slid back into my hair.

"I'm so sorry. So, so sorry."

I didn't wonder what he was apologizing for. I turned my face in his hand and pressed a kiss to the warm center of his palm, just as his other hand wrapped around me and pulled me even closer. I closed my eyes and let out a long breath. "I love you," I mumbled against his skin, too afraid to give the words the clarity they deserved. I lifted my eyes to his and felt the pulse in his thumb leap.

"I love you, too," he said, and the crack on my heart went deeper, because I was about to walk away from the man I loved to say a final goodbye to the man I used to love. It wasn't fair, that Colin should have me in the room with him when he had such a tenuous grip on his mortality. It should have been Mila. It should have been someone who had loved him through everything, someone he had shared this part of his life with.

But it was just me.

I squeezed Jude's hand on my face before I stepped back. I couldn't keep touching Jude because I knew it would make my resolve that much less solid.

The hallway felt impossibly long, like I was in an alternate reality and my destination kept getting moved farther from my touch, despite my advance toward it. The blues and grays of the hallway blended together, blurring in my vision once I reached the door to Colin's room. The handle was cold and the curtain was drawn over the window so that passersby couldn't look in.

When the door opened, a rush of warmth enveloped me. The walk to the bed somehow felt longer than the walk down the hall, but I did it, pulling back the privacy curtain to give him a smile.

He looked awful, lying in bed with machines hooked up to his whole body. He tried to open his eyes, but they fluttered immediately closed. He was so weak, so tired, and I could sense he was ready. Ready to leave the earth and its punishments upon his body.

I couldn't let him see me break. I knew that. The last thing he needed to be burdened with as he left this world was my grief.

Taking a seat in the closest chair to the bed, I wrapped my hand around the rungs on the plastic bed. There were wires in one of his hands, and other wires that disappeared under his gown. The scene was unchanged from a few days earlier, when I'd sat at his bedside, but Colin's face was now bloated and his skin was a color I'd never seen. When his eyelashes fluttered again, I leaned in and said, "I'm here, Colin."

I watched him lift a finger against the white waffle-knit blanket and impulsively, I grabbed his hand and squeezed, hoping he could feel me since he couldn't open his eyes.

He made a noise from his throat, but the room was loud from the beep of machines and the air conditioning kicking on, and the television show he had been watching. I found a remote, switched the television off, and leaned closer to Colin. "I'm here for you," I said gently at his ear. "It's okay. You're okay."

I felt the gentlest movement in the hand that held mine, so I squeezed it again, hoping he was lucid enough only to know that he wasn't alone. I'd known bone-deep loneliness, but this was something else. It would be the last time he'd be lonely.

"Just relax," I said softly, when I saw him struggling to lift his eyelids again. I couldn't believe that this was it. Colin wouldn't leave this bed again. He'd be surrounded by strangers when he took his last breaths and they'd wheel him from this room to a cold, dark place until he was moved underground. He should have been laid to rest at the top of a mountain.

"I'm here," I repeated when his breath through the oxygen mask shuddered.

I looked him over, taking in everything about this Colin. The curls were dulled considerably, and most of them were plastered to his head from sweat. Seeing this, I picked up a washcloth and ran it over his forehead. His eyelashes stopped fluttering then, and he seemed, overall, much more relaxed than he had been when I'd first sat down.

The hospital robbed Colin of all his scents. He smelled clean, but he didn't smell like the man I'd known and loved. Brushing a hand across the curls that spilled over his forehead, I wondered if I would be like Mila—cutting and running—or if I would stay, if things had been different. If

I'd stayed with Colin, I would have stuck by him through it all. It seemed criminal that Mila wouldn't be here for this. I looked up at the door more than once, expecting her to breeze in. Foolishly, I'd thought it would be the thing to make Colin better. To make him whole again.

But Colin couldn't be cured by love any more than anyone else.

Colin shuddered and shook, and I squeezed his hand harder than I had ever squeezed another. With one hand holding Colin's, I ran my other hand over his knuckles. Colin himself might have looked different, but little things like this brought me back to how we'd begun—in the hallways of our high school, Colin with his smirk and me with confusion. He'd looked at me and seen someone worth knowing. No matter what we'd gone through since then, I couldn't wipe that from my memory. Or all the times he'd made me laugh—given me a reason to laugh. He'd loved me once, in a way equal to how I'd loved him. Love may have left our hearts, but his place had always been there.

I dropped my head to the bed, my forehead right beside his arm. "Goodbye," I whispered into the blankets as the tears slid down my cheeks, creating wet spots under my face.

And then I heard it, muffled but still discernible. "I'm sorry."

Lifting my head, I blinked. His eyes were still closed, but there was a frown line on his face. I knew, despite the oxygen mask over his mouth, it had come from him.

The door opened and Jude stepped in. I knew we needed to say our goodbyes and then leave, to allow time for his family to grieve. But I couldn't fathom walking away from him, knowing it would be the last time I'd see him.

"Come here," Jude said, and though it was a request and not a demand, I felt compelled to go to him. His arms were open and I stepped into them, letting him fold me in his hug as we stood at the foot of Colin's bed. Watching him struggling. The beeps on his machines were the only sound around us. It was so similar to how I'd last seen Ellie that I bit down hard on my lip.

"He's really going," I said, tears still pouring from my eyes.

"He is."

I stepped from his arms and gave him a look that let him know I'd be waiting. Jude smoothed his hands over my hair and then nodded.

One last look over my shoulder was all I had left in me.

Once I was in the waiting room, I pulled open my notebook and decided to do something I hadn't done in a long time, not since before the love had left my heart: I wrote for Colin. There's something to be said for pouring out your heart on paper when you're surrounded by a dozen people quietly sniffling, ripping tissue after tissue from the dispensers placed strategically throughout the waiting room.

I fell in love the first time at sixteen,
warm hands clasped together,
spinning circles at the state fair,
our laughter the only sounds we heard.

Up and down the makeshift sidewalk
we strolled,
his arm around my shoulders,
my wind-messy hair on his.
Sweat and sugar made us sticky
and he fed me blue cotton candy
with his fingertips,
his smile stretching his cheeks
in a way that was everything
I needed.
I wanted to live forever in that moment,
sweat trickling down my spine
and soaking my tank top

and his body warm against mine
in the May heat.

"God, you're beautiful," he said,
swiping thumbs across my face,
stretching my skin to my hairline.
I licked my lips and reached forward,
pushing my lips to his,
tasting soda
and cotton candy
and him.

The sun beat down on us,
warming our skin while
the people shoved
around us.
I decided in that moment that
I never wanted
anything,
anyone
more than this,
than him.
Sixteen years old
with all my tomorrows
planned with him in mind.

How do I say goodbye
to the person who saw me first,
gave me my first kiss,

who loved me
when I didn't think I was lovable.
Your soul is leaving,
but your body remains.
An empty vessel,
but one that taught me
how to love
and be loved.
You gave me a place in your life,
and I'll hold a place for you in my heart.

CHAPTER EIGHTEEN

I didn't go to his funeral.

Instead, I curled up in Jude's bed. For two days.

When Jude asked me if I wanted to go to Colin's funeral, I looked at him with my heart in my eyes. "No. I said my goodbye. I don't want to watch him be lowered into the earth, knowing he should be up on a mountain."

Jude understood, so we stayed in bed, watching mindless television while we counted the days until my flight. It was always looming there, in our periphery, reminding us of the little time we had left together.

The day before my flight, sick of us moping about, Jude tossed a backpack to me. "We're going for a hike."

It had been literally years since I'd last gone on a hike, and I shook my head at him. "I'm tired."

"That's fine. Be tired on top of the mountain with me."

I looked at him with an eyebrow raised, but he wasn't budging. So I pulled myself out of the bed and gave him a look, which he ignored.

Reluctantly, I tied my hiking boots I'd brought with me as a just-in-case. Like I'd been packing, planning for us to do this. And as if I'd known I was going to write my heart out, I brought my notebook with me.

Jude packed up snacks and water in his pack before hooking a water bottle to my pack. "It's just a day hike," he told me.

"I figured," I replied, but didn't finish my sentence. I figured because my flight left at five the next morning. We only had time for this day hike, unless Jude planned on trapping me at the top of a mountain and keeping me from going. Part of me relished the idea, but after Colin had died, I was left with an overwhelming sense of being carved out. I didn't understand how I could be so emotionally devastated by someone who had hurt me years before, but Jude told me, "The fact that he was able to hurt you should tell you how much he mattered to you."

He wasn't wrong. I may not have been in love with Colin, but I couldn't erase our six years together like it hadn't happened.

"Is this the hike you were planning on, when you told my grandpa?" I asked him when we exited his car at the trailhead.

"Yup." He tightened my straps and then held out a hand for me to hold as we ascended the rocky slope.

Along the way, Jude stopped to crouch, pointing out different animal tracks. So much of this was familiar, the way he showed me different plant species, and how they were good for humans or how they weren't. Part of me wished we had done this sooner, so we could go camping in the wilderness. Because that's who I was, someone who yearned to be out where things grew wild and free.

Despite the relief the hike gave me, I felt like I was still holding on to grief with a stubborn grip. I thought of how not even a week earlier, I'd been standing on top of my apartment building, contemplating what it might be like to just step out into air. I knew that wasn't okay. I knew I needed to go back to therapy, like I had after Ellie had died, and I'd make an appointment as soon as I could. Because that's what I was realizing: I didn't want this grief to define me as it had for so many years now. My name meant sadness, but it didn't have to be how I lived my life.

I looked at Jude as he held back a branch so it wouldn't smack me in the face. He looked back at me like he always did. Kind, patient, and whole. I smiled at him, and he smiled back and it made me a little bit lighter than I'd realized.

I didn't want to carry this weight anymore. I wanted to shed it. I wanted Jude, which was what I'd always wanted. Who I'd wanted. I thought of our conversation on the hood of his car in Wyoming, before we'd returned to reality. And while Jude took a break to fill up our water bottles, I sat and pulled out my notebook.

If you can't love yourself,
let me love you enough
for the both of us.
I can't, I tell him.
He asks why
and with a deep breath,
I say,
Because you deserve more
than empty hands
and a heart with holes.
And a heavy I can't shake;
a burden that is mine alone.

The feelings were true. But I didn't tell him. I'd never told him. So my words could say what my voice could not. I ran my fingers over the words, letting the graphite push into my fingerprints. The words looked runny but were still legible. On an impulse, I ripped that page out and folded it into a square. I closed my notebook and then my eyes and just breathed in the mountain air, letting it take space in my lungs beside the grief I couldn't shake.

When Jude returned with our water bottles, I shoved my notebook in my backpack and stood. "I thought you packed enough water."

He shrugged. "I did, but nothing beats fresh, filtered spring water."

After tasting it, I knew he was right. And it was then that the gravity of me leaving the next day hit me. There would be no mountains to climb with Jude. And just like that, more grief weighed me down, like weights around my ankles and on my shoulders.

The climb to the top of the small mountain he'd picked felt much longer than it was. My shoulders were heavy with my pack, and heavier still with my grief. I took more breaks, sitting on hot rocks as I shrugged the pack off my shoulders. I wished I could shrug my sadness as easily.

"You can do this," Jude told me with all the confidence in his eyes. "Push through. I know you can."

The lump in my throat was hard to swallow. When he looked at me like that, like he was so sure of me that I should be too. And so, I was.

When we finally reached the top, Jude reached a hand down to me to pull me up the last few steps. I didn't let go of his hand once I was on top of the rock with him, looking over the miles we'd climbed and the vast wilderness that was spread out in front of us. After several seconds, just inhaling the thin air as the wind shattered against our bodies, he said, his voice as soft as water, "Let it out."

"Let what out?"

He turned to me, his eyes soft and his hands holding mine. "The sadness that's choking you. I can see it. You sigh as if the weight of the world is pushing you deeper into the soil. So," he said, spreading an arm out wide. "Let it out."

I let go of his hand and crossed my arms. "That's silly."

"If it helps you, it's not." He wasn't smiling, just looking at me with that quiet and patient confidence he often wore. "Scream. Shout. Cry. Let it out. There's no one but you and me, and it's okay. It's okay to feel the hurt you're feeling, and it's okay to let it go."

My eyes filled and I stared at him. My tongue pressed against the roof of my mouth and I felt the world go unsteady beneath my feet.

"Think of all the times we sat up on a roof together. This isn't much different. If anything, you can be freer out here." When I still just looked at him, my eyes filling with tears that felt cold in the cool air, he added, "If you want, I can go first."

I nodded, feeling the first tear cross the threshold of my lower eyelid. And I watched as he turned away from me, closed his eyes, and then let out a shout that wasn't words, but was repressed agony. He held himself tall, but when the sound left his mouth, I saw his jaw tremble. I'm not sure how long he stood there, on top of the world, letting his aching pour invisibly from his mouth. But when he was done, he turned to me and his eyes looked clearer. Cleaner, somehow.

"What did you shout about?"

"Colin. You."

"Me?"

"What you went through. Alone." If I wasn't already in love with him, I would've fallen right off that mountain in love with him then. He reached for my hand again and he said, "It's okay, Trista. It's just us."

It's just us. So true, in more than one way. I closed my eyes, thought of how I'd screamed in my apartment until a neighbor had banged on the walls that separated us. My grief couldn't have been contained within those four walls, and I'd sought out the top of the building to let it be free.

But even then, I'd felt myself being pressed down. My heartache being stifled in the confines of the city around me. Out here, in the forest, there was no one but us. And I was safe.

So I opened my mouth and let it out. It was tentative at first, a shout of anguish that was smaller than I knew I felt. A whisper in the roar of my thoughts. But then it came again, louder this time, howling from a place that had awakened inside of me. My chest burned, a ball of fire exploding across it. Over and over, I screamed. I yelled. I let all of it out, emptying myself of everything I'd kept inside for years.

When it stopped, my throat was raw and my face was hot. And I had the same sensation I'd had after I'd first vomited. I was empty. But unlike then, I was still, somehow, full. It was the first time I had felt empty and full.

Opening my eyes, I looked first at Jude, who looked at me expectantly, waiting. He was always waiting.

"I love you," I told him, and it was easier to say now that I wasn't being crushed by everything else.

"I love you," he said, right before I walked into his arms, arms that waited for me. Always.

I rubbed my cheek against his windbreaker, letting its coolness calm my heated face. I pulled the folded poem out of my pocket and tucked it in the open pocket of his windbreaker, hoping he'd read it and understand why tomorrow I'd be saying goodbye.

"Thank you for holding me when I needed to be held."

"I will. Always." His arms held me tight against the wind that whipped at us from all directions, and I felt his steadiness consume me.

Back at Jude's apartment, we tossed our packs on the ground and fell into bed—limbs reaching and hearts pounding. He took his time taking my clothes off, like he was savoring each second of our last night together. My early flight loomed above us, but we didn't talk about it. We didn't talk about anything.

His hands tangled in my hair as he pulled me to him, his fingers curling at the nape of my neck. He held me like he was afraid to let me go, and I realized then that he was always inventing new ways to hold me. With his hands at the base of my neck; with his lips as he swallowed the goodbye I didn't want to say; with his arms around my waist as he lifted me up and into his arms. He kissed me from my neck to my navel, and when he slid inside of me, our eyes met and held.

It was a love to live on, the way we met again and again, until we were soaked with sweat and fraught with trembles.

He kissed my forehead and brushed the hair from my eyes so he could look at me more clearly. His eyes spoke to me, telling me he wasn't ready to let go. I wasn't ready, either.

And so he didn't, holding on to me the rest of the night until the morning, when I awoke to my pack at the foot of the bed.

"I put the stuff from your pack in your bag," he said, and his eyes were tired.

I stared at the pack before looking at him.

"Are you ready?" he asked.

That word. "Let's go," was all I said.

CHAPTER NINETEEN

The airport was quiet. The world hadn't awoken yet, our demons buried for the time being. Jude was holding me just outside of security, and I was holding him too. I didn't want to let go just yet. I had my ticket in my backpack, and a stomach full of stones as I thought about leaving.

I held him long after I should have. My flight was minutes from departure, but I wasn't ready to say goodbye, for a third time, when all I wanted was to stay.

It was becoming harder for me to walk away from him, my tomorrow.

"You have to go," he said, in a voice that was hoarse from the early hour of the morning.

"I know," I said, but I didn't know why. Why was I walking away from him again? To board a plane to a place that hadn't felt like home, despite living there for two years? Stalling, I asked him, "When was the last time you were on a roof, Jude?"

"With you," he told me, not seeming the least bit taken aback.

"The last time I was on a roof was when Mila called me, when I thought you died." It felt so long ago, but it was hardly a week before. "I don't think I would've jumped. I found myself on top of a building when Ellie died." I looked up into his eyes, holding his gaze. "I think I went up on that roof to find you, Jude. I've never felt closer to you than when I was on a roof."

He closed his eyes and pressed his forehead to mine. "Trista," he said, his voice heavy with feeling. "I don't want you hurting. Ever."

"I don't want to hurt anymore," I told him honestly. I held his arms in my hands.

"Trista," he repeated and pulled away. He cradled my face in his hands. "It'll be too late for you soon. They're not going to let you board the plane."

"Would that be a bad thing?"

He nodded. "Because you're not ready." Silently, I heard what he didn't say: *And I want you to be ready.*

I opened my mouth to tell him goodbye, but he shook his head.

"I just need you to know something. I don't want for much, because all my needs are met. But," he said carefully, running his fingers between mine, "I want for you. And it's the wanting that keeps me up at night. The wanting that makes me feel incomplete. You're not the only person who feels like they're walking around breathing half the air they normally would, feeling like no matter what they do, they're missing a piece that makes them whole." He swallowed and I felt the ache in my stomach return.

It was going to hurt like a bitch, to do this. To pick up my backpack and turn away from him. I had to do it quick, rip off the bandage and walk away. My arms tingled from the very prospect of it, but I had to do it. I had to let go.

"Okay," I said and sucked in some air. "Goodbye."

"Goodbye," he said, his voice calm but his eyes sad. I couldn't look into his eyes and feel his pain, because my own pain was already trapping me into a tighter space than I could breathe in.

I pulled away and stepped back until just our fingers were touching, and then I turned and walked stiffly away, as an ache bloomed bright in my heart.

Security took less than a couple minutes thanks to the ungodly hour, but the walk to my gate felt like climbing that mountain—impossible.

I closed my eyes and heard Jude telling me I could do it, which was the only reason I made it to my gate just as they started calling the first boarding group.

I felt shaky then, like I felt when I hadn't eaten in a while, so I sat down and dropped my backpack. I couldn't believe I was doing this, that I was walking away from him again, letting this plane take me thousands of miles away from him. To a place without the Rocky Mountains, to a place without Jude. A place that wasn't home, because Jude was.

For the fifth time that day, I struggled to remember why I was doing this.

The second boarding group was called, and I glanced at my ticket. My boarding group. But I wasn't ready to get in line just yet, telling myself I'd be the last one on the plane. Thinking of Jude's eyes had me pulling my notebook out of my bag. It still smelled like the mountain we'd climbed, and sticking out of the bottom was a little daisy. I plucked at it, holding it up and thinking of Ellie as I twirled its stem in my fingers.

When I looked back down, I saw pulling the stem out had pulled out a paper too. I stared at the piece of paper that stuck out, thinking that I hadn't put anything in the notebook—there weren't loose papers in danger of falling out.

So I flipped the notebook open, and stared at the poem I'd written Jude.

If you can't love yourself,
let me love you enough
for the both of us.
I can't, I tell him.
He asks why
and with a deep breath,
I say,
Because you deserve more
than empty hands

and a heart with holes.
And a heavy I can't shake;
a burden that is mine alone.

I felt confused as I'd stared at it, remembering how I'd put it in Jude's pocket while we stood on top of the mountain. But then I saw, through the paper, that there was writing on the back. So, I flipped the paper over and when I recognized Jude's writing, I sucked in a breath to fill my lungs.

His mouth opens
and his heart unfolds
and he says
We deserve nothing
except what we choose.
And I choose you.
Your hands aren't empty
when I hold them.
And your heart has no holes
when I fill them.
So accept the heavy I bring you,
in your hands
and in your heart
and I'll help carry your heavy, too.

A drop of water hit the paper, bleeding into his words before I realized it had come from my eyes. I reread it, over and over, imprinting it in my brain.

I didn't want to leave Jude. I didn't want to leave Colorado. I wanted to find myself up high upon a mountain, letting the thin air fill me whole. I wasn't perfect—I wasn't the woman I wanted to be for him. But

I realized that I didn't need to keep waiting. Time is the biggest thief of all, it's what Jude had said to me once. And I didn't want to waste any more of it.

He thinks you're worth it. My grandfather's words hadn't left me yet, and had seemed to replace the ones Doug had branded on my skin. I didn't want to suffer; I didn't want to live with an insatiable ache.

And suddenly, I didn't ask myself again why I was leaving—because I wasn't. Not this time.

I shoved the paper back into my pack and then zipped it up. I would have run, but my legs were barely stable as I walked away from my gate, down the long walkway to security. I followed the signs to baggage claim, my heart moving faster than the feet that carried it. It all but galloped in my chest as I strode through the entrance to baggage claim and took in the silence, the empty.

I went to arrivals, where I had been last, and looked for Jude.

The airport was filling up now, when it had been nearly empty when we arrived. But I saw him, sitting on one of the black chairs by a door.

He didn't see me at first, because his eyes were closed and his hands were folded over themselves in his lap. I tried to imagine what he was thinking as I approached him, but then his eyes opened and I stopped thinking about everything except getting closer to him.

"Trista?" he asked, standing slowly and looking at me like I was the last person he expected to see.

"Jude." I stopped a foot away from him, looking up at his eyes as he squinted at me. All my fears and my reasons for leaving left me in a whoosh and there was just us, facing one another as the world moved around us. I swallowed and put my hands on his chest. When his hands covered mine, I said, "I'm not ready for everything I want to be ready for. I'm not perfect. I need help. But," I watched his eyes grow wide, "I *want* help. I'm ready for you to help me." I let out a breath, feeling the words tumbling from me wildly. "I'm ready, Jude."

THE END

221

EPILOGUE

JUNE 30, 2016

THREE YEARS LATER

I waited on the path, pushing the tip of my boot into the dirt until it made a crescent moon-shaped hole. Up ahead were a group of hikers who were excitedly chatting about the prints they saw along the side of the road. I smiled to myself, because I knew how they felt.

I crouched to admire a cluster of daisies just off the path, not taking for granted the strength in my legs, the way they held me solidly until I stood back up and sucked in the air. The weather was stunning, with very few clouds in the sky, and the wind that usually accompanied this hike was dulled to a gentle breeze, making it a much easier hike than it usually was.

I heard a jingle behind me and turned, seeing Jude approach me as he stared down at his camera's viewfinder.

"Get anything great?" I asked.

He looked up, his concentration clearing as he smiled at me and held the camera out. In the photo was a cluster of mountain goats, hanging off the edge of the rock like it was no big deal. While most of them were looking everywhere but at Jude in the photo, one of them stared straight into his lens, his coat clean and his horns curved. He looked almost majestic, like he knew that this was his domain and we were just passing through.

I flipped through a few of the photos, checking out all the things Jude had photographed for his website, and landed on a photo of me when a breeze had picked up and sent my unrestrained hair about my head. I was laughing, with one hand holding back some of the hair and my eyes were closed.

I gave Jude that look, the one he was used to by now, when he took a photo of me that I hadn't expected. "Thanks," I said, but I wasn't really upset. I looked different from when I had years before—a healthy kind of different. Shortly after I'd made the decision to stay, Jude had brought me with him to the gym a few times a week and had driven me to my therapy appointments until I'd sold my car in Maine and purchased another. I wasn't one hundred percent over everything I'd been through and all that I had done to myself, but I was healthy and my muscles were strong. And while I still had days that the self-loathing closed in on me, they were few and far between. And most significantly, I didn't feel as empty as I had before.

About a year before, Jude had purchased a truck and a fifth-wheel trailer, which we took on the road in the summers, living like drifters as we toured the national parks. I helped Jude with his website, but had expanded my web design business online, with Jude's help.

"You look so . . ." He stared at the photo as he contemplated his next words and then smiled at me. "Full, of life."

Because I was. I'd left Jude in 2011, intent on finding myself, but I'd lost her along the way. It took a while for me to realize that I was a work in progress, always learning, evolving, and that there was no end to finding myself. I was just lucky enough to have Jude along for the ride with me. I brushed my hand over his hat—the Rockies one—and grinned up at him. "I have hair in my face; you can't even see me." I waggled a finger in his face. "You're full, too. So full of shit, your eyes are brown."

Jude laughed, the sound I never tired of, and wrapped an arm around my shoulders as we continued our ascent. "Do you remember what you said five years ago?"

"How could I forget?" I stepped around a rock and looked up at the hike that awaited me. "I thought that was why you brought me here, because I said I'd be here."

"Or maybe I just like climbing Mount Washburn. You're an added bonus as a companion."

I rolled my eyes and shoved against him gently. So much had changed in three years, and nearly all of it was good. I was taking better care of myself, both inside and out. I was climbing every week from the time the snow thawed until it started up again. And through all of it, Jude had been steady. Like the rock we climbed, willing to hold me up and lead me to the top. I was grateful, so grateful. My hand came to my shoulder, where his hand was resting, and I squeezed it, turning and giving him a smile that I felt down to my soul.

"Five years ago, you said you'd be climbing Mount Washburn, and now you are. Again."

I leaned into him. "I'll be happy if we don't see a bear this time."

"I'll wrestle it, if need be."

"Good." I let go of his hand to stop and admire the tracks near our feet, preserved in mud that had dried over. "Your wrestling skills may come in handy, because these look like bear tracks." While we were paused, I pulled off my windbreaker and shoved it in my pack.

Jude stooped to run his fingers over the tracks. "Little bear," he said and looked around. "Which means its momma is near it too."

"I'd like to make it to the top before we run into her," I said, heavily hinting that Jude stop admiring the tracks so we could move on.

He stood and faced me, the shadow of his cap washing down his face. "Let's go then," he said, running his fingers over the ink along my collarbone. It was my surprise to him before we embarked this summer on our trip. Just one word, that meant so much to us both: Ready. Jude had loved it so much that he'd had it tattooed over his chest, above the scars that decorated it like war wounds. It was hard to think of him as even the slightest bit weak when he carried so much of me through the last handful of years. "Let me know if you need a break," I said seriously, looking him square in the eye.

"I will," he promised and grabbed my hand as we climbed the rest of the way.

Once at the top, Jude paused against a giant rock to take a breather. He didn't often get winded on these hikes, thanks to us taking them slow. But when he did, I was always reminded of how important his health was. When I thought about Colin and how hard he'd always pushed himself, I worried even more about Jude.

"I'm okay," he'd tell me, but it was still hard to think about the fact that he could end up like that, spending his final breaths hooked up on machines, in a bed that had held many bodies before him. But I mostly shoved that to the back of my mind, when Jude's words repeated in my head like an echo. *"Fear is healthy. It's when you're drowning in it that it's not. Fear grounds you, but it can bury you too. Take a little bit, but then push on."*

So I did.

The wind howled and people around us laughed as their hats were sent up in the air. Jude pulled out his camera and captured the moment, frozen in time on his viewfinder. He turned to me on a laugh and our hands touched. He never stopped reaching for me, always reminding me he was there, waiting for me to figure it all out. My hands went to his like we existed on the same magnetic field.

"Ready?" he asked, holding up his camera.

Smiling, I nodded, and he wrapped an arm around me as he had five years earlier, shielding me partially from the bite of the wind. He held his camera up, pointing it at our faces as he took the first snap. He pulled it back and looked at it, but he looked disappointed somehow.

"What's wrong?"

He turned the camera to me so I could see our photo. We were both smiling, our cheeks pink as my hair swirled around us both.

"I still don't see what's wrong." I turned to him, looking at him curiously.

"The last time, you were wearing this hat." He pulled it off his head and put it on mine, smoothing down the hair that hung out of it.

"We don't need to be exactly the same as last time," I told him, but held on to the hat and the memory it gave me.

"We couldn't be the same people," he said. He shoved one hand into his pocket and looked at me. "We've grown so much, you and me. Separately and together."

"Mostly together." I smiled at him and brushed away the hair that slapped against my face from the force of the wind this high up.

"Mostly together." He nodded, but he stopped smiling as he stepped closer and spun my baseball hat around so that I was wearing it backwards. He pressed his forehead against mine and I wrapped an arm through his as I closed my eyes and relished this moment, a moment I couldn't have fathomed five years earlier, when we'd stood in this very spot together. He pulled away and I missed his warmth, but his mouth was covering mine and he kissed me hard enough to have me gripping his arms for balance. Then he pulled back, a breath away, and said against my lips, "I want to keep growing with you. Let me love you, Trista, through all of our tomorrows."

I opened my eyes and in his hand was a ring. In his eyes was his love, spilling over. On his lips were promises that I never dreamed of. "Yes," I said immediately, staring into his soulful eyes, eyes that had inspired a hundred poems.

He didn't say anything as he slid the ring over my finger and then curled my fingers so he could warm them with his whole hand. But I felt the shake in his hand and wrapped my arm around his neck, pulling him down so I could press my mouth against his. "Are you ready to chase adventures with me?" I asked against his lips as we stood still in that moment of time.

He laughed into my mouth and I felt his smile curve my cheek. "I'm ready."

AUTHOR NOTE

When I decided to write this story, I initially shied away from the subject of bulimia. Not because I didn't want to talk about it—I did. But I hesitated writing about it because it's a tough conversation to have, as an author and as someone who struggled with her weight for years, and still does.

The first time someone made a joke about my weight, I was eleven years old. Uncomfortable by the way the group of friends stared at me, I just turned away and pretended to be distracted by something else, to avoid letting them see how that made me feel. I was always on the skinny side growing up, so much so that my family nicknamed me Toothpick. After experiencing some hard years in elementary school, I found myself struggling to figure out my place in the world once middle school hit and I began to gain weight. One of my good friends committed suicide and I watched my remaining friends forging friendships with other people, and slowly, one-by-one, they left me until one day, I realized I was sitting alone in the lunch room.

Ironically enough, it was after I watched a video in health class about eating disorders that I decided to see how purging made me feel. At school, I would eat my lunch as usual before going to the bathroom and vomiting it all up. After school, I'd eat an entire loaf of bread before purging while I watched endless segments on some home shopping channel. My father, who I lived with during the school year, was at work until late at night most nights. it was easy for me to hide the fact that I was slowly shrinking, becoming so gaunt that I was five-foot-eight and wearing girls' size seven swimsuits when I should have been shopping in the juniors' section.

I abhorred feeling full. Whenever I'd start to feel shame for who I saw myself as, the feelings would build and build until I nearly choked on them. I felt like purging was the only way I had control over myself, and each time I vomited I had a false sense of relief that my feelings were gone, too.

I was conscious of the dangers of bulimia, which makes it even worse that I continued doing it after I vomited blood one day. I still remember the metallic taste in my mouth, and how I spent twenty minutes brushing my teeth afterwards. But I didn't stop doing it.

Honestly, I'm not sure that I ever would have stopped had it not been for the summer I flew to New Hampshire, to spend time with my mom. When I stepped off that plane, her face fell and I knew immediately that she knew something was wrong. We never really talked about it in depth, but I spent that summer seeing my cousins every day, swimming all hours of the day, and eating all of my mom's cooking. I gained healthy weight, and returned to Colorado with color in my face and a body I wasn't ashamed of. A month later, I met the person who has remained my best friend for sixteen years, and never fell back to my old habits.

The reader doesn't get to see Trista heal from her bulimia, but that's because I feel like healing from something like an eating disorder is very personal. I didn't believe that her overcoming her bulimia was the root of her issue—it was overcoming her sadness, ultimately, that was the most important, because her sadness was what triggered everything else.

I didn't do traditional therapy for my bulimia as a teen, and I never stepped inside of a hospital to get help. That doesn't make my treatment any less effective; it just makes it different. I don't want to send the message that recovering from bulimia nervosa is easy or even simple. It's been sixteen years and I still struggle with the urge to vomit when my emotions become too much, or when I've eaten until I feel full. And while I haven't purged in many years, I know now that I'm never alone, even if I think I am.

I hope that if you ever feel that kind of loneliness, or that kind of hurt, that you seek help. There are people who can help you recover. If you or someone you know is struggling, please reach out. You're not alone.

In the United States:

National Suicide Prevention Lifeline
(24/7)
1-800-273-TALK (8255)
http://suicidepreventionlifeline.org/

National Eating Disorders Association (NEDA)
(M-Th, 9:00 a.m. – 9:00 p.m.; F, 9:00 a.m. – 5:00 p.m.)
1-800-931-2237
https://www.nationaleatingdisorders.org/

International:
Choose your country
http://www.suicide.org/international-suicide-hotlines.html

ACKNOWLEDGEMENTS

As always, the first line in my acknowledgements belongs to my kids and husband. Writing takes a toll on me, but it also puts a certain kind of strain on those who rely upon me. I'm thankful for the bunch I have, and all the love and support they give me.

To Sona Babani, my best friend forever. Thanks for driving a million hours just so we can sit on my couch and play games on our phones. I love you. Awna byenna sherma.

Jade Eby, my beebee. You're a big part of the reason I was able to publish two books this year. I'm so fortunate to have you in my life, to talk about books, cats, and creepy shit together. You're beautiful and talented, and I wish the whole world would read your words. I can't wait to support you through your next release.

Karla Sorensen, ass kicker extraordinaire. Thanks for beating me up and being mean. It worked, because I finished. I hardly remember what it was like to write a book without having you encouraging me. Keep being baseballs. I don't say it enough, but you're pretty okay. #manifest

Jena Campbell, you're like a walking, talking, hands-to-its-chin emoji. I love that you're my cheerleader and that you are so giving and selfless and helpful and amazing and maybe you could just build a basement in your house so I could never leave it. #machete

Whitney Giselle Belisle, thank you for loving tent guy and for encouraging me to write this story. One day I'll write a kick ass dentist in my book, but I can't name her Whitney because that might be weird . . . considering we have the same first name. Thank you for encouraging me, and believing in this story. Comma splices forever.

Thank you to Lex Martin, as always, for sending me hysterical messages as you read my stuff. Thank you for being passionate about this story and telling me what I needed to hear. I hope to squeeze the shit out of you one day.

To all the authors who have supported me through the process of writing this book: Ella James, I'm still so stunned by your support and the kind words you said. Thank you for everything. Karen Cimms, thank you for taking the time to give me such helpful feedback. I made a lot of very necessary changes to this book thanks to your input, and the book is a billion times better for it. Kandi Steiner, all of your messages while you read *Into the Tomorrows* gave me life. You are one of the most positive and genuine people I've met in this industry and I'm so lucky to know you. KL Grayson, I just love your face. You're always so positive and uplifting, and I can't wait to write with you!

Thank you to Murphy Rae with Indie Solutions by Murphy Rae for giving me a chance. Your edits were thorough and honest, and I'll work harder on my commas. Thank you to Alexis with Indie Girl Proofs, as always, for being so thorough. I am grateful for your messages as you read, and your complete honesty. To Amanda Marie, with AM to PM Book Services—I'm so thrilled I got to meet you in June, and talk to you about books! Thank you for the proofread, and for being so very lovely. Ginelle Blanch, thanks for making time for me, to pick up on the things I missed. Your dedication is impressive, and your willingness to work with my schedule is much appreciated.

Thank you to Cassie Hanjian, my immensely supportive agent.

To Crystal Crawford, let's always "act casually" because it's the best. Let's drive through another cornfield someday.

To my beta readers: thank you to Briana Pacheco for your email—I loved it so much. I still reread it. You're amazing. So, so amazing. Thank you, Kristen Johnson, for making time for Tent Guy! Amy Bosica—your emails make me feel like I actually know what I'm doing and you've made me cry. Bravo. I'm ever so grateful for you three.

To the readers who have become friends, thank you all for being there for me, giving me your thoughts on my covers, your honest opinions about my writing, and making me laugh when I needed it. Christina Harris, Tiffany Elain, Tina Lynne, Kimberly Dodd—you're my people.

Thank you to Tribe for all the support you give me. xo

Mary Ruth, thank you for all the beautiful teasers you make for me. You're an artist.

Cynthia Aponte and Samantha "SamPA" Hanson, you two make me laugh every single day. I'm lucky to know you both—so, so lucky. I'm so glad we formed our little group chat.

Thank you Talon Smith, for being like an adult Sour Patch Kid—first you're sour and then you're sweet. But for serious, one of the most important things to me is trust, and you've proven yourself to be trustworthy. When I meet you, I'm gonna make it rain M&Ms and seatbelts.

Thank you to my Barbetti Babes—I love each one of you so freaking much. If I could, I'd buy all of you tacos. Thank you for traveling far and wide to meet me at signings, and for giving me all the feels.

To Debbie Snyder for margaritas and movies and being an ear when I need it. You're an honorary aunt to my kids, and they're so lucky to have their favorite Kevin.

To J.R. Rogue for writing the custom poem used in my epigraph, thank you for sharing your art. I love the way you arrange words.

I have one million bloggers to thank, for going out of their way to pimp my books AND me! I value your support and your time, so I thank you for all the times you shared my books with your followers. I know many of you also gifted copies of my books to your friends and/or hosted sponsored giveaways for my books. I truly thank each of you from the bottom of my heart. Here's a short list of the MANY who support me.

Samantha and Dusty from Reviews by Reds

Ali, Tiffany, Debbie, and Leah with Black Heart Reviews

Tina with Typical Distractions

Sanzana from Urban Book Hangover

Natasha from Book Baristas

Mary Ruth with The Reading Ruth

Kristen with Literary Misfit

Talon with Under the Cover Blog

Zoe from Literary Lust

Shannon with The Sisterhood of the Traveling Book Boyfriends

Deniz with Books & Tea

Christy with Captain Reads a Lot

Nicole with Nicki's Book Obsession

Amy with Once Upon a Book Blog

Linda with Second Bite Book Reviews

Wendy with Cheeky Chicks Book Hangover

Natasha with Read Review Repeat

Cynthia, Marci, and Tina with Restless Book Obsession

Erin and Katie with Southern Belle Book Blog

Alexis from Three Girls and a Book Obsession

Belinda and Lily from Hopelessly Devoted to Books

Giselle from Hopeless Book Lovers

Autumn from Paperrdolls

Claire from Claire Fully Reads

Tawnya from One More Chapter

Thank you to all my readers. One of the best things about being an author is the relationships I form with the readers who reach out. I love getting to know you on my Facebook fan page, in my reader group, on Twitter or Instagram and even via email. You rock my world.

Finally, thank you to my Savior and Lord, Jesus Christ, for giving me strength when I am weak.

He heals the brokenhearted and binds up their wounds.
Psalm 147:3

MORE BOOKS BY WHITNEY BARBETTI

Ten Below Zero

Bleeding Hearts Series

Into the Tomorrows (Book One)
Back to Yesterday (Book Two)

He Found Me Series

He Found Me (Book One)

He Saved Me (Book Two)

Box Set (Books One & Two)

ABOUT WHITNEY BARBETTI

Whitney Barbetti is a mom to two and a wife to one, living in eastern Idaho where she spends her days writing full time and keeping her boys from destroying her house. She writes character-driven new adult and contemporary adult romances that are heavy on the emotional connection. You'll most likely find her curled up with a good book and a giant glass of wine, with Queen playing through her headphones.

You can connect with Whitney here:

Website
http://www.whitneybarbetti.com/

Facebook
https://www.facebook.com/whitney.barbetti

FB Readers' Group
https://www.facebook.com/groups/457841991024544/

Instagram
@barbetti

Twitter
@barbetti

COMING SOON:
Back to Yesterday Book Three
Spring 2017